The Convergence of Current Events,
Biblical Prophecy and the Vision of Islam

FROM

9/11

TO

666

RALPH W. STICE

ACW Press
Ozark, AL 36360

From 9/11 to 666
Copyright ©2005 Ralph W. Stice
All rights reserved

Cover Design by Alpha Advertising
Interior Design by Pine Hill Graphics

Packaged by ACW Press
1200 HWY 231 South #273
Ozark, AL 36360
www.acwpress.com
The views expressed or implied in this work do not necessarily reflect those of ACW Press. Ultimate design, content, and editorial accuracy of this work is the responsibility of the author(s).

Library of Congress Cataloging-in-Publication Data
(Provided by Cassidy Cataloguing Services, Inc.)

Stice, Ralph W.

From 9/11 to 666 : the convergence of current events, Biblical prophecy and the vision of Islam / Ralph W. Stice. — 1st ed. — Ozark, AL : ACW Press, 2005.

p. ; cm.

Includes bibliographical references.
ISBN: 1-932124-65-9
ISBN-13: 978-1-932124-65-1

1. Eschatology, Islamic. 2. Islam—Psychology. 3. Islam—21st century. 4. End of the world (Islam) 5. Great Commission (Bible) 6. Bible—Islamic interpretations. 7. Prophecy—Islam. 8. Islam—Relations—Christianity. 9. Muslims—United States. 10. Eschatology. 11. International relations. 12. World politics. I. Title.

BP166.8 .S75 2005
297.2/3—dc22   0507

To Bill, who made this book possible.

To the American Church: I love you enough to tell you the truth.

To the 1.3 billion Muslims around the world: may you find the rest you seek in Christ.

To the man at Island Alliance Church in Stevensville, Maryland, who asked me to autograph his notes after one of my seminars. It was then that I realized I might have material worth putting into print.

Acknowledgments

I would like to thank Robert Livingston, author of *Christianity and Islam: The Final Clash* and Joel Richardson, author of *Antichrist: Islam's Coming Messiah*. Both of these men allowed me to profit from their extensive research as I wrote this book. Livingston has compiled an extremely solid biblical case for an Islamic antichrist and I highly recommend his work. Richardson has delved into Islamic documents to describe the messiah that they await. His book will prove to be a valuable resource on this topic as well. Thank you, men, for allowing me to benefit from your hard work.

Preface

This book has been written in response to the demand by many of the listeners around the country who have attended my seminars on *Islam and the End Times*. Due to the gracious provision of a longtime friend, I have been able to even more thoroughly scrutinize the thesis that I have created over the past decade of ministry among Islamic people. This work represents the sum of hundreds of hours of investigation and writing that buttresses daily interaction with Muslims. A plethora of books are available that examine the issues raised here; most are far better researched by people who have far more time on their hands and assistants to help in the process. I do not write to duplicate the efforts of such authors.

I have written, rather, to give the American evangelical Christian church a resource for tying together the mountain of information available to them in the post-9/11 world. Scores of books talk about the rumblings within the Islamic world and the perils of our dealings with it. Hundreds of others explore biblical prophecy in great detail. This work represents one of the few books that link the two together.

I am an ordained pastor, but also a former journalist. I have served as a missionary in Islamic communities for the past 10 years, but I also am an avid reader of the secular media on this topic. I seek to combine my dual identity within these pages. I hope that you will be pleased with the result.

I quote from a wide variety of sources, and the reader will soon notice a reliance on *The New York Times* and *The Washington Post*, two papers that I scour each morning. I know that this qualifies me as a heretic in some quarters. I would only say that I reference those publications because they are two of the few daily sources that tackle international news and are readily available to me. Please notice that I quote everyone from George Will to Maureen Dowd, and all sorts of voices in between. Realize as well that many of the articles quoted do not include opinion by their authors, but quotes from Al-Qaeda agents and French politicians, from U.S. military sources and Egyptian journalists. Whether you mine such quotes from *The Rolling*

Stone or *The Washington Times*, the important task remains to present a well-rounded picture. Please do not assume a "liberal bias" in my work simply because I draw on a multitude of sources, many of which you might not frequent.

Understand as well that each book or article cited stands as one of perhaps several that I have read, and the highlighted nugget represents a synthesis of opinion on a given matter. In other words, I did not search for one or two sources to back my ideas. Rather, I convey facts and opinions that surfaced frequently in my research, and you could find 10 articles proffering similar views for every one that I note.

As you read, please do not interpret this book as an attack on Muslims. I have read my share of screeching works that evidence little of Christ's love for these people. I want all of my readers to have a greater love for Muslim people as you understand the slavery they are born into and the inherent danger of several core beliefs in their faith. I do believe it is possible to care deeply about these people, yet maintain a clear-eyed view of their religion and its aims. We do not have to go to an extreme of either: "I hate Muslims and we should bomb them all," or "Islam is a religion of peace and should be considered one of many ways to God." Jesus can enable us to love those who are diametrically opposed to us politically, theologically and even morally.

For those of you who stand outside the body of Christ and will miss many of the references I make in these pages, please excuse me for writing to my family. That group is not a closed one. I invite you into a relationship with Jesus so that you can be sure of your eternity and know His peace in today's turbulent times. Please contact me for information if you want to know more about following the spiritual shepherd who promised abundant and eternal life. He's the greatest! Also, I plan on a sequel for a broader audience that will contain less "insider" language that might puzzle you in this work.

And to you, my Muslim reader, before reacting negatively to any book that would link your faith to the antichrist, consider prayerfully the arguments made herein. I write for you, ultimately, that you would see the path down which your faith proceeds so that you can get off before it's too late. I write out of concern, not scorn; to educate, not to smear. If you have made it this far past the title page, perhaps you are a genuine God-seeker. May He bless you on your journey.

Table of Contents

America 2017:
Life under an Islamic Antichrist

In the beginning, God created the heavens and the earth (Genesis 1:1). In the end, God will create a new heaven and a new earth (Revelation 21:1). In the time before that re-creation, God will allow one fearsome world ruler called "the beast" to emerge from among 10 kings to rule the earth during a time of great distress, as Revelation 17:17 promises, "For God has put it in their hearts (the 10 kings) to execute His purpose by having a common purpose, and by giving their kingdom to the beast, until the words of God should be fulfilled."

If we believe God and His Word, then we can be sure that the world will undergo a time of chaos and war unlike any time previously experienced. One central figure arises again and again in Scripture called the beast, the antichrist, the king. He could be alive this very moment, waiting for the proper time to assert his authority. The extent of his dominion will reach all nations, even the peaceful shores of the United States of America. This book will reveal a preponderance of evidence, both biblical and historical, to advance the thesis that an Islamic person will fill this role of world champion. When he does come to power in God's time, his control will stretch into the Western world, according to Scripture. What would his reign look like in the U.S., say, 12 years from now, and what events might have already started the clock's ticking? This fictional prologue, based on the research presented in the following 11 chapters, paints a picture of what life would be like in the near future under the rule of an Islamic antichrist.

2017: No God but Allah in America

The call to prayer sounds from Bangor, Maine, to Baja, California. The Mahdi government has constructed makeshift mosques in most American towns, but not every outpost has been touched, yet.

Despite the lack of gleaming houses of worship, daily prayers to Allah were ordered to be offered. Of all the increasingly constrictive requirements of the Mahdi administration, this proved to be the most nagging daily one—the 4:45 A.M. wail that now rouses millions of Americans each day. When Mahdi first proposed a plan for world peace seven years ago, he seemed like an excellent option for dominant leadership. Now, it had come to this: waking up hours earlier than customary to the haunting ancient Arabic chant:

> "God is most great." (repeated four times)
> "I witness that there is no god but Allah." (repeated twice)
> "I witness that Muhammad is the messenger of God."
> (twice)
> "Come to prayer." (twice)
> "Come to prosperity." (twice)
> "God is most great." (twice)
> "There is no God but Allah."

Then, during the preaching portion of worship on Friday afternoons, Islamic clerics across the land repeated a phrase that sounded like whimsy a decade earlier: "The Koran is stronger than America!"[1] To the astonishment of the world, no one could argue with that now.

The Necessary Precursor: The Invasion of Iraq

If one fact could be highlighted about world history that would stand without debate, it would be how quickly one event can change the military and political landscape, a tipping point, if you will—a government official is shot, an agreement is signed, a boat lands. The sweeping change over the United States could hardly have been anticipated on the day when Saddam Hussein's statue was flung to the ground and America reigned as the dominant superpower.

Yet, some Islamic analysts had warned about the consequences of the Iraqi invasion: "I believe the slightest spark could set things off," one moderate official in neighboring Jordan had cautioned, noting that the anger in the Arab world toward the United States was the biggest threat to global stability, and an Islamic revolution could spread from Iraq around the world.[2] The spark had indeed produced an inferno of rage that had charred the nations and permanently altered the world landscape.

What had begun as "the first American-Arab war," according to Mohamed Kamel, an Egyptian university professor, ended as the last, great war. The painfully slow American "exit strategy" was perceived as simple occupation by former friends in the Middle East. As Kamal continued, "America never had a colonial legacy in this part of the world, but it is about to have one."[3] That legacy proved to be too much for the Islamic world to stomach.

America was strong and brash just 14 years ago, led by a president who urged Islamic fundamentalists to "bring it on" as his mighty army battled a seemingly unending wave of holy warriors. Convinced that its model of capitalistic democracy was the final, best way of life, the U.S. stepped into the tumultuous Middle East ready to reshape and guide the needy nations there to the source of salvation known as "freedom and democracy." Regrettably, that preemptive action was precisely the one for which Osama bin Laden and his associates had hoped.

The Bush administration's plan had seemed so enlightened, so justified, so benevolent, so positive, so American. Spreading capitalism and democracy to the Middle East seemed like the perfect antidote to the suffocating regimes in Iraq, Iran, Afghanistan and others. The benefits were abundant—the Middle East would taste the sweet milk of freedom and the United States would have a region full of friends who would ensure stable relationships and the resulting continual flow of oil to American gas pumps.

What other choice did President Bush have? To stand by while terrorists continued to plot attacks on the U.S. and other Western nations? No, the events of 9/11/01 called for war, and U.S. troops were needed to clean out old dictatorships and replace them with freely elected governments. Terrorism would dry up like a puddle in the desert as the region stabilized under the contagious influence of democratic nations headed by presidents friendly with Washington.

Yet, as two British writers astutely pointed out in their tome on anti-Americanism in the twenty-first century, "many of the worst effects of American power are the result of the best-intentioned actions." This occurs especially, they note, because America has long seen the world as simply an extension of itself: "If the world is America," they wrote, "then it follows as a natural corollary that the interests of America should be the interests of the world. And all those who act against the interests, or culture, or worldview of America are in fact acting against the welfare and security of the world."[4]

What no one in Washington had allowed themselves to acknowledge was that Muslims do not think like Americans. The vast majority had never wanted a Western-style democracy, a secular regime or a long-term occupation while they learned the rudiments of occidental culture and governance. No, devout Muslims reject man-made laws and view democracy as a lower form of atheism because it puts the will of the people over the will of the Divine.[5]

Violent opposition to the grand American plan that had been hatched in a capital city that was psychologically, materially and spiritually light years from Baghdad continued, day by bloody day. Heeding the numerous calls to get a cleaner, closer shot at the infidels, jihadists flooded into Iraq and made life miserable for the foreign soldiers. Rather than thinning the ranks of terrorists, the Iraqi invasion had actually swelled their ranks and revived the movement.[6] As one veteran journalist in the Middle East predicted, "the terrorists' greatest hope is that their hysteria catches on in the West—just as the spirit of the jihad infected the Crusader—and touches off a crazed counterassault on the Muslim world. This hysteria, if it ever came, would feed on another illusion: that there is only one Islam, if we could only get all the veils off it."[7]

As the death toll had mounted in Iraq, the coalition was whittled to just a few participatory forces. The United States eventually found itself standing alone in its resolve to transform the Middle East. The long-predicted complete rupture among Western nations had been accomplished.[8] Goliath stood squinting in the sunlight, alone, vulnerable, confused, friendless.

The already tenuous relationship between the U.S. and its Middle Eastern allies had been permanently broken because of the invasion. As one State Department official put it in 2004: "Not only have we validated and emboldened our enemies, but we have shamed our friends. Arab moderates who trusted our ideals feel betrayed and abandoned."[9] This break with former friends both near and far would pave the way for a later unifier, a new superpower.

If American intelligence agents had listened carefully to all camps within Islam both immediately after 9/11 and during the Iraqi occupation, they would have realized that fundamentalist visions did not stop with a Middle Eastern empire. No, their goals sprang from the core of Islam, founded 1400 years before. For this reason, it might be more accurate to call fundamentalists "purists" rather than "radicals." For, as one of the leading Al-Qaeda militants said regarding his intention to assassinate the prime minister in Iraq, the fight against the infidels would continue "until Islamic rule is back on earth."[10]

As expatriates retreated from Islamic areas of the world in the years after the war in Iraq, exactly as jihadist leaders knew they would, politics and religion also mixed in unique Islamic fashion as fundamentalists, now free to influence elections and thrilled to employ U.N. support for transparent balloting, reaped the blessing of Allah and rode vote totals to power in Morocco, Egypt, Saudi Arabia, Syria, and Jordan, as Arab experts who had tracked the expansion of the Islamic Brotherhood worldwide had predicted.[11] The first decade of the twenty-first century shone as a glorious era indeed for Muslims, an empire reborn, yet awaiting unification. Al-Qaeda had evolved from a terrorist movement to a political force, winning long-term control in governments throughout the Islamic world, verifying a forecast made soon after 9/11 by certain security experts.[12] Those who had trumpeted the triumph of democracy in Washington had never bothered to gauge the true temperature in Islamic lands, the boiling hot anger directed at corrupt, secular dictators that were glee-fully discarded when ballot boxes were placed at polling places.

Some prophets had foreseen the chaos of 2010, a world divided along cultural and religious lines, with the new development of nuclear arms available to both sides. Now the stakes ran extra high. As one retired Army colonel said in 2004: "Although today's terror-ists are an indisputable menace, they do not yet threaten global peace or our survival. But the political transformation of Al-Qaeda into a radical pan-Islamic movement would divide the world between the progressive West and a number of belligerent, deeply reactionary, nuclear-armed states, and raises the possibility of far more serious conflict."[13] The key component needed, the last link in the chain, the sole remaining puzzle piece was a godly, charismatic Muslim leader to unite this disparate collection of countries.

Mahdi: The Man to Stop the Madness

That is where Mahdi stepped in. After the nuclear madness that briefly erupted in the battles over the Saudi oil fields, the world looked for a leader who could bridge the gap between East and West. Mahdi fit the need perfectly with his command of English, political savvy and knowledge of the Western world. The long-held Islamic dream of a virtuous caliph to guide the masses and lead them to world triumph had finally come true.

Through a series of power grabs that began after the fall of the royal Saudi family and resulting world uproar, Mahdi had cemented his position as undisputed monarch of the world, even though he would insist that Allah himself was the real ruler of the Earth and he simply acted as his intermediary. He was aided in his takeover by the sometimes miraculous assistance of Isa, the self-proclaimed reincarnation of Jesus Christ.

A Palestinian with both Jewish and Arab blood, Isa appeared out of almost nowhere in early 2010 to urge the world to practice Islam, as Muslims had predicted for centuries that he would. Signs and wonders buttressed his teaching, convincing many of his apparent divine origin. When urged to challenge Mahdi for world rule, Isa demurred, stating that he was only a common servant of Allah and ready to do whatever was necessary to spread Islam. He would become Mahdi's right hand man as their sovereignty extended even to the former "home of the brave."

America had been neutralized by a combination of forces: world opinion, its need for oil, the threat of nuclear holocaust and Mahdi himself. As the American agenda of de facto world rule became apparent after the fall of Saudi Arabia, an unprecedented alliance turned to him for a checkmate. Drawing on his familiarity with the U.S. and his impeccable Islamic pedigree (a direct descendant of Muhammad), Mahdi had sagely billed himself as the master power broker, balancing the new Islamic confederation's threat of nuclear destruction with the Western desire for world peace.

By gaining concession after concession from the U.S. in return for a limited flow of oil and a freeze on nuclear and chemical weapons production, Mahdi headed an Islamic-European union that overwhelmed one of the world's great empires and turned the wealthiest nation in history into an economic middleweight. Told for the first time in its history that "the American way of life" was not sacred and would no longer be maintained at the expense of the rest of the world, Uncle Sam stood shocked on the sidelines like a demoted quarterback holding a clipboard.

As time passed, political compromise morphed into cultural totalitarianism as Mahdi found cause to continue the transfer of power from U.S. institutions to Islamic clerics. The core goal of Islam, that "religion be wholly Allah's" (Koran, Sura 8:39) re-emerged as one-fourth of the world's population sensed the probability of their faith's triumph. From 2014 onward, Mahdi and his cabinet rushed to the finish line.

The result was an America in 2017 that looked little like the America of even 2007. The Mahdi kingdom still permitted the citizenry to do what they did best—work industriously and make money—but the spheres in which they operated were transformed by Islamic law. Treasurers overhauled the entire banking system in accordance with the Islamic interdiction of interest on loans. New bosses slashed executive salaries as their first step in assuming control over mammoth companies. A flat tax of 20 percent was imposed on all goods, services and income as part of the traditional Muslim *jizya* tax on conquered peoples (Koran 8:41). On the factory floor, supervisors granted breaks to their workers throughout the day for prayer, and skeleton crews labored on Friday afternoons as the bulk of the labor force attended services at the mosque.

Sharia law, once seen as the sort of tough-on-crime measure long craved by the stateside public, had turned into an awful experiment gone bad, a freedom-sapping enforced religion, the most un-American system one could devise. What sounded like perfect justice had led to the loss of freedom of conscience, the most precious liberty for any human being.

Earlier Islamic revolutions, as in Iran, for example, had provided the chilling logic now followed in the former land of the most free:

> "If you deny the rules you are denying the rule-maker. If you put the rule-maker away you are against the Leader. If you oppose the Leader you are against the Holy Prophet. If you are against the Holy Prophet you are against the Holy Book, and the Holy Book comes from God. Someone against God must be killed."[14]

The sexual revolution was halted as those caught in (or sometimes just accused of) adultery were stoned. Even petty thieves
nabbed by the police had their hands amputated. Repeat offenders
faced a worse fate. In a clever adaptation of the "three strikes" laws
that had gained popularity in the U.S., Mahdi offered the Islamic version: first offense=amputation of the right hand from the joint of
the wrist; second offense=amputation of the left foot up to the
ankle, third offense=imprisonment for life.[15] The severity and cer-
tainty of almost instant judgment and punishment had nearly cured
America's crime problem in even the most dangerous inner cities,
bringing muted cheers of relief from many citizens, as Mahdi had
promised.

How events had led to the United States of Islam was another
"frog in a pot" proverb, where incremental change results in a deadly
scalding. Mahdi had declared at first that Americans were free to
practice their faiths, citing Koranic passages that laud the "people of
the Book." Drawing from Islamic history, he required that Christians
and Jews only pay the *jizya* tax and wear a distinguishing symbol, as
previous conquering rulers had done.[16] That emblem was the subject of much debate. For decades, governments in Islamic lands had
required identification cards that listed one's religion. In that vein,
proposals for certificates, armbands and patches were thought to be
too cumbersome, expensive and antiquated. Mahdi designated a
committee to create a hi-tech solution that would identify all
Muslims. The group decided on a laser imprint of the Islamic creed
in Arabic script, a common feature on Middle Eastern flags. Those
who did not have the mark were treated as second-class citizens, and
later, worse.

In the early days of the Mahdi era, non-Muslims were free to
worship in their churches and synagogues, but no new non-Islamic
houses of worship were permitted to be constructed. When
Christian and Jewish groups protested this sly method of eventual
extinction, Mahdi realized anew the power of the American evangelical church and its ability to rally substantial support against the few
governing authorities he had placed in the U.S. He concluded that
Americans had forfeited their chance at freedom of worship, publicly changing his opinion of Christians, even as the founder of
Islam had done when confronted with Christian and Jewish
refusal to follow the new faith. Mahdi had known all along that

the continuation of religious freedom in the U.S. would prove impossible to control, but he permitted it initially to gain prestige and bolster his reputation as a reasonable man and a restrained Muslim. He cannily annulled all non-Islamic worship because it "was in conflict with the rule of law and endangered the precarious order that had recently come to the nation."

It helped to have Anglophone speechwriters to explain his policy shifts. Those changes made sense to many, even some faithful worshippers who reluctantly traded freedom for order and fell prey to the carefully crafted arguments of Islam, Judaism and Christianity being "cousins" and the worship of the "one true god, the god of Abraham, Moses and Jesus" taking a slightly different, Arab twist. It was a bit stunning, actually, just how many Christians capitulated to the new rules, some even citing Romans 14 and obedience to governing authorities. Mahdi and his deputies had masterfully peddled the stream of thought that had infuriated Americans just a generation earlier. They stopped short of calling the U.S. "the great Satan," but they built a powerful case for a need to remake a "morally corrupt, socially degenerate society." Drawing on the writings of evangelicals, they sounded the same alarm that Christian leaders had for the past half-century, only this time the law was the answer, not Christ.

"The Apostasy Comes First"

Careful readers of Scripture, however, were not astonished by the surrender of their previously committed neighbors. Paul promised nervous believers that the Day of the Lord would not come "unless the apostasy comes first, and the man of lawlessness is revealed, the son of destruction" (2 Thessalonians 2:3). Those reluctant to slide into this stream of renunciation put up a fight at first, responding to the new ruler's first wave of propaganda with the response: "Christ alone." To counter this resistance, Mahdi and company repeated the mantra that Islam was nothing more than an improved extension of Christianity. They did so frequently enough to cause many churchgoers to succumb, convincing a huge slice of the American populace that morality could be enforced and, in fact, needed to be.

Another factor abetting Mahdi's campaign was the widespread discouragement that permeated the Christian community. Stupefied by the events around them that indicated an apparent lack of care from their God, these churchgoers pondered the abandonment of their faith as it was shaken to its roots. Their previous confidence in the rapture of the Church had been shattered, and the decimation of that key doctrine left the remainder of their belief structure vulnerable to soothing arguments about God's importance in life and government. This subset of "believers," too, yielded quickly to the repackaged Christianity that Mahdi and his lieutenants preached. Millions bowed to an age-old lie: that might proves right; that is, the quick triumph of Mahdi and Isa proved the divine endorsement of their faith. A Christianity long constructed on American military might and pre-Tribulation rescue crumbled more quickly than a sand castle at high tide. When the twin props of wealth and comfort were dislodged beneath them, most American churchgoers' faith was found wanting, assembled on the wrong foundation.

The prophecies of Matthew 24 had turned true. People's love had grown cold, many had been deceived by someone saying, "I am He," and others had been so busy eating and drinking and marrying that they were not sure how to react to the new world order.

Isa had made several U.S. tours to explain the religious platform of the new ruling authority. His abilities to heal hundreds at rallies and to cite a combination of scriptures from both the Bible and the Koran had persuaded tens of millions that he was, in fact, Jesus returned. A crucial failure to test the spirits resulted in a massive acknowledgement of Isa's power as a proof of his divine seal. Isa had the gentle manner that one would expect of Jesus—the compassionate eyes, the soft hands of a healer. He was the kinder, gentler half of the new ticket, a simple man who dressed in flowing robes, completely uninterested in money, fame, or the latest fashion. He could turn stern as well, when needed, just as Jesus had done in the Gospels. He had tanned good looks, and his beard and long hair looked far less threatening than it had on the other Muslim clerics pictured in press photos that had circulated for decades. Isa was crucial to the pacification of the U.S. He was not as needed in other countries where his name was not similarly honored. He proved to be an essential vice president in the Christian world, however, and his combination of religious rhetoric and supernatural abilities calmed many an audience from Oslo to L.A. He spoke with authority and clarity in improving English that was as endearing as it was sincere. Theologians scrambled to reconstruct their eschatological timelines to include this sudden return of "Jesus."

The Occupation of America for Allah

To complete the colonization of the U.S. for Islam, Mahdi beamed a worldwide call to occupy infidel lands, which met a mixed response. Some Muslims, fearing contamination from the remnants of a hedonistic Western culture, stayed home and enjoyed daily contact with friends and family. Others more inclined to thrill-seeking jumped at the chance to kick the humbled giant and rake in his spoils, permitted in Koranic law as soldiers of Allah to take booty (Koran 8:1, 41; 48:20-21; 59:7). These conscripts were eager to experience the land of milk and honey and to taste its fruit, all the time whipping the morally corrupt West into shape. Jets packed full of men shouting "Allahu Akbar!" had landed throughout 2015–2016, and they emptied an ardent workforce onto the tarmacs of JFK and O'Hare, Logan and Dulles. These young people, mostly men, shrieked with delight when charged with the enforcement of *sharia* law from sea to shining sea, their eyes afire with the fury of a holy god, moist with the joy of a dream come true, the glory of Allah covering the Earth at long last.

The hordes of lanky Islamic youth that had come to the States had catapulted from a class of unemployed no-names that no government had cared about to the official enforcers of the new global regime, a heady promotion indeed. The "combination of low productivity and high birth rate" in Islamic nations had created "an unstable mix, with a large and rapidly growing population of unemployed, uneducated, and frustrated young men."[17] Rather than sinking into history as another lost generation, this age group had chosen another path, the path of militant Islam, and now that decision was being validated beyond their wildest dreams.

Repeating the long-held slogan of the Islamic Brotherhood, now legal and flourishing throughout the world, these zealots skipped happily through every day's work of enforcing Allah's will on planet Earth. When they assembled for morning meetings, their collective cry sent chills down anyone near enough to hear it: "God is our purpose, the Prophet our leader, the Koran our constitution, jihad our way and dying for God's cause our supreme objective."[18] That was a long way from "I pledge allegiance to the flag."

This generation's enthusiasm to purify "the great Satan" reached its zenith when confronted with certain stubborn followers of Jesus Christ. These brave men, women and children had refused to repeat the Islamic confession of faith while in jail. They likewise never reported to city hall to receive the required laser tattoo. These few cells of the faithful had held out through the initial persuasive speeches, and even after the administrative transition to forced conversion. They met in secret and worshipped Jesus as God in flesh and the Savior of mankind, and in the process discovered the intimacy and power of the Early Church, a longtime goal of Western evangelicals. They also learned that only intense persecution and suffering could produce such coveted body life, a lesson that many of their overseas brethren had ascertained long ago.

An unfailing formula began to emerge as these two immovable objects collided: the thinner, hungrier and angrier the jailer was, the more likely he would make an example of the infidel family before him. These interrogations and resulting disappearances sometimes made the headlines, sometimes did not. Enough accounts of executions were leaked to keep the public terrified, much as Al-Qaeda terrorists had done for the decade before the Mahdi government. The powerful images brought celebration worldwide—often-obese Americans, the men stripped of their shirts, paraded down main streets while their guards shouted, "Remember Abu Ghraib!" occasionally beating the men in strategic places with their batons. Stumbling into a public square, weary and exhausted, the last of the true disciples of Christ kneeled in front of stone altars, exposing their necks to the sharp swords of the police.

At times, only the men were slain, their wives and children then awarded to one of the many newly immigrated Muslim bachelors. Occasionally the whole family was beheaded in front of crowds comprised primarily of new immigrants, cold-blooded killings justified by the charge of all the family members proclaiming Christ's Lordship. Videotape shot at the scene was relayed around the globe, documenting not only a complete reversal of the world's power structure in just one decade's time, but a powerful new testimony to curious billions who wondered about a faith that produced serenity before the executioner's blade and instant death.

The stark contrast was more vivid than ever before: a faith that beheaded people for their beliefs compared to one that spoke about forgiveness of its enemies, calmly facing extermination.

That calm came from a mystical, divine peace flowing from the presence of the Holy Spirit and the promise of an oft-quoted Scripture in 2017: "I saw the thrones on which were seated those who had been given authority to judge. And I saw the souls of those who had been beheaded because of their testimony for Jesus and because of the word of God. They had not worshiped the beast or his image and had not received his mark on their foreheads or their hands. They came to life and reigned with Christ a thousand years" (Revelation 20:4). It wasn't every day that a family got to fulfill biblical prophecy and prepare the way for a 1000-year reign.

Chapter One

"We Should Have Warned Them": Why This Book Was Written

I was standing in the kitchen of my apartment in Nanterre, France, when my daughter called me to come look at the television screen. The sight of a plane lodged in one of the World Trade Center's two towers looked like a clip from a movie unfamiliar to me. As I realized that the image was live, my mind went down the mental road I am sure many others traveled that day: "Accident, how in the...? Clear day, what happened? Those poor people!"

As I heard the panicked American voice faintly behind the French announcer's, I wondered if this was not, indeed, an accident. Minutes later, when the second plane hit its target, I turned to my wife and said somberly, "We should have warned them." I did not possess any intelligence briefings from the CIA or FBI about the elaborate plan of Al-Qaeda operatives to crash several airliners into American landmarks on September 11, 2001. I had not encountered any of the terrorists in a flight school or served them in a bank. I had not attended meetings of their inner circle or had a hint of their dastardly intentions. I did, however, have a thorough knowledge of Islam, its evolution and the goals of fundamentalists. Many years of conversations with Muslims sprang to mind as I saw the plumes of smoke rising from the Twin Towers and the screams of eyewitnesses in New York. Exhaustive reading stored in my brain's hard drive gave me a detailed context in which to interpret what I was seeing. As proof of God's miraculous design, my brain made dozens of calculations in the split second before I felt guilt for not informing my homeland about the gravity of Islam's growing jihadist wing.

A few miles from my apartment, automobile horns blared in celebration as the news spread of the Twin Towers' incineration. The

grimy 19th arrondissement, where I used to receive Arabic tutoring
in a decrepit McDonald's, hosted spontaneous rejoicing as I shook
my head in sadness, confusion and culpability.[19] A few days later, a
Muslim leader of Algerian origin went on a French version of "Meet
the Press" and said that all of the Muslims in France had mixed emotions about 9/11. They were sorry that so many people died, but
happy that America suffered a blow, "because we Muslims around
the world suffer such blows every day."

For years I had felt the pulse of a very angry Islamic world, having interacted with fundamentalist preachers, former members of
terrorist groups and hyper-devoted Muslims who dreamt of world
conquest, all in settings quite distant from the relatively calm United
States. I hadn't needed to venture very far to sense that pulse; it
vibrated all around me. Living in a joyless, turbulent suburb of Paris
for four years, I had Muslim neighbors who regularly espoused the
rage of a sometimes violent religion and the anger of a people suppressed and hated, the same fury that powered Osama bin Laden
and his mercenaries. I heard similar vehemence during four years'
residence in another predominantly Islamic neighborhood in Côte
d'Ivoire. The agony of Muslims worldwide expressed itself in both
communities, and the eerie atmosphere of tension before a destruc-
tive explosion touched my family in both places.

Islam and the West: The French Experiment

In France, periodic episodes of violence erupt, intermittent
bombs detonate, but the big bang is still to come. In Côte d'Ivoire it
exploded in September 2002 when Muslim rebels seized the northern half of the country. On September 11, 2001, this fury decimated
two commercial steeples, thousands of families and world peace.
The same disenchantment with political powerlessness and poverty,
perversity and pain runs through all acts of aggression undertaken
by Muslims today, and that discontent blended well with the nearly
constant gray skies in northern France. My city of 100,000 followed
the state-imposed master plan for the ring of towns around Paris—
myriad high-rise apartment buildings quickly constructed to house
the descendants of the menial laborers that France had imported in
the 1960s and '70s. Brought to the continent to perform the tire-
some tasks that the French had neither the numbers nor appetite
for, these North African Muslims from Morocco, Algeria and

Tunisia had remained on French soil when their retirement years arrived. They not only settled in France, they multiplied, at a rate that confounded the natives, and along with that numerical growth came a more strident cultural voice. The first generation of imported workers had practiced a moderate, peaceful, invisible Islam, occasionally rallying for workers' rights but not calling for the overthrow of the French government. These *maghrébins* (North Africans) didn't even insist on state help or permits for mosque construction, as they prayed privately or in simple common rooms in the shantytowns they inhabited.

Any Muslim person in France over the age of 50 can tell you that his peers were neither secular nor overtly religious. They maintained their Islamic heritage, yet kept a low profile as they treasured the employment for which they had long searched. Overjoyed by the generous benefits of a socialist state and European pensions, many of these men amassed enough money to keep an apartment in France and build a large house in Africa as well. They sometimes kept wives in both places, too. That's where the trouble started. After several years in France, these laborers pressed for the importation of their wives and children to their new country. France eventually agreed to this massive immigration in the 1970s, and Muslim families proved to be extremely fertile in Europe. France witnessed the emergence of its first significant minority, a development that later would rock its society, for the next generation was not so content to work on assembly lines or to dig subway tunnels. These now-French citizens did not accept the second-class status afforded them by the sometimes blatantly racist Caucasian majority. As factories became more automated and rail lines reached their limits, job opportunities dwindled.

The historically uniform school system offered few options for success to this new generation of light brown *maghrébins*. Often growing up in households where Arabic alone was spoken, where the lonely books standing on the shelves included the Koran and a few keepsake volumes from the motherland, this second generation struggled in perhaps the most difficult secondary school environment in the world. Few made it to the last year of *lycée* (high school), fewer still passed the baccalaureate to continue on to university. French cities soon filled with angry unemployed young people who felt cheated, not blessed, by their family's new country. As a result,

Islamist groups that promise a pristine society, full employment and
the triumph of Islam (once the current stifling system was overthrown) found a happy hunting ground in cities like mine, where
the national unemployment rate of 20 percent among young people
was at least double for those of North African heritage.[20] French
authorities have identified seven terrorist training centers around
the country, two in the Paris region, to make it convenient for men
and women from my city to be discipled in the world vision of bin
Laden. Suburbs like the one in which I lived have been labeled a
"breeding ground of volunteers" for Al-Qaeda,[21] a "wellspring" for
terrorism.[22] Security experts have singled out two primary pipelines
for fundamentalist recruitment in French suburbs, and they attract
hundreds of potential jihadists while operating under the international radar screen, due to France's absence from the list of Al-
Qaeda strongholds,[23] The Islamists call themselves Salafists in
France, reflecting the name of a branch of Wahhabite Islam, a particularly radical school of thought. The Salafists control 30 mosques,
primarily in the Paris and Lyon regions, and expulsions of imams
who preach jihad and non-integration into France occur on a
monthly basis.[24] It was in this setting that I tapped into the passion
of Muslims around the world.

France, I believe, serves as an excellent laboratory for the experi-
mental amalgamation of two volatile substances: Western civilization and Islam. Those of us who have lived there have stood on the
front lines of the announced "clash of civilizations" that has erupted
in the twenty-first century. With the largest chunk of Muslims living
in a Western nation (15 percent), France has drawn the attention of
the world as it seeks to facilitate a moderate Islam within the freedoms and traditions of a European country. As one writer observed,
"A French failure to integrate Muslims could lead to a general
European and Western failure."[25] French Arabist Gilles Kepel argues
in his latest book *The War for Muslim Minds* that the future of Islam
will be determined by the interpretation of that faith decided upon
in the next several years in European countries. The many tensions
within the larger Islamic community are compressed into the lives
of immigrants and their sons and daughters on the continent, where
they are free to debate the form they choose to live and practice.
Kepel confesses to be an optimist regarding Islam's accommodations
to "modern life."[26] Others are not so sure. Myriad questions surface

as these two cultures collide, among them the compatibility of Islam with secular democracy (separation of church and state) and human rights (especially the rights of women and of non-Muslims). In France, the entire country awaits the answer to an even more far-reaching query: which mode of Islam will emerge? If fundamentalism dominates, it could lead to religious and civil war, most French fear.[27]

The French government, and most prominently former minister of the Interior and current minister of Finance Nicolas Sarkozy, constantly battles to maintain the delicate balance between freedom of conscience and religion and suppression of terrorist ideology and activity. Sarkozy recently told colleagues at an International Monetary Fund meeting that he hoped to oversee the creation of an Islam "made in France," referring to measures such as state financing for the training of imams and mosque construction, unheard-of allowances in a republic founded squarely upon the complete separation of religion and government. As he said, "Why should we let Saudi Arabia build mosques here and Algeria export radical imams to France? I want an Islam of France, not an Islam that happens to be in France."[28]

France's concern with a "foreign" Islam has prompted the police to shutter several informal mosques of the Wahhabite variety. Authorities carefully monitor the activities of Muslims attending these mosques, and then the government, if it determines that the teaching therein represents a danger to national security, simply closes the buildings and posts security guards at all the entrances. Such closures highlight many of the struggles in France. Should the government encourage Muslims to express their faith or tightly supervise it? Will the Islam of the '60s and '70s return, or will a new-found radicalism carry the day?[29] Can Islam be managed and pacified, tamed to coexist with other faiths and political philosophies? Watch closely in years to come, even if that means buying an international newspaper now and then or turning on BBC News.

Some French emit optimism, confident that its schools and culture will continue to have a "civilizing" effect on the latest wave of immigrants, as it has for decades on other blocs of newcomers. I often asked French people what they thought the solution was for the tension between the natives and the North African immigrants. The answer was summarized by one landlord with whom I was negotiating a lease: "Do you see that group of children?" he asked as he pointed to a group of six-year-olds. "The current generation is too far gone, but once that group goes through school, they will behave correctly." *On verra*, we shall see. I wish France the best, but I see all the elements of an explosive social cocktail.

In addition, those of us who have lived in France have had contact with ethnic groups that feed a huge portion of active terrorist cells around the world, namely Moroccans and Algerians. I do not wish to typecast either nation or its people, and I have dozens of tremendous friends and acquaintances among both groups. I thoroughly enjoyed the English students I had from these groups and admired their courage as they sought to better themselves with mastery of a third language. However, the crude facts show a significant slice of terrorist cell membership from these two countries. Morocco, with its tradition of strong royal control, close ties to the U.S. and moderation in its practice of Islam, has surprised many analysts in recent years with its exportation of terrorists. Observers cite grinding poverty and perpetual unemployment among the causes for the flowering of this new generation of jihadists, as well as the present king's crackdown on political parties that lean towards Islamism.[30] Algeria, saddled with a history of fierce combat against France and internal terrorism after the annulment of elections in 1991-92, has sent many troubled young men and women abroad. My Algerian friends blamed a culture of violence introduced by the French as the reason for their clan members showing up on terrorist rolls around the world. Both of these countries contribute men and money toward the fulfillment of Al-Qaeda and other terrorist groups' goals. Their citizens were my neighbors, my friends, my students. I know them, and their hopes, fears and goals in life. I have lived next door to people whose fellow countrymen terrify the world; I regularly have spoken face-to-face with Muslims who had participated in fundamentalist movements, giving me an insight no scholar or journalist living in the U.S. can share, no matter how many exclusive interviews they garner during week-long trips overseas. Observing such people at close proximity over four years' time has given me a unique window into Islam and its place in the modern world.

Those of us who have resided in France and observed the current collision of cultures are able to offer an honest, up-to-date, frank eyewitness account of Islam's solubility in a world dominated by the West. In my immediate neighborhood, about two-thirds of the residents prayed to Allah, most having immigrated from North Africa. Tensions ran high as the formerly restrained French police battled the temptation to install a sort of martial law on city streets. Their traditional low-key presence had done little to maintain order in the "disfavored zones," and certain hazardous neighborhoods rarely, if ever, saw a policeman on foot, horse or in a vehicle, as a fearful force skipped particular stops in their circuits. Petty theft and drug dealing predominated. French girls wailed in the park behind my apartment as young bandits snatched their cell phones. Drug dealers nonchalantly walked their pit bulls to the basketball courts, where they transacted business while my son and I played one-on-one. Informal gangs loitered in apartment lobbies, annoying and occasionally bullying or robbing the residents.

Sometimes the rage of the jaded young *maghrébins* turned toward the state. Commando assaults on schools and police stations were frequent. A two-week period in December 2003, for instance, witnessed a concentrated wave of crime that ruined the Christmas holidays for my neighbors: a preschool destroyed by vandalism, a nighttime police patrol pelted with Molotov cocktails launched from a passing scooter, a police station incinerated by arson, and several cars burned to a crisp in an underground garage. All of these attacks took place a mere five blocks from my former apartment.[31] My city had the feel of a community that had a foot in two universes: one in traditional, exquisite France, the other in some criminal netherworld out of a Batman movie. When going to the supermarket two blocks away, you could buy fresh French bread or witness a beating in the parking lot. When taking the traditional long lunch, you could sip wine over a delicious steak-frites or stroll into a sandwich shop and see bearded men in gowns reciting the Koran at their tables. High schools struggled to stay open as classrooms were torched and professors stabbed. Sporadic arrests of the lobby bullies produced caches of arms and drugs. Speeding cars and scooters, at times eluding police, careened down the street to the right of my balcony in dangerous zig-zag chases almost every weekend.

The Ministry of the Interior recently selected my neighborhood as one of two in France for an experiment in Draconian law, budgeting for beefed-up foot patrols, random identification checks, and frequent vehicle searches, as well as canine squads to patrol apartment buildings and enforce curfews.[32] The French hope this radical pilot program will curb the explosion of crime that petrifies its citizens and propels extreme right, law-and-order politicians to national prominence and unprecedented vote shares. To many French people, "Arab" and "criminal" are synonymous, "Muslim" and "delinquent" two sides of a coin, yet knowing personally many Islamic people and seeing the conditions in which they lived helped me to sympathize with their frustrations. That disgruntlement produced an indignation that they directed not only at the French.

Anti-Americanism at Its Peak

In my efforts to befriend my Islamic neighbors for the sake of Christ, I battled ingrained stereotypes of Americans. One of my son's first playmates at age nine would constantly taunt him about Americans loving violence and dropping bombs on people at will. After taking a steaming pot of mint tea to his father in an effort to establish a relationship, I heard the transmitter of these views, the boy's father, confess to me that he had never liked Americans. Fortunately for me and my wife, he would make an exception in our case. To God be the glory. This man was not alone in his hatred of the United States. Other acquaintances asked me why my country did not do more to help the poor countries of the world, why it backed a "savage, murderous" government in Israel and cruel dictators in their homelands, why it had a president who prayed for guidance then ordered bombings that killed innocent people. These hostile Muslims did not have to look far for reinforcement of their views. The Caucasian French happily joined them in protesting the United States' domination of the world and its agenda for the planet's future. French journalists focused on Palestinian suffering and loss and repeatedly denounced American foreign policy in the Middle East. I am convinced that this European corroboration of anti-American sentiment exacerbates traditional Islamic repulsion for the "Great Satan." The long-held belief that the world's peoples differentiate between America and Americans contains some truth, but I can tell you that when conversations begin, those lines blur as anger surfaces and a convenient target appears. Americans abroad rarely wear patriotic clothing and restrain their use of English for a reason. In the heat of the moment, a hater of the U.S. does not make the distinction between politics and the person with the stars-and-stripes bandana in front of him.

This double stream of anti-Americanism issuing from both the French and Islamic communities materialized on a daily basis. Teenagers sometimes shouted at my children when they heard them speaking English. Visiting American friends were screamed at in shopping malls when people heard their American English. Short-term missionaries had bottles hurled at them on the subway. One would have to be deaf, dumb and blind not to sense this tense atmosphere. I'll never forget the hail of rocks and profanity launched at my children when they visited the playground behind our apartment building early in our term in France. As my daughter and son interacted in English, a few of the children began to shout "(expletive) Bush" in their limited English and hurled pebbles as my confused kids left the tire rope swing. Unhappy with a rigid society that boxes many of its minorities into dilapidated skyscrapers? Just heap a few epithets on the head of the American president and perhaps you will feel better. Or, drive a tractor into a McDonald's. Or, participate in the plot to fly two planes into the World Trade Center.

The deep and complex problems of two societies—French and Muslim—were often attributed to globalization, or, Americanization, many would opine. Obviously, this setting made for an interesting context in which to do ministry. Hearing the rants of the poor and powerless gave me great insight into today's terrorists and the reasons for Islamic fundamentalism's revival and spread. I find a glaring lack of similar life experience among those who write authoritatively about Islam in the modern world. I have shared the street with these people; I know them. As I write, I recount real exchanges, not imagined scenarios or academic studies.

I have more recently gained a greater understanding of the American view of the Islamic world as I edit transcripts of trials before Immigration judges. I realize that when these judges deport Muslims and others back to their countries, they have absolutely no idea what conditions in many of these countries are like, despite a pile of State Department Country Reports at their elbow. My coworkers forgive my chuckling as I hear well-educated men and women on cassette recordings tell converted Muslims, for instance, that they exaggerate their fears back home, or that they can pursue educational opportunities almost equal to those in the U.S. Other "aliens" are told they should have an easy time finding a job, given their experience gained stateside, or that they should report further persecution to their local police. These feel-good scenarios would be hilarious were the reality in countries like Pakistan and Egypt not so tragic. We cannot change our heritage, our national identity. We are all doomed to seeing the world through the angle provided to us by our home culture, yet world events now force us to walk a mile in the worn shoes of the poor and misguided as we try to understand the groundswell of destitute god-fearers that threaten the world as we know it.

Islam's Plan for the World

In addition to the collective irritation on the part of Muslims worldwide (for reasons I will explore later), a global plan for the glory of Allah also must be exposed and dissected in this book. I have read and heard much about how wonderful the world will be under the reign of Allah, through the intermediary of a godly global leader, the last in the line of successors to the Prophet. Posters and graffiti throughout the Muslim world proclaim: "Twelfth Imam: We Are Waiting For You."[33] Who is this figure and what is he supposed to accomplish? I will attempt to answer that question in a later chapter. To return to the United States in July 2003 and hear supposed government experts offer uninformed and inaccurate analyses of Muslims, Islam, Al-Qaeda and bin Laden has shocked and disheartened me. For instance, to postulate that the terrorists' war on the West is about power, not religion, could not be more untrue. That perspective results from seeing the conflict through a Western lens, a dangerous view indeed.

In Islam, political power and religion are joined, as modeled by its founder, Muhammad. Bin Laden desires most deeply to bring glory to Allah and impose his will on earth. This stimulus also propels suicide bombers, who face the choice of a wearisome life in search of a wife, employment and daily bread, coupled with a demanding faith, or the paradise that awaits martyrs in jihad.

As one author who interviewed the families of scores of martyrs has stated:

> "In Islam, martyrdom is not something to be feared,
> Muslim authorities agree. In fact, it is to be welcomed as

the most beautiful testimony of faith. Muslim scholars have written extensively on the duty of believers to fight and to be ready to die to overcome oppression and corruption in the world. And Muslims around the world, especially in the Middle East, regularly hear imams extol the virtues of martyrdom at Friday prayer....In order to understand the new danger facing the United States, Americans must examine Islam's reverence for martyrs and its teachings about war."[34]

In all of the hullabaloo after 9/11, at least a few people rightly analyzed the motivations of the perpetrators. Jane I. Smith, a professor at Hartford (Connecticut) Seminary, observed: "Apparently, one can assume what was done was done by people out of a genuine and sincere belief that they were helping bring about the will of God....And that, in turn, may be the most frightening thing about it." She went on to call the hijackers' last written communication "truly pious," which it was, in a twisted way.[35] The essence of Islam needs to be discussed more rigorously to determine the origin of the burning, demonic element that produces fanatical hatred and a love of death. As bin Laden said shortly after 9/11: "We love death. The U.S. loves life. That is the big difference between us."[36] Where does this bizarre and fearful view of life and death come from? I echo the brave writers who urge us all to stop diverting investigation of the possible causes of terrorism because "something here, if thought about too deeply, undermines categories we use to live our lives, undermines our faith in the essential goodness of human beings. Three years after Sept. 11, too many people have become experts at averting their eyes."[37] In short, this new war is ALL about religion. We must dig into Islam to discover its roots, while considering the demanding circumstances in which most of the world's Muslims live. As renowned Middle Eastern expert Bernard Lewis has noted: "For bin Laden and those who follow him, this is a religious war, a war for Islam against infidels, and therefore, inevitably, against the United States, the greatest power in the world of the infidels."[38] We should have paid better attention to the diatribes of Khomeni, who was discounted as a madman but has had a lasting influence on the Islamic world. Whether or not you agree with him or take him seriously, he remains a revered figure,

the George Washington of modern, pure Islam. He clarified the link
between the core of his faith and world conquest with statements
like this one, which have inspired Muslims for 25 years now:

> "The first Muslims…used to accomplish important business
> on the occasion of the hajj or at their Friday gatherings. The
> Friday sermon was more than a sura from the Qur'an and a
> prayer followed by a few brief words. Entire armies used to
> be mobilized by the Friday sermon and proceed directly
> from the mosque to the battlefield—and a man who sets
> out from the mosque to go into battle will fear only God,
> not poverty or hardship, and his army will be victorious and
> triumphant."[39]

Fortunately, the 9/11 commission's report finally figured out that
we battle not against terrorists but an ideology. As one columnist
noted, "It seems like a small distinction—emphasizing ideology
instead of terror—but it makes all the difference, because if you
don't define your problem correctly, you can't contemplate a strategy for victory."[40]

He continued:

> "The commissioners don't say it, but the implication is
> clear. We've had an investigation into our intelligence fail-
> ures; we now need a commission to analyze our intellectual
> failures. Simply put, the unapologetic defenders of America
> often lack the expertise they need. And scholars who really
> know the Islamic world are often blind to its pathologies.
> They are so obsessed with the sins of the West, they are
> incapable of grappling with threat to the West."[41]

That's where missionaries like me come in. We are neither
"unapologetic defenders of America" nor "blind to (Islam's)
pathologies." This is why dozens of people in the audiences who
have heard my presentations on Islam ask: "Have you spoken with
anyone in the State Department? Why don't we ever hear this?"

Missionaries have a clear-eyed, in-depth, unique knowledge of
Islam and its followers. We speak their languages and have gained

entrance into their hearts. We are removed enough from American hyper-patriotism to analyze the missteps of our homeland and how they inflame the Islamic world. The problem with U.S. intelligence is not only a bureaucratic conflict among competing agencies, but a lack of familiarity with the Islamic worldview, at ground level. As Reuven Paz, an Israeli terrorism expert has said, "The intelligence community in the United States does not understand Islamic culture. I'm saying that after being in Washington for the past two years. I know they have so much information…but they cannot understand it or use it."[42]

Perhaps part of the problem is the paltry $5 million in our budget dedicated to foreign public opinion polling, less than the research costs in many U.S. senatorial or gubernatorial campaigns.[43] With such limited knowledge about how the rest of the world thinks, our leaders' ignorance of global opinion leads to nasty surprises when we interact with other nations and peoples. More than ever, mediators between American and foreign cultures must give the confused a crash course in international perspectives.

It's time to assemble all the pieces of this puzzle before our world explodes in a conflict of civilizations. This book represents a summary of the seminars I have presented around the country in the past two years; I write at the request of my audiences, who have requested a written record of my views and predictions. In those seminars, I present many warnings, the most dire of which I will develop in this book. In our struggle against Islamic terrorism, one of the many quandaries that our country faces can be summarized in two parts: 1) if this conflict is truly a "war for hearts and minds," then we face certain defeat. We live in an era dominated by thinkers that recognize no absolute truth, thus one's worldview should not be imposed on another because each have equal validity. I, however, would argue that Islamists can only be transformed by a revolutionary conversion experience to Jesus Himself, not a GI's ad-hoc distribution of used sneakers off the back of a Humvee in Iraq. Evangelism, obviously, is not in the State Department's repertoire, nor should it be. As the Smart Culture Cards issued to military personnel headed to Iraq order: "Don't engage in religious discussions."[44]

Furthermore, Christian missionaries who are not restrained by a government employee's need to remain religiously neutral confront opposition from dozens of governments, namely those in Islamic nations who have no interest in aiding the fulfillment of the Great Commission (Matthew 28:18-20) given by Christ. Such workers for the Gospel rarely gain entrance into Muslim countries for long periods of time, and when they do get a visa, they are forbidden to proselytize. Islam clearly sanctions horrific punishments for apostates both in this life and the next. Built-in societal, cultural and religious mechanisms hold Muslims in an iron grip, preventing them from discovering truth on their own. So, conversions will be limited, few hearts and minds will be changed, and only a small remnant will be won, to use biblical terms. We are cornered by our own secular government and the Islamic republics we seek to impact. I would add that conditions remain desperate enough for impoverished billions that they will not be swayed by any propaganda campaign of Western origin, no matter how clever, splashy or well-funded. The battle to change minds and encourage a wave of moderate Islam will continue to be unwinnable.

2) the best strategy for the United States, in light of 1), would be to withdraw most of our forces from the Middle East for a time, allow certain nations to install theocratic governments and then stand by as they inevitably fail. Citizens of those countries would quickly discover that moderate, modernizing Muslims are best equipped to run a country in today's world. V.S. Naipaul's Nobel-prize winning book, *Among the Believers: An Islamic Journey*, repeatedly makes the point that theocratic governments based on *sharia* law inevitably disappoint because flawed human beings must still impose the law and control the ruling structure. Disillusionment rapidly sets in and many begin to question Islam, especially the fundamentalist version. For proof, I would ask: have you ever talked with an Iranian about his country? It's hard to find a single one who thinks it is proceeding on a sound, productive path in the modern world. Most educated Iranians become quite emotional when discussing the destruction of their homeland. Another more current example would be Afghanistan. How many pro-Taliban Afghans could we find who would argue that the revolution there was a success and the country better off as a result? Unfortunately, we do not have the luxury of watching such regimes bloom and wither in a few years' time; we have too many "interests" at stake (read: oil), so we must intervene in the region to ensure a continual flow of petroleum

to our nation. I do not doubt for a minute the sincere desire of the present administration to spread "freedom and democracy" in the Islamic world. I do doubt that Muslims will ever find our troops to be a welcome presence during this process. They will always be repugnant, especially when stationed on or near holy ground in Iraq and Saudi Arabia. Our best-intentioned plans in the Middle East will continue to do more harm than good to our national security.

I also write because Americans have little contact with destitute Muslims and cannot possibly comprehend the dire situations that impel many of them to foment revolution. Most Muslims who live in the U.S. come from an elite class in their home countries and practice a more secularized, far less zealous adaptation of Islam. These doctors, engineers and traders are often happy to be in the U.S. and are critical of fundamentalists. They comprise the most visible face of Islam in our offices and on the airwaves. They do not, however, represent a majority of Muslims worldwide, the average Muslim. In reality, they constitute a tiny fraction of Islam's followers, and their views on life, their faith, the West and the future represent a minority viewpoint, albeit the one we hear most often. I, though, have had the privilege of living among the incensed masses. I have heard their cries for help and watched them suffer. A compassionate portrayal of their complaints rarely gets airtime or column space in American publications.

In an uncertain age where the terror threat index changes colors like a chameleon, the American public deserves a thorough examination of all these subjects, an analysis that is neither fanatically critical of Islam nor vulnerable to its latest public relations campaign. The time has come for a balanced look at this second-most-popular faith and its people, which will help us to better understand what is occurring in countries around the world where Muslims are making themselves seen and heard as never before. What motivates a people to revolution? How far will that revolution spread? To hear top administration officials say that Islam is a "religion of peace" and then note that terrorists "hate freedom" has pushed me to the boiling point. In addition, my fellow countrymen, friends and relatives fight and die in Iraq with no clear plan for an exit, continually surprised by Third World culture and Islamic tendencies. One faux pas after another has created an imbroglio that dominates the headlines, sways elections, aggravates tensions and swells the ranks of confirmed terrorists.

I write because, as a *Newsweek* analysis of the 9/11 Commission Report said: "Grimly, what the new 9/11 report makes clear is that nearly three years into the war on terror, America is still not close to understanding the enemy."[45] I believe I know that "enemy" better than many, having spent time with them in a wide variety of settings over the past decade. Few of the American "experts" who offer interpretations of Islam and terrorism seem to have spent much time with typical Muslims in overseas contexts. I see gaping holes in the theories of those who predict the future of Islam based only on world history or socio-political analyses. In short, precious little information exists in print that is drawn from the street level of worldwide Islam.

Richard Clarke, the former head of counterterrorism at the National Security Council and author of *Against All Enemies: Inside America's War on Terror*, repeated a popular view on engaging the "enemy," Islam's "radical" wing of "jihadists" in a recent editorial:

"In addition to 'hearts and minds' television and radio programming by the American government, we would be greatly helped by a pan-Islamic council of respected spiritual and secular leaders to coordinate (without United States involvement) the Islamic world's own ideological effort against the new Al-Qaeda."[46]

This begs the question: are we sure that this subset of Muslims is "radical" and unpopular? Do we think such a council of Muslims could even be assembled, let alone respected by the hungry, unemployed millions who want revolution? Are we sure that world conquest by violent conflict is not part of Islam? A primary thesis of this book will be that certain combustible elements have existed in Islam since its inception, and we will be powerless to nullify the effect of those core teachings and beliefs and the resulting behaviors. These seeds of conflict can never be modified because they have been implanted into the faith; they are part of Islam's genetic code, and that DNA is being cloned around the world at a rapid rate. For instance, the Koran, Allah's incarnation on earth, features a healthy dose of exhortation to war against non-believers, to the tune of one in every 55 verses, as Don Richardson has highlighted in his recent work *Secrets of the Koran*.[47]

Incorrect Reactions to Islam's Re-emergence

One reaction to these truths about the warrior nature of Islam is to color all Muslims as wild-eyed terrorists. I write also to correct the notions of some of my fellow evangelicals who have reacted to fundamentalism's rise by stereotyping Muslims as evil, half-human creatures who constantly think of death and destruction. This caricature oversimplifies reality, lacks accuracy and can prove to be quite harmful. We human beings, if truth be told, share many of the same aspirations and desires in life. Our upbringing determines much of how we view the world and how it can achieve its ideal state. Muslims cannot be faulted for being raised in a faith that calls for worldwide domination by almost any means. They should not be culpable for worshiping a book penned by a man who raided caravans to feed his band of soldiers and killed many opponents who blocked his imperialistic goals. In addition, those who worship Allah, even halfheartedly, have almost no exit out of the faith. Growing up in a free and fluid society can lead us to believe that anyone can change their path in life or their religious affiliation. Having ingratiated myself into two Muslim cultures, I can testify that leaving Islam is like slipping out of a straitjacket. Rare is the person capable of bursting out of this constricting community. The chokehold that Islam places on its followers should arouse compassion, not scorn, among followers of Christ.

Another equally dangerous evangelical reaction to the fundamentalist threat is to re-broadcast the idea that the world is assuredly going to Hell, very quickly, but we will escape its annihilation when Christ snatches His people out of the morass. This idea has proven so popular that 100 million books have been sold featuring the eschatological view that Christ will return twice—once to gather His flock before nuclear exchanges broil our planet and another time to set up His kingdom on earth. The authors of the series promoting this interpretation of biblical prophecy landed on the cover of *Newsweek*, but only after outselling almost every other book in the past few years. The reason for the popularity of the *Left Behind* series? The *Newsweek* profiler offers: "In an age of terror and tumult, (future scholars) may find these books' Biblical literalism offered certitude to millions of Americans amid the chaos of their time."[48]

I shudder at that word "certitude." If Americans are certain about a school of prophetic interpretation that was hatched just 140 years ago and subsequently taught primarily in the United States, then we had better expand our reading list! I don't want to plunge into theological arguments, but I have been stunned in my travels to discover how few believers in other countries subscribe to a pre-Tribulation Rapture of the Church. This predicted sequence of events finds its roots in a dispensational theology that has gained far from universal acceptance, yet appeals to the American yearning for a happy ending with minimal discomfort. Believers from other churches around the globe accept suffering as part of the Christian life; they have lived through it. They know that God often does not spare His people from agony, that His word in fact promises such anguish for those who follow Christ closely. These believers have watched their pastors be executed, they've prayed for personal friends who have been imprisoned for their faith, they've watched their churches burn. They find it absurd to believe that the Church somehow will escape earth's final hour of tumult, the culmination of Satan's rage against the redeemed.

I seek to counter this escapist mind-set through this book because, if the Church is also "left behind," then I want her to be well informed of what could transpire, rather than have her toss her faith away at the first sign of trouble and persecution. I would love for Messrs. LaHaye and Jenkins to be correct, but I don't think that they are. Why not prepare for the worst, then be pleasantly surprised if we do acquire a front-row seat in Heaven while the world explodes and new believers are slaughtered? We can even order perfect popcorn! I said once that I should have warned Americans about terrorism and the global reach of Islamic anger. I give that warning now and risk assuming the role of the prophet Jeremiah so that the U.S., and particularly the American church, will be forewarned about the difficult days ahead, the "time of Jacob's trouble" (Jeremiah 30:7). I think this period will have a distinctly Islamic flavor.

I have seen a swell of world anger directed at my nation, and I cannot stay silent. I have heard hours of venomous spite heaped on my country's head and I must relay the message, however distorted it might be. I am under obligation to warn peace-loving Americans about the true gathering storm in the Islamic world. Saddam Hussein was *not* at its epicenter; he actually impeded it. Now he, too, has been brushed aside. I feel like a man who has traveled to a far country and seen a tidal wave approaching his homeland. Upon my return, I want to describe to you the height, depth, color and roar of that breaker, its curl and the fear it induces. As I've read my Bible, I have figured out why that whitecap looks as it does, and why God has allowed it to gather force.

This book will not serve as another primer on Islam. Other authors have done a far better job than I in explaining the basics of that faith. I do not claim to be an expert on Islam nor do I speak fluent Arabic. I am, however, electrified by the convergence of Islamic and biblical prophecy, and I have seen a vision of the future that I must offer for consideration. Meeting Wahhabite missionaries in West Africa, conversing with former members of a terrorist group while in France, reading about Muslims' confidence in the triumph of Islam, I have formed a Last Days scenario that could quite possibly become reality in the next decade. I would be in sin were I not to share it.

Moreover, I can no longer hold my tongue or pen as I witness the curious, continuing conspiracy of silence regarding certain secrets of the Islamic faith. I hope to overturn a few of its concealing rocks and examine the disquieting ideas underneath, among them: 1) the anti-Jewish bile that dominates Islamic discourse and has been a part of the faith from its founding, 2) the Islamic agenda for the future, which calls for world obedience to Allah, in fulfillment of several Koranic commands, 3) the Islamic vision of the End Times, which awaits two men, including Jesus, for its realization.

In all of my news-gathering, reading on Islam and personal exposure to Muslim teachers, I seldom hear these topics tackled. The hour has arrived to expose them and then determine the implications for all of us. Most importantly, we need to figure out how God might use these features of the Islamic faith in His master plan. In all of this investigation, I guard a love for and appreciation of Muslim people, a God-given affection for them. I am convinced that the Lord loves them, too. Coupled with that love is a judgment of a faith that does contain truth but ultimately proves false. This brilliant lie has held more than a billion people in its grasp. It might soon lasso several more billion. This combination of empathy and anger arises from my decade of living shoulder-to-shoulder with Muslim people.

Life As an Embedded Missionary

During my term in Côte d'Ivoire, I observed worship at the mosque several times, learned the language of the Muslim people there (Jula) and became part of their community to the point of being playfully invited to address the faithful during the all-night celebration of the Night of Power, the 27th night of Ramadan, marking Mohammed's first revelations from the angel Gabriel. I and a missionary colleague were later criticized in a Friday message given by the imam of our city's largest mosque. Thousands of Muslims were told to avoid two white men who spoke Jula, would greet passers-by saying "Asalaam aleykum" and then try to corrupt a Muslim's faith! I considered it an honor to be singled out for such shunning.

My years in the Third World city of Bouaké gave me great insight into the lives of the world's majority, who struggle in desperate poverty. News reports from other cities in developing countries have convinced me of the amazing similarities between Bouaké and Baghdad, Abidjan and Cairo. Living among these flat broke families and witnessing their courageous struggle to earn a living taught me much about life. Those years would give any observant person a profound perception into why desperately poor people perform desperate acts, often in the name of Islam.

Through daily interactions with Muslims, I compiled a solid profile of how they think and feel, how they view the world, what they are seeking in this life. That accumulated data more than doubled when I moved to a ghetto outside of Paris. Here, I encountered a different version of Islam, a more bitter and angry twist on the faith. It was far harder to make friends in France. North Africans unaccustomed to kindness from white people viewed me with suspicion, and I was told more than once that Muslims had pigeonholed me as an undercover narcotics cop. Why else would a Caucasian befriend Arabs? Once past the initial wariness, and after a thorough quiz on U.S. foreign policy (which I always passed when I did not endorse it unreservedly!), I was able to sit and drink tea with neighbors and hear their stories. My network ranged from a former member of the Islamic Salvation Front in Algeria to a Tunisian engineer, from a mentally disturbed Moroccan to a French-born university student who confessed to be a woman without a country. These friends taught me much as well, viewing life and God through a far different vantage point than their West African brethren. Singed by racism, intrigued yet troubled by fundamentalism, they had varying degrees of devotion to religion. Provoked enough in conversation, they revealed a scary sense of honor, brotherhood and revenge that I would never forget.

I was privileged to visit secret places in Paris—not the sewers that tourists walk through—but a different underground. I sat pensively in an office while scanning a map where pushpins indicated the future sites of mosques and Koranic schools in the metropolitan area. I celebrated the end of Ramadan in a huge Islamic rally that filled a large meeting hall. I toured a storefront school of Arabic that was fresh off winning its first French convert.

My knowledge of Islam, thus, boasts more than what can be gleaned from books, pamphlets and Web sites. It is deeper, richer, a priceless firsthand awareness gained from a decade among these people, eating in their homes, visiting their workplaces and listening in their houses of worship. My ear has been to the ground as Islam has thrust itself onto the world stage. I have seen Islamic anger spilled out in my living room, in the mosque, in a crowded market. I have heard the yearning for a better day, when Allah will triumph, both in person and through voluminous reading that has taken me to other Islamic lands.

No one's understanding of this detailed religious system and its followers can be complete. I do encourage you, reader, to trust me as I try to explain this people and their place in our world today. You can, perhaps, find better guides in the world. Yet I stand humbly as a bridge between my American past and the Islamic present. The best guides know something of both worlds.

Chapter Two

The Twigs Are Tender, The Leaves Are Out: Closing In On the End Times

People who have attended my seminars have later confessed to me their unfavorable attitudes before hearing my presentations. When they hear the subject of *Islam and the End Times*, they shut down, unwilling to hear yet another version of how the world will self-destruct. Before breezing through this chapter, I beg you to track with me and follow my construction of a context for the ascension of an Islamic antichrist in the near future.

Oh, and you can relax as well. This chapter won't lead to the founding of a new denomination or cult!

Doomsday prophets have cried wolf too many times over the past 30 years. Scores of books have been published with arguments for the imminence of Armageddon, seminars have spread from coast to coast, movies have been made and distributed, and yet we are all still here!

The accumulation of this sometimes-frantic false prophecy produces an understandable, albeit undesirable, effect: weary of so many unfulfilled predictions and an overemphasis on the Last Days at the expense of here-and-now kingdom living, millions of Christians have tuned out any more mention of the Great Tribulation and World War III. I identify with this End Times fatigue, coming as I do from a generation that grew up with Hal Lindsay, the first movies about the Rapture and intensive Bible studies on the book of Revelation. Cults have risen and fallen based on eschatalogical prophecies, too, and imagined disasters such as the Y2K scare have conditioned us to be even more reluctant to believe that the world will implode shortly. For all of its problems, planet Earth seems to possess remarkable powers of recovery as she lurches along. Life does go on.

The danger in this rusting of our spiritual antennae is that we will become like the generation of Noah—merrily eating, drinking, going through life's traditional cultural milestones and caught completely unaware by the last chapter of time (Matthew 24:37-39). I write, in part, to ward off this deadening of our mystical nerve endings, which I believe are supernaturally fabricated to keep us all in a perpetual state of alertness. Evidence of this built-in readiness can be seen in the success of the *Left Behind* series and recent movie titles such as *End of Days* and *Armageddon*.

I offer this chapter as dispassionately as possible. Please do not picture an over-caffeinated televangelist screaming about the last hours of Earth. Wipe away the images of the gentleman who was wrong 20 years ago when he claimed that Jesus would return in 1990 in the cassette series that you ordered from a 1-800 number, believing it your Christian duty to do so. Instead, let's calmly and rationally evaluate a portion of Biblical prophecy to consider anew if world events are pointing towards the final act, as described in Scripture. I have narrowed my focus to Matthew 24 because the predictions there pour straight from God's mouth, they minimize confusion, and they can be measured. Jesus gave us phenomena to track in order to raise not our terror level of awareness, but our joy at the coming of His kingdom. One gauge in particular, which I will examine in detail, lends itself to precise analysis, I believe.

The same people who have entered my seminars with a skeptical, dazed, even hostile attitude have always emerged nodding their heads in agreement that the picture I paint of the proximity of Christ's return makes sense. I want to convert you as well, not to scare you, but to convince you that the present day merits vigilance and preparedness.

To submit the argument that the current surge in Islamic fundamentalism will lead directly into the End Times, we must first construct a frame of reference that would favor the occurrence of such an event. In other words, proof must exist that we live in the Last Days, evidence independent of Islam and its movements. Sitting on the Mount of Olives a week before His crucifixion, Jesus painted a picture of "the end of the age" for His inquisitive disciples. Beginning in verse 5 of Matthew 24, He tells them, and us, to watch for wars and rumors of wars (vv. 6,7), famines and earthquakes (v. 7), widespread persecution of believers (vv. 9,10), false prophets (vv. 5,11), and lawlessness (v. 12). He concluded His list of signs with a parable from the fig tree, pointing out that when its branch "becomes tender, and puts forth its leaves, you know that summer is near." In the same way, He added, "when you see all these things, recognize that He is near, right at the door" (v. 33). How many leaves can be seen in 2005? How tender are the twigs? Documentation can be marshaled to prove that all of these phenomena sweep our world today in unprecedented levels, or that they have appeared at a constant rate over the past two millennia. Without question, our globe has hosted a stunning number of wars and skirmishes throughout human history; legendary famines and earthquakes have plagued certain societies for centuries, false prophets have appeared with regularity. In addition, each generation thinks the next age group gives new definition to "lawlessness," and Christians have been martyred since the earliest days of the Church.

Let's consider, briefly, the evidence that some of these omens appear more ominous than ever before, being sure to guard our intellectual integrity and admitting that catastrophic events have always been with us. I will close this chapter by focusing on the most easily measurable sign in the passage, the famous verse that calls for the gospel of the kingdom to be preached to all nations before Christ's return.

Wars and Rumors of Wars

For decades, observers could make the case that our world was filled with "wars and rumors of wars." Two horrible, bloody world wars lured most of the globe into conflict in the twentieth century. After those epics, the Cold War spawned many armed engagements as the United States and Soviet Union supplied one side or another with firepower in their race for global supremacy. People groups around the globe have agitated for independence for years as well, from the Basque people in Spain and France to the Kurds in central Asia. A careful monitoring of current events, however, does seem to point to a new progression of armed conflict, powered by unlikely twin forces: democracy and Islam. As several nations rapidly gained independence after the fall of the Berlin Wall in 1989, other emboldened people groups petitioned for sovereignty, challenging historic borders and fighting, if necessary, to redraw them. Thus, Eritrea broke away from Ethiopia, the Kurds battled for an expanded homeland and several peoples fought for control in a newly configured Democratic Congo.

Islam motivates many other groups to engage in battle for a separate state where *sharia* law will predominate (Chechnya) or for a theocratic regime in a currently secular state (Algeria, Afghanistan). Still other Islamic states seek to conquer less Islamized regions of their own countries and thus bring the entire country under Allah's sway (Sudan).[49] In a later chapter I will explain the combustibility of these two forces—democracy and Islam—and reveal how ambassadors of "freedom" will actually help to create countries that suffocate liberty as fundamentalist Islamic governments proliferate, an unfortunate, ironic twist as the world becomes more democratic.

Are there wars and rumors of wars in 2005? The United Nations defines a "major war" as one in which 1,000 battlefield deaths occur each year. The globalsecurity.org Web site states that 16 such wars rage at present, with 20 minor conflicts threatening to erupt into the fiercer category. About one-half of these clashes feature Muslims, a percentage that will almost certainly increase.[50] One ghastly change in the nature of these regional disputes is the proportion of civilians who are slaughtered, rising from just 5 percent of the death toll in World War I, for example, to an incredible 75 percent today. Those affected non-combatants would certainly maintain that war touches the world in a more all-encompassing fashion in modern times. Such terrorizing conflict led one observer to summarize the global scene as follows: "The millennium ended with much of the world consumed in armed conflict or cultivating an uncertain peace."[51]

Whether or not we can determine that our world has degenerated into a more divisive, violent place, one trend is indisputable: the disintegration of nations into smaller states, which has created a momentum that will continue to birth independence movements. Robert Kaplan, an astute and award-winning author whose books have guided American presidents, makes the point in his work *The Ends of the Earth* that freedom fighters are redrawing the world map to more closely resemble the chaotic cartography of the seventeenth century rather than the neat divisions of the late twentieth. In his travels throughout the Third World, he found several disaffected peoples who desired independence and prepared to take action. He makes a powerful argument for a coming, unprecedented reconfiguration of nation-states via secession and bloody uprisings.[52] As a student of African history, I can vouch that the retreat of Cold War rivals and colonial powers from the continent energized many rebel groups to take the offensive and carve out a kingdom. I have listened to such revolutionaries on my front porch, when they asked me for their support in 1999, three years before they grabbed half of Côte d'Ivoire. Their standoff with government forces has yet to be satisfactorily resolved, as essentially two nations operate within the borders of one previous state.

Calculations on the number of wars and the resulting statistical comparisons to previous eras should not be used to sound any trumpets and herald the return of Jesus. However, an undeniable wind of freedom does blow around the globe as the number of nation-states grows. Insurrectionists around the world have taken up arms to create sovereign areas for their people groups as perhaps never before. Jesus did not predict an increase in wars, simply a globe racked by wars and rumors of wars. Sadly, that condition has afflicted our planet for centuries, and certainly does now.

Famines and Earthquakes

Verse 7b highlights two other characteristics of "the beginning of birth pangs": famine and earthquakes. Famines have plagued various peoples since the beginning of time, as have earthquakes. Both biblical historians and writers in other ancient cultures noted the occurrence of these calamities in the millennia before Christ, and they continue to this day. We all have faced the moral dilemma of channel surfing only to tumble upon footage of a bone-thin child holding a cup while waiting in line for a daily food ration. If we continue to surf does it mean our hearts have grown hopelessly callous? If we choose not to give to the intervening charity, do we violate Christ's command to care for the poor? It's a lot to think about at 5 A.M.! Evidence of the fall of all creation when man sinned, famines are not new and have not been eliminated in our modern world.

Despite generation after generation of concerned scientists who have optimistically predicted the end of world hunger, a tricky element called human nature has halted progress in feeding all peoples. Bread for the World Institute, a nonprofit anti-hunger education and research organization, revealed in its latest annual report on the state of world hunger a "backtracking"—not an advance—on the ambitious goal set by world leaders in the mid-1990s: cutting hunger in half by 2015. Hunger has indeed decreased throughout the developing world from the 1970s through the mid-'90s, but the number has jumped by 5 million annually since then. The Institute found that political leadership lacked the will to effectively fight hunger in almost every nation concerned. The report also blamed trade rules and crushing international debt for the regression in this crucial battle. Many African nations, for instance, spend more on debt repayment than they receive in aid. In most instances, world trade agreements do not empower Third World farmers, either, to grow enough food to feed their fellow countrymen. Details of their woes can be found on many Web sites and in scores of books.[53]

Unfortunately, other facts of modern life have combined to exacerbate famine in the past decade, among them the HIV virus and the rapid urbanization of our planet. The HIV virus not only kills people, it aggravates famines as well. More than 40 million people live with the infection, and many of them work in rural agriculture. Farms cease to be tilled as heads of households die and women and children are unable to make the land profitable. Fewer hands are available to raise crops because of the world's rush to the cities as well. In 1800, just 3 percent of the world lived in urban areas; by 2030, 60 percent will crowd into cities, with the most dramatic increases occurring in developing nations.[54] In short, very few young people want to farm as their fathers did, from the U.S. to the Ukraine. I can tell you from personal experience that young people in the villages of developing nations do not want to work the earth for small profits when they can strike it rich in the city (they suppose) as a trader, a tailor or a taxi driver. I never once met a teenager in Côte d'Ivoire's rural communities who wanted to stay in the bush when he or she matured. To further their education, these young people had to move to the cities, where there were functioning high schools. Alas, those cities did not have the infrastructures to support the population boom that has resulted. Despite advanced agricultural methods in prosperous countries, the combination of fewer people remaining in the profession and the screaming demands for foodstuffs in the world's slums produce a constant hunger that can evolve into famine in the developing world.

To add more bad news, civil strife and erratic weather patterns also have worsened world hunger. The United Nations reports that food emergencies have been declared in 35 countries, among the worst being Sudan (one million people displaced in warfare), Zambia (flooding), Zimbabwe (redistribution of land crisis), Sri Lanka (drought), and Iraq (uncertain distribution channels), among others.[55] Inconsistent climatic conditions that cause drought could result from global warming, although a lively debate in the scientific community rages on. Whatever their origin, increased floods, heat waves and other extreme weather have contributed to prolonged dry spells and crop ruination that multiply the effects of famine in recent years.[56] AIDS, drought, civil war, overfed, uncaring politicians and global warming all combine to sustain conditions for famine. Jesus said the poor would always be with us. Regretfully, famine will persist as well, despite the capacity we now have to eliminate world hunger. End Times or not, we should all, as followers of the man who multiplied the fishes and loaves, be grieved by the fact that the number of hungry people in the world increased during the last half of the 1990s by 18 million, to a total of 842 million, *reversing* a steady drop over the past three decades, according to a recent study by a United Nations agency. More than one in seven people in the world endures chronic hunger, which is measured by a daily intake of fewer than 1,700 calories and a lack of access to safe and nutritious food.[57]

"In various places there will be famines" certainly rings true in 2005. News of devastating earthquakes jumps onto our front pages quite frequently as well. A rapid scan of the frequency and locations of earthquakes could yield just about any "proof" that we seek to argue for an appearance of Last Days tremors. Those who would make a case for a skyrocketing total point to reliable figures published by the U.S. Geological Survey, failing to add that the number of seismograph stations worldwide has increased even more rapidly. Major earthquakes, which register greater than 7.0 on the Richter scale, "have remained fairly constant throughout this century," according to the USGS. The number of stations measuring such quakes has ballooned from 350 in 1931 to more than 4,000 today, thus making us more aware of the quakes that do occur.[58] The 50 earthquakes that strike daily around the world do seem to have rumbled recently in areas that have not typically experienced such upheavals. People from West Virginia to Iran will tell you that their communities have not felt the ground shaking beneath their feet until the past few years. The locations for tremors in the past decade do strike observers as curious, as long-dormant faults move without warning.

One fact cannot be debated: the number of people killed in major earthquakes has shown an appreciable increase in the past few decades, with more than one million total deaths from quakes in the twentieth century. This grisly trend results, of course, from the larger numbers of people in an increasingly urban world; as a result of humanity packing into smaller spaces, earthquakes now kill people more efficiently than ever. Some experts predict a tenfold increase in such deaths during the coming century.[59] I would add that these higher numbers of deaths could be limited if public opinion were aroused to battle the too-common practice of corrupt government officials granting permits to bribe-paying developers who escape building inspections. All of the deadly "acts of God" have an evil underside of human nature that multiplies the effects of such tragedies, as apartment towers erected without any heed for building codes quickly collapse when the ground shakes, killing most of the dwellers within. The next time you read about the large numbers of casualties in a developing nation after an earthquake, remember this often overlooked factor.

Persecution of Christians

In addition to natural disasters such as famines and earthquakes, Jesus also said that His followers would perish from persecution in great numbers before His return. Again, the statistics point to an increase in this phenomenon, despite only occasional press coverage of this outrage.

Paul Marshall, senior fellow at the Center for Religious Freedom, Freedom House, in Washington, D.C., traveled a short time ago to 20 countries to document the suffering of our brothers and sisters in Christ. His thorough examination of persecution around the world, *Their Blood Cries Out*, has been cited in Congress and provoked reactions in several other countries.[60]

In his book, Marshall details the horrible suffering of millions of believers worldwide. From his research, called "an exhaustive survey that cannot be ignored" by the U.S. Senate, he estimates that 200 million Christians face "violence, imprisonment, torture and death for their faith."[61] Let that number sink in a bit before you read on, and let us all admit that we had no idea the problem was so vast.

The Christian Church faces a nasty confluence of factors in the early twenty-first century that have aroused opposition to her. As Michael Horowitz, senior fellow at the Hudson Institute, a Washington think tank, explains: "Minority Christian communities have become chosen scapegoats in radical Islamic and remnant Communist regimes, where they are demonized and caricatured through populist campaigns of hate and terror."[62] The few remaining Communist regimes, in places such as China, Vietnam and Cuba, have heeded the tremendous influence of Christian churches in the overturn of Communism in Eastern Europe. For this reason, these countries have stepped up their surveillance of the Church. As a 1992 article in the Chinese state-run press advised regarding the emergence of Christianity in that country: "we must strangle the baby while it is still in the manger."[63] Someone should remind Chinese officials that this strategy did not work 2000 years ago for King Herod, and it will not work now.

In addition, the revival of militant Islam has led to the targeting of Christians throughout the Middle East and Asia. In lands such as Saudi Arabia, Qatar, Sudan and Mauritania, laws mandate the death penalty for apostasy. Anyone who leaves Islam to convert to Christ is subject to beheading. Fresh news accounts of the genocide in Sudan have brought a welcome focus on the cruel face of this anti-Christian spirit in some forms of Islam. Between 1.5 and 3 million Christians have died already in Sudan, and another 100,000 are bought and sold as slaves there today.[64]

Sadly, it appears that the twenty-first century will surpass the bloody twentieth century, when more Christians were killed for their faith than in all the 19 centuries that preceded it. The current state of believers in many nations certainly matches Christ's vision in Matthew 24: "you will be hated by all nations on account of My name." Organizations such as Voice of the Martyrs (www.persecution.org) highlight the struggles of Christians in the 40+ countries where followers of Jesus face daily persecution. I would not recommend such reading for peaceful sleeping, although I do believe we need to awaken from our slumber regarding this ongoing outrage.

False Prophets

Not only will true believers be hated, hunted and killed in the Last Days, other people of faith will be led astray to a Christ-less eternity by legions of false prophets. Do more spout their heresy now than in previous eras? That's another difficult sign to verify. False prophets have existed as long as there have been men and women who claim to have special insight from God or some other spiritual entity. Christ's words in Matthew 24 hint at a boom of this movement in the Last Days. Again, data abounds that can prove or disprove a resurgence of false teaching, but our age has undoubtedly witnessed a new spiritual quest by millions who have decided against classic Christianity and instead sought truth and meaning in other varieties of Christianity and non-Christian faiths. For example, due to the increased contact between Asia and the Western world after World War II, as well as a renewed spirituality in the 1960s and '70s, Eastern religions have surged in popularity in Europe and North America.[65] Changes in American immigration laws accelerated this exchange between the two hemispheres, and the resulting "new religious movements," referred to as "cults" in an earlier time, have mushroomed. Approximately 500-600 "alternative religions" have gained followers in the U.S. One writer noted that the "emergence of parapsychology...and the rise of alternative branches of the psychological disciplines...established a scientific basis for the introspective search which Eastern and Occult religions claimed as their special expertise."[66]

This growth, of course, has not been restricted to the U.S. One medical doctor who has studied cults extensively wrote in *The Harvard Mental Health Letter* that "cults represent one aspect of a worldwide epidemic of ideological totalism, or fundamentalism." He continued: "The current historical context of dislocation from organizing symbolic structures, decaying belief systems concerning religion, authority, marriage, family and death...is conducive to the growth of cults."[67]

This rise in false prophets has infected the Christian Church as well. Thirty-four thousand separate Christian movements now gather adherents around the globe; more than one-half of these are independent churches that have become, in effect, their own denominations.[68] Free from an accountability structure that often helps to ensure doctrinal purity, these unaffiliated churches can easily adopt heretical ideas under the guidance of one charismatic leader who begins to mix Christianity with other systems of thought. I can testify to the outbreak of such unregulated groups that insist on freedom from denominational strictures in Africa. This separation proves healthy in many instances, but the cult-like tendencies and false teaching that seep into certain groups can damage people spiritually, emotionally, and sometimes even physically. I have interviewed several Ivorians who have left such assemblies. Their descriptions of cultic practices such as group sex, signing over their savings to church leaders and living in communal compounds chilled me. Again, God can choose to work through new wineskins in the church, and many wonderful stirrings of His Spirit have occurred through anointed prophets in Africa and other parts of the world. However, when entire congregations are deliberately burned to death during church gatherings or bankrupted through swindling clergy (both of which have occurred in Africa in the past few years), the roots of such evil can often be traced to a man or woman who has become both intoxicated with power and allergic to accountability. Scripture tells us to test the spirits to verify that they are indeed from God (1 John 4:1). Beware the preacher who has "heard from the Lord" and has a fresh vision for what the Church should be. Rather than passively accept the proliferation of false teaching in this era, let all of us who name Christ's name be diligent to teach truth and to guard people from this epidemic of phony prophets. We must be more active than ever in helping God-fearers to anchor themselves in the Bible, even more so in this climate of cult cloning.

Lawlessness

In conjunction with these counterfeit teachers and the misleading of many, Christ foresaw an increase in lawlessness that would cause people's love to grow cold (Matthew 24:11,12). Citizens around the world complain of rising crime rates, and a majority of Americans insist that our country grows less secure each year, despite statistics that point to the contrary.[69] While crime rates actually have dipped in the past few years in many American cities, different forms of crime have abounded both here and abroad. We can rejoice that many urban areas witness fewer violent crimes than they did 10 years ago, but other forms of lawbreaking among the higher classes, such as fraud and corporate corruption, have garnered headlines. When we hear the word "lawlessness," we immediately picture angry mobs raiding stores and dark, filthy city streets where muggers rule the turf. We must not forget, however, how crime has found its way inside the board room as well. In fact, many more people are affected by even one act of accounting chicanery, with the life savings and pensions of hundreds or thousands vanishing, than the thievery of one hapless mugger. Organizations that track such white collar crime report that rates have spiked, even as violent and property crime has ebbed in the U.S.[70]

In other countries, the crime report provides no encouragement of any kind, no trend towards safer neighborhoods. The United Nations has identified criminal activity as one of its primary global challenges in the twenty-first century, as entrenched forms of a variety of illegal activities restrict certain nations' development. It fascinates me how little we hear about this problem of the human heart when the developing world is discussed. In short, sin hinders a nation's progress. For instance, a number of researchers have turned their attention to Africa and its elite class's "massive involvement" in criminal activities such as drug smuggling, financial fraud and coercion/violence, which they say poisons entire societies and hinders their advance.[71]

Africa is not alone in its wrestling against unlawful acts. Two authors that have tracked global crime rates reported in a recent article that our world is witnessing a "steeply rising global rate of combat-unrelated violence." A 34-country sample uncovered a 50 percent increase in such crime in just one decade's time; Latin America suffered an 80 percent increase, and the Arab world spiked an incredible 112 percent.[72] The reasons for this escalation? The survey tabbed: aggressive cultures, ineffective justice systems, the huge slice of 18-24-year-olds in developing countries, reduced social inhibitions, population density, anonymity, poverty, urban social disintegration, greater awareness of income irregularities, the media's emphasis on violence and aggression, and the increased availability of guns and drugs, a dispiriting catalogue of causes, to be sure.[73]

When people ask me about my time abroad, they almost always focus on my family's safety, assuming that we lived in peril in Africa and tranquility in France. The reverse was true on most days, but petty crime thrived in both places, especially in the Parisian suburbs. Violent crime remained more rare due to a paucity of firearms. In each locale, my neighbors would tell me that the younger generation committed more crimes than the previous one due to the breakdown of societal morality and a newly fluid sense of right and wrong. Does our current epoch reveal an expansion of lawlessness? Most of the world would answer in the affirmative.

In summary of the auguries given by Jesus in Matthew 24:4-12, remember that entire books treating every one of these signposts individually are available for your further study. Web sites galore have sprung up to "prove" that earthquakes are on the rise and that law-abiding citizens comprise a minority in today's world. As is the case with many statistics, facts and figures gathered by both professional and amateur investigators can be used to bolster the case for both sides of the question of whether we live in the Last Days. I would never stake my belief that we live in the time of Matthew 24's fulfillment on such Web sites. I do believe, however, that solid numbers exist to support the notion that the world resembles the portrait painted by Jesus in that chapter.

The One Sure Sign: The Fulfillment of the Great Commission

For my part, I prefer to focus on the one time-sensitive sign that Christ gave, not only because my life's work has been wrapped up in it, but also because it can be more accurately measured than the other indicators. I refer, of course, to the prediction given in verse 14: "And this gospel of the kingdom shall be preached in the whole world for a witness to all the nations, and then the end shall come." Jesus told us that the story of His coming, ministry, death and resurrection must be proclaimed to all ethnic groups. Note that He says it must be preached, not embraced necessarily, by the "whole world." We do know from Revelation 7:9 that at least one representative from every tribe, nation and tongue will worship around the throne of God and before the Lamb in Heaven. This portends that, no matter what occurs in our world, Christ's church will succeed in completing the mission that He gave to her. A vast multitude will glorify the one true God, and this mosaic of redeemed souls will feature at least one representative from every people group on Earth.

Remark again that Scripture does not tell us how many souls from each people group will share in this breathtaking scene, just that every tongue will be heard in that heavenly chorale. The assumption that multitudes from each ethnicity will join us in praise, while certainly a desired outcome, cannot be proven from Scripture. God's Word promises at least one, but no more. Thus, the goal of the Great Commission needs to be more precisely defined.

Are we anticipating the conversion of the bulk of the population in every geographical nation? Jesus not only did not guarantee that result, He reminded us that the road in following Him is a narrow one, and *few* are able to tread it: "For the gate is small, and the way is narrow that leads to life, and few are those who find it" (Matthew 7:14). This fine point proves crucial as we evaluate Matthew 24:14. We must first decide what the world will look like when this Scripture is fulfilled. Will an abundance of Christian leaders preside over societies using the Bible as its legal and moral basis, or will the "triumph of the Gospel" be a less visible phenomenon, where just a handful of people in some cultures receive the Word with gladness?

Armed with a master's degree in missions, I can verify that the first vision has been favored when preachers talk about the spread of the Gospel. American optimism often flavors the image we have of a planet that has been thoroughly saturated with the message of Christ. However, having lived in far less evangelical societies, I would submit that the second picture better mirrors reality, that non-Christian majorities will always control global politics and a redeemed remnant is the most we can hope for in the majority of nations.

Missiologists differ on the objective of this Great Commission. One common viewpoint postulates that Matthew 24:14's fulfillment will result in a "viable" church in every one of the world's cultures, a church of healthy size capable of evangelizing its own people. By this definition, we certainly remain at least 40 or more years distant from the realization of Christ's global mandate. Approximately 6,900 people groups can be defined as "least reached" (less than 2 percent evangelical Christian) and more than 1,300 of those live "where the Gospel is not generally available."[74] Three thousand ethnic groups do not even have one Bible verse in their own language and dozens of countries prohibit the entry of evangelical missionaries, thus impeding any effort to establish a viable church in their lands.

To consider one concrete example, God will have to turn Saudi Arabia upside down for a sustainable church to emerge in each of its people groups. Christianity cannot be openly practiced there and is so little tolerated that Christians who die on Saudi soil cannot even be buried officially, for fear that such infidel corpses would pollute the holy land. A reproducing church in each clan inhabiting the birthplace of Islam remains a fantasy for now. Another example would be the nation of Morocco, where a recent clarion call to all followers of Jesus Christ produced just 250 pilgrims at a nationwide conference.[75] Countries such as these, held in the vise of Islam, will need to be completely and thoroughly transformed before healthy, sizable churches can materialize in them.

Other End Times "experts" exhort the Christian Church to mission by claiming that every single human being should have at least one chance to accept or reject the Gospel. This worthy goal should drive all of us in the daily ordering of our lives, but Scripture never promises that every person will have a chance to respond to Christ. Those who have spent any time in less Christianized lands struggle with the sovereignty of God when considering this dilemma—every day dozens of people perish around them who have never heard that Christ died for them. By God's grace, I have never struggled with this reality. I rarely question Him regarding His plan. I have been moved many times, though, to ask God what He will do with the millions of subjugated Muslim women who will be judged without ever having had the freedom to even seek out Christian teaching. For these women, among whom I have lived, their whole life passes without the liberty to pursue religious instruction apart from their husbands. They have been forbidden from visiting my home and contacting my wife, even if they hunger for truth. Such difficult realities I leave at the Lord's feet; He is just.

Setting aside the scenario where every single person among the Earth's 6.4 billion human inhabitants has a chance to hear a clear, understandable Gospel presentation in their heart language (again, a noble objective, I believe), we need to consider other more realistic frameworks for the fulfillment of the Great Commission. If we contemplate other possibilities of how the "unreached" will become "reached" and change the criterion from a viable church in each ethnic group to at least one believer in each group (a more exact Biblical idea), then we create an entirely new equation. For if just one person from each ethnic nation must believe on Jesus in order for Him to return, then we are handcuffed when attempting to predict a date, which Scripture says will be the case (Matthew 24:36). That conversion in the last untouched group will be a matter of the heart, done in a quiet place, unseen by the human eye or a missions tracking service.

If we could monitor the advancement of missions work like a telethon total, then the wonderful people at Wycliffe Bible translators could notify us all by e-mail regarding their final translation of the Bible. Thankfully, that sterling organization aims to complete the mammoth task of rendering the Bible in every language within the next two decades, as its literature states: "Vision 2025 mandates that Bible translation work should be at least in progress (if not completed) for each and every language that needs it by the year 2025." This target date appears to be quite feasible, praise the Lord, with the New Testament already available to 80 percent of the world's population in its native tongue.[76] The fact that Wycliffe is closing in on this praiseworthy milestone should both encourage and challenge us all. Given that the annual rate of Scripture portions translated has doubled in the past 50 years,[77] the success of this bold initiative might arrive even sooner than anticipated.

However, if the climax of the Great Commission's completion depends on one individual's heart cry, coming earlier than an every-known-language-translation date, then we are unable to pinpoint the exact time of Christ's return, as God desires. Moreover, a date for that final people group to have one of its members surrender to Jesus looms much closer than we might have thought previously. Despite the fact that closed countries do not allow missionaries into their lands to establish churches, the Gospel does cross their borders via radio and satellite TV at a record rate. Modern technology advances beyond the pace of security, as we all know.

I witnessed this electronic seed sowing while in France. Flyers appeared throughout my city announcing satellite transmissions of Christian programs on television channels beamed into North Africa, where millions would have the opportunity to hear the truth in the comfort of their own homes, shielded from government authorities. Those broadcasts produce tangible fruit. One visit to a Campus Crusade for Christ response center in suburban Paris took me into a secret, thrilling world where phones rang constantly and letters arrived by the bushel as dozens of North Africans relayed requests for more information about the Gospel. That memorable morning reminded me of God's power amidst seemingly impenetrable borders.

In His all-wise plan, God identified a ready audience for satellite TV among Muslims, who might be the biggest fans of this technology in the world because they hunger for an electronic diet more varied than the one state channel they can capture by standard antennae. When they emigrate to foreign countries, their dishes provide them with a taste of home and the melody of their native tongue and music. Those receptors sprouted like inverted mush-rooms in my neighborhood in France, despite an official ban on them in many apartment complexes. When visiting with North African friends there, I often only saw the images and narration from pan-Arab satellite channels on their screens. The Internet also attracts large crowds of Muslims wherever its tentacles reach. Cybercafés flourish in Islamic communities as young people yearn for contact with the outside world; many inquirers anonymously stop in Christian chat rooms to pose questions and later pore over Web sites that explain the real story of "Nabi Isa."

Gospel literature also continues to be scattered worldwide, with teams of short-term missionaries attempting to place Christian tracts and a *Jesus* film video in every car headed by ferry to North Africa from France and Spain, for instance. A rich variety of such literature is now available in the Arabic language, as well as in the native tongues of Islamized peoples, a heartening development of the past 20 years. Beyond the slice of the globe where I have lived, radio reaches the illiterate who cannot profit from pamphlets in their tongue. Programmers estimate that a whopping 99 percent of the world's population has access to Christian broadcasts, a fact that causes me to conclude that the moment when a listener in that last ethnic group decides to follow Jesus will soon arrive. In addi-tion, a full 90 percent of the world's population has either all or part of the Bible, the *Jesus* film or gospel recordings in their language.[78] Almost the whole world has heard the story, dear reader. The clock is ticking.

The story of the *Jesus* film merits a book in itself. Campus Crusade for Christ leaders report 5.6 billion viewings of the produc-tion as of 2003, in languages known by 90 percent of the world's population. The number of people who have watched the film has almost doubled since 1999! If that rise in viewership continues to skyrocket at that rate, one can understand my optimism about the Gospel's advance. Even if that figure represents an inflated total due to repeated exposures to the movie, Campus Crusade estimates that two-thirds of the world has seen this superb portrayal of the Gospel on film.[79] (I will share my stories of projecting that film to unreached peoples in another space.) *The Passion of the Christ*, another adaptation of the Gospel account of Jesus' life, has set box office records in nations full of previously unevangelized peoples.

The Lord has curiously used man's evil desires for His glory, as Muslims who are eager to view a supposedly anti-Semitic film leave entranced by the love of Christ.

As Steve Douglass, president of Campus Crusade for Christ International recently stated:

> "Amazingly, many Middle Eastern and North African nations (including Lebanon, Egypt, Qatar, and other even more closed nations) have allowed the showing of 'The Passion of The Christ' in movie theaters. The original motive for this may have been that officials felt the film would show Jews in a bad light. But God used this and is touching many hearts with the message of the Prince of Peace through the film!"[80]

He continues:

> "A staff member from a very sensitive nation recently wrote, 'The film is so popular here that they have been canceling the other films to show "The Passion" in all the theatres…well over 50 percent of the people watching it are local Muslims. I will close with a question asked by a national, "Do you have the New Testaments in Arabic? I and ALL my friends want to read it." This staff member said the film was being projected 19 times a day in that nation's four cinemas. He added that a friend told him, 'Everybody is talking about this movie.'"[81]

Theaters in Jordan, Syria, and the United Arab Emirates also report record crowds. The film's frequent impact can be encapsulated by the response of one young woman in Qatar. Leaving the cinema in tears, her parents asked her why she could not stop crying. She cogently replied, "Because He taught them to love their enemies!"[82] The powerful absurdity of this moral cannot be underestimated in cultures that call for revenge in order to preserve one's honor. This woman understood that the only way out of the downward spiral of violence and hatred in the world is the love and forgiveness taught by Jesus. Only a person filled with Christ's gracious Spirit can call a true cease-fire in the Middle East.

Leave it to the Lord to use a hatred for His people to reveal His splendor, the glory of His only begotten Son who died for the world. Would you or I have picked this strategy to impact the hardest spiritual soil on the planet? Probably not, but praise Him, His ways are not our ways! Could it be that He has engineered a sweep through the Islamic world for one last opportunity to respond to His truth? Even as I write, the last unreached people groups of the world are watching films and DVDs that are prompting them to give their hearts to Christ. An unprecedented movement to evangelize the world sweeps churches in other parts of the world, including the incredible renewal in China, where the Church has gained a vision to disciple all people groups from their country down to Jerusalem, which would encompass many Islamic peoples who have never heard the Gospel.[83] This vision, along with the awesome arising of a passion for Muslims in Latin America, for instance, will help to fill in the gaps as cross-cultural workers with American passports have more doors closed in their faces and face greater resistance even when on site. God Himself will wrap up the completion of His Great Commission in the next several years. With this kind of colossal Gospel dissemination, we realize that the objective of one person coming to Christ from each language is not only achievable, it is impending. In fact, it could happen any day now, all the more reason for us to lift our heads up. We cannot possibly know when a radio broadcast reaching deep into Nepal or a screening of *The Passion* in Saudi Arabia convinces a person in an untouched people group to follow Jesus.

If the idea of the Lord saving just one person from each people group troubles your heart, I appreciate your concern and would urge you to do all that you can to ensure that growing church bodies are planted in every land. I would be the last person to declare a moratorium on missions; my God-given calling and career motivate me to do otherwise. I, too, grieve when I read that just five cents of every hundred dollars given by American Christians goes to "financing pioneer church planting among unreached peoples."[84] With such feeble backing, does it surprise us that just three missionaries work to plant churches among every one million Muslims? Are we doing all we can as the American Church to accomplish the Great Commission? I wonder. Greater percentages of giving need to go to the front lines and a higher share of missionaries needs to re-deploy to true pioneer areas.

As I often tell audiences, world missions can be compared to a meal. We in the Christian church have eaten our meat and mashed potatoes as we have impacted responsive continents with the Good News. All that is left on our plate, naturally, are the peas and carrots, which we have purposely avoided—the most hostile and least accessible people groups. The worldwide Body of Christ must now decide if she is ready for one last powerful thrust into often dangerous places filled with people who are antagonistic toward Christians. To borrow from American football imagery, it's as if the Church is lining up for one final play, just one yard from the goal line. Will we dig dip to push the ball into the end zone or collapse in fatigue or fear?

Through the power of God's own Holy Spirit, we WILL accomplish this goal. Yet, ironically, we might not even know when, as a God-seeker in the heart of an Amazonian forest repents after hearing a radio broadcast or a weeping woman in a 100 percent Islamic region trusts Christ for forgiveness in a cybercafé after having her questions answered in an Internet chat room. From all indications, that final representative to complete the heavenly chorus pictured in Revelation 7 will be added in the next decade.

The leaves are out, the twigs are tender. Summer approaches. What is the climate like in the Islamic world?

Chapter Three

The Role of Islam in the End Times

With our spiritual sensors heightened and our energy directed at fulfilling Christ's Great Commission, we now must examine more closely the setting for Earth's final chapter. We have established a feasible timeline and have begun to outline the plot; now we need to fit a stage. Where do Scripture and current events point to, geographically, for this planet's final battles?

One strategy for drawing this map would be to identify key players in the End Times, such as the antichrist predicted in numerous biblical passages, and see if we have any clues as to their origin and the theaters of their actions. To prepare us for that task, the cultural blinders that have heretofore led us down futile rabbit trails must be exposed.

False Antichrists

Okay, I'll go first. As a teenager, I heard many supposedly well-informed guesses about the identity of the antichrist. Reflecting my anti-Catholic surroundings, the most prominent conjecture in the crowd in which I traveled was the Pope. I can only imagine the confusion, for example, when some writer excitedly tagged John Paul I as the embodiment of evil, only to revise his prognostication when that Pope died just 33 days after assuming his position. Today, talk of the Vatican being the control room for the Tribulation has waned, although plenty of Web sites still finger the Pope as the future Beast. Given the efforts John Paul II made to reconcile the Catholic Church with other Christian traditions and the almost universal respect that he earned, only the most diehard anti-Catholics continue to cling to this prejudice. Even though the Pope reaffirmed many traditional

Catholic doctrines, few people would doubt that he led a thoroughly Christian life and was an insightful interpreter of the mystery of following Jesus. His successor, Benedict XVI, appears to adhere to similar doctrinal positions. Yet, the Protestant hatred of Catholicism endures, and many evangelicals persist in their Pope-watching to monitor any antichrist-like tendencies. I meet several people from this camp every time I present my seminars. This enduring school of thought continues not only due to anti-Catholic history, but a Western bias for centering End Times activity in historically prominent Rome, a foundational city in our civilization's history. Among the arguments I've heard are that Rome will be the "great city" referred to in Revelation, the metropolis that will serve as the quintessence of the world's evil and thus undergo the unmerciful judgment of God. It will earn this fate as a result of the Pope leading a 10-member European confederation to establish world domination, the thinking goes. These seemingly permanent theories prove how powerfully our religious culture colors our understanding of the antichrist. I am especially amused by the interpretive gymnastics performed by so-called scholars who try to move and rename Babylon from its Iraqi roots to Italy.

Religious animosity has not been the sole source of our often narrow field of vision when seeking to identify the antichrist. Political antagonism has also produced a variety of American antichrists, most of them Democrats in recent times. As the Republican party wooed white evangelicals in the 1970s and '80s, I heard antichrist theories about politicians such as Senator Ted Kennedy, one in fact based on a bizarre calculation of the numerical values of the letters in his last name. Kennedy fit many of the criteria for antichristhood: he was liberal, Catholic and from a powerful family. The very mention of his name, when associated with a presidential candidate, is thought to be sufficient dead weight to sink a campaign. Poor man! I hereby proclaim his candidacy for antichrist dead in the water.

The suspicions about different political entities evolving into the antichrist haven't stopped at our borders. I clearly remember hearing sermons that anointed the European Common Market as The Beast, especially when it had 10 members several decades ago, matching the 10-horned monster described in Daniel 7. Now that the European Union has ballooned to 24 member states, amateur prophets have gone back to the drawing board, determined to demonize some European leader or alliance, largely due to the weakening of evangelical Christianity on that continent and consequent emergence of post-modern thought. Rather than pray for these dear lost people, we besmirch them, determined to find an antichrist among them. For example, in the research that I have done on Franco-American relations, I have discovered numerous sermons by American preachers in 1789 that labeled France as the antichrist. Reacting to the revolution and its installation of Reason, not God, as the guiding light for the French people, these firebrands spearheaded a nationwide repudiation of all influences French: from the cessation of French language teaching in many universities to a call for rupture in our diplomatic relations. And you thought "Freedom Fries" was the first shot fired in this cultural conflict!

All of these conjectures, from Ted Kennedy to the European Union, reflect the Western-centeredness of American prophetic interpretation. This school of exegesis reached its peak during the Cold War, as biblical pundits scoured passages in Deuteronomy to prove a final showdown between an eagle and a bear. Surely, those nasty Russian Communists would produce the antichrist. They fit the checklist in full: godless, cold-hearted, powerful and fierce. The assumption has been that the United States are the good guys, the defenders of the faith, and any threat to them qualified for inclusion in the antichrist club.

Despite His rich, gracious blessing on the U.S., God does not claim American citizenry, nor will He unfurl His plan exclusively on our land or through our enemies. When we tab antichrists solely due to their standing vis-à-vis our nation or subculture, we have become myopic, which explains the imposter Beasts exposed during my lifetime, from left to right: the Pope, Russia, Communism, Ted Kennedy, China, the European Union. This skewing of prophecy does not represent a moral fault, just the nature of culture. We read and interpret the Bible through the only lens we have, which is Western. The mindset of the majority of Bible interpreters has narrowed their field for exploring the mysteries of prophecy even before they begin. Like children trying to whack a pinata, they have been too blinded by their own prejudices and frames of reference to make contact with the giant target looming in the pages of Scripture.

The Geographical Setting of Biblical Prophecy

A survey of prophetical books, however, divulges scant mention of lands that comprise North America, Russia or China. Whether we feel at ease with the facts or not, the geographical setting for Armageddon centers around the Holy Land, and I'm not talking about Nashville. As we dust off our atlases and read the names of the nations surrounding Zion in the pages of prophecy, we find a long list of overwhelmingly Islamic countries.

This book does not focus exclusively on Biblical prophecy, so I will not offer a thorough primer on its interpretation. Just remember that as the prophets saw the future, they saw events as one sees mountain ranges, which, when viewed in one dimension, seem to bunch together, but in fact lie hundreds of miles apart. In the same way, events written about in a single chapter of Scripture might occur thousands of years apart. This explains part of the confusion about the mission of Christ when He came. The disciples grouped prophetic passages together, linking the coming of Emmanuel with the establishment of God's unopposed kingdom on Earth, head-quartered in Jerusalem. We are apt to repeat this mistake when we ignore the ancient words about former kingdoms and insist that most or all of the events described in Daniel or Matthew or Malachi have already occurred. Isaiah, for instance, undoubtedly wrote about the nation of Judah's peers at the time when he declared warnings against them, but he also saw hundreds, then thousands of years into the future when he wrote of a baby being born of a virgin, and later, a land where the lion would lie down peacefully with the lamb.

With this understanding, let us pinpoint the modern nation-states that biblical writers mention repeatedly in prophetic passages. I won't pretend to be able to go further and hazard a guess for the date of fulfillment of each announced event; my goal remains the location of the region where God's plan has unfolded and will eventually culminate. Don't be too impressed. This exercise does not equal rocket science in degree of difficulty. All that you need to plot this out at home is a current map of the Middle East alongside a few ancient maps, often found in the back pages of a decent study Bible. Perhaps you will wonder, as I have, why teachers of the Word have said so little about the catalog of Islamic countries that jump off the pages of Scripture. In brief, why have analysts of the Bible worked so hard to establish Russia, China and the United States as the key players in the prelude to Armageddon while ignoring the tumultuous nations that have surrounded Israel for millennia? Ignoring Islamic people when discussing eschatology is like omitting the Yankees when discussing baseball.

One quick example can prove my point. The largest book of prophecy, Isaiah, homes in on Assyria, which comprised part or all of modern Saudi Arabia, Jordan, Iraq, Iran, Turkey, Syria and Lebanon. Isaiah also highlights the ancient kingdoms of Edom and Moab (Jordan) and Arabia (Saudi Arabia), and pronounces woe on Babylon, found in Iraq, and Egypt, whose modern borders resemble the nation of the prophet's time. Damascus is mentioned by name, and Philistia is condemned, home of the Gaza Strip today. (Joel and Amos also identify Egypt and Jordan for special judgment from God for opposing Israel.) In all the judgments that God pronounces through Isaiah, he looks not to distant shores unknown in the time before Christ, but to the neighborhood around His chosen people, and when He speaks of His earthly kingdom in chapters 60-62, it is in the context of punishment of those same nations, which now comprise the heartland of Islam. My point? If you believe the pages of Scripture, you absolutely must agree that the countries around Israel will be the site of Armageddon. Currently, those countries host populations that are nearly 100 percent Islamic, with interpretations of Islam that grow increasingly radical and anti-Semitic by the day.

To zero in on just one of these countries, consider contemporary Syria. Until recently, one would not identify this country as a hotbed of Islamic fundamentalism. In fact, if this nation deserved the chastisement that Isaiah and other prophets have foretold, a neutral observer would quickly conclude that the brutal Baath government most merited such reprimand. Yet, in just the past couple of years, Syria has become the site of a "dramatic religious resurgence." The government that vanquished 10,000 Islamic militants two decades ago has shed its reputation as the Arab world's most secular state. Mosques overflow with adherents, women wear the veil in record numbers and young men train in paramilitary units to protect Muslim preachers and prepare for combat abroad. Syria, now more threatened than ever by the U.S./Israel duo, is "fostering the very brand of religious fundamentalism that it once pruned so mercilessly."[85] And, as researchers continue to gain information about the insurgents in Iraq, they find more and more links to neighboring Syria. This once low-profile bastion of secularism has transformed into a launching pad for anti-Western ideas and armed men. In a word, Syria has prepared herself for extensive participation in the Last Days as an antagonist to Israel, a clash predicted long ago by Scriptural writers.

Jordan, too, right next door to Israel, recently has combated a resurgence in Islamism that has seeped into its halls of power. Despite a moderate king who thankfully offers a frank, honest perspective on the region for anyone who wants to listen, nearly half the seats in his country's parliament are filled by members of the Islamic Brotherhood, a notoriously extreme political party.[86] Other country studies could fill a library and are beyond the scope of this book. Rest assured that the fundamentalist wave described in chapter 5 will crash on the land promised to Abraham, and then see Yahweh's judgment in response.

Another example of the prominent role of Islam in the End Times is the anti-Israel coalition found in Ezekiel 38. There, the prophet speaks of a Jehovah-hating league comprised of Magog, Persia, Ethiopia, Libya, Gomer and the house of Togarmah and his bands. The names unfamiliar to the modern ear, such as Magog and Gomer, have sent prophecy buffs scurrying for explanations for centuries. Even now, a score of Web sites speculate on the identities of Gog and Magog. I grew up hearing that they encompassed the Soviet Union, but hear far less talk of that since the demise of Communism. I favor the summary given by missions expert George Otis in his definitive book on Islam and the End Times: "A thorough historical review does present us with two important facts about this confederacy: 1) its inherently Islamic character, and 2) its lack of correspondence to modern political boundaries."[87] Otis goes on to venture a guess at the modern equivalents of these enemies of Israel, rightly observing that Ezekiel referred primarily to peoples, not nation-states. Otis associates this fearsome alliance with the Turkish people and Muslims living in the modern "stan" nations (Kazakhstan, Kurdistan, etc.). This coalition will be led by a charismatic figure who will rally the world against the Judeo-Christian legacy. To peek at a passage that actually refers to the Beast, turn to Daniel 7-11. In chapters 7 and 8, Daniel's terrifying vision includes the kingdoms of Persia, Media and Greece. Media and Persia today contain Iran, and the Greece of Daniel's era included parts of Turkey and Eastern Europe.

Later, in chapter 11, Daniel hears from an angelic being with a human appearance (an Old Testament appearance by Jesus?) and learns of four kings of Persia to come, the last of whom will "arouse the whole empire against the realm of Greece" (11:2). This vision seems to be set in a time period after the one of chapter 8, where Greece is mentioned as a supreme power. In other words, it seems that someone from Iran will overcome a kingdom labeled as Grecian. Could this "Greece" be the Western world, founded upon the system of thought and government created in Athens? Could this be the clash of civilizations proclaimed in today's headlines, Islam vs. the West? Could the Persian who provokes this final conflict be the Ayatollah Khomeni, who introduced the world to fundamentalist revolution with his followers' overthrow of the Shah of Iran in 1979? I don't want to stray too far on a speculative tangent and thus weaken my primary argument and credibility. I only seek to verify the geographical location of the final battles for world power, not take detailed stabs at very difficult prophecy.

The focus of many prophetic passages has been the coming war between Israel and her enemies. Our newfound interest in the Middle East should have been aroused far earlier, immediately after the creation of the state of Israel in 1948. That event set into motion many tensions that trouble our world to this day, and it also satisfied the biblical requirement of Yahweh's people living in their own land before the Last Days. Most interpreters of prophecy will tell you that the countdown to Armageddon began in 1948. The fulfillment of Scriptures like Zephaniah 3:14-20 is a modern marvel, and it roused the dormant volcano of ancient hatreds that will explode in The Last Days:

> "Shout for joy, O daughter of Zion! Shout in triumph, O Israel! Rejoice and exult with all your heart, O daughter of Jerusalem! The Lord has taken away His judgments against you, He has cleared away your enemies. The King of Israel, the Lord, is in your midst; you will fear disaster no more. In that day it will be said to Jerusalem: 'Do not be afraid, O Zion; do not let your hands fall limp. The Lord your God is in your midst, a victorious warrior. He will exult over

you with joy....I will gather those who grieve about the
appointed feasts—they came from you, O Zion; the
reproach of exile is a burden on them. Behold, I am going
to deal at that time with all your oppressors, I will save the
lame and gather the outcast, and I will turn their shame
into praise and renown in all the earth. At that time I will
bring you in, even at the time when I gather you together;
Indeed, I will give you renown and praise among all the
peoples of the earth, when I restore your fortunes before
your eyes,' says the Lord."

Other passages zoom even closer on the location of the key
actors in the End Times. The prophet Obadiah tells us that the final
conflict over Mount Zion will be between the houses of Jacob, representing Israel, and Esau, representing Edom, as Genesis 36 tells us.
The final holocaust thus explodes on the lands of Israel and Jordan.

"Then the house of Jacob will be a fire and the house of
Joseph a flame; but the house of Esau will be as stubble,
and they will set them on fire and consume them so that
there will be no survivor of the house of Esau, for the Lord
has spoken....The deliverers will ascend Mount Zion to
judge the mountain of Esau, and the kingdom will be the
Lord's."—vv. 18, 21

Daniel, among others, zooms even further in, evoking a titanic
struggle between the antichrist and God Himself, with events in the
temple at Jerusalem serving as the center of the battleground for this
final war when, I believe, the entire world will ask: Who is God,
Allah or the God of the Bible? For a brief period of time, Allah will
appear to be dominant, only to have Jehovah crush him. Will you be
capable of clinging to your faith in the meantime?

Will you believe that El-Elohim reigns supreme during the
assuredly short-lived dominion of the small horn in Daniel 8:11-14?
There, the prophet reported that the horn had:

"magnified itself to be equal with the Commander of the
host; and it removed the regular sacrifice from Him and
the place of His sanctuary was thrown down. And on

account of transgression the host will be given over to the horn along with the regular sacrifice; and it will fling truth to the ground and perform its will and prosper. Then I heard a holy one speaking, and another holy one said to that particular one who was speaking, 'How long will the vision about the regular sacrifice apply, while the transgression causes horror, so as to allow both the holy place and the host to be trampled?' And he said to me, 'For 2,300 evenings and mornings; then the holy place will be properly restored.' "

The Bible tells us that no matter what happens in Jerusalem and vicinity during the epic conflict of the Last Days, we know for sure that El-Shaddai will intervene and destroy the enemies of His people. Those of us who have studied God's word have heard much about this final outpouring of His wrath. What we have neglected has been the role of Israel's neighbors in this showdown, the undeniable presence of Islamic countries throughout apocalyptic literature.

As a young man, I heard much about the Holy Land and its attractions, its mystical hold on the pilgrims who go there and the renewed spiritual passion on the part of those fortunate enough to make the trip. Despite having gone to church since I was a child, though, I knew precious little about the hostile enemies surrounding this land, save for an occasional slide of an Arab shepherd selling goats near a tourist stop in Bethlehem in the presentations about the wonders of Israel. Muslims received negligible attention in the presentations I saw in the 1970s, with throwaway lines like, "And there's a typical Bedouin selling all sorts of items, from live animals to wooden carvings of camels—beautiful carvings, really." Now the whole world wants to know what's inside the mind of that trader. Study of his native language has skyrocketed in American universities. Seminars on Islam have sprouted up throughout the U.S. Congressional hearings seek to determine the future course of the faith in which the uncomplicated Bedouin was raised, and national security rests on the outcome. It's a shame that such topics went unexplored for decades, but 9/11 has made everyone curious about the man in the turban. Looking back, I'm not sure how the violent relationship between Israel and her enemies was not brought into discussions of the End Times. I believe it had more to do with ignorance than racism. I don't think people like

Hal Lindsay, to name one, gave the Muslim bloc much attention as a world power. My, how times have changed!

Despite our weariness with the turmoil in that region, conflicts rage on, and they have begun to implicate the U.S. Or, perhaps it would be more accurate to say that we implicate ourselves as we flex our sole superpower muscles and seek to "solve" the Middle East's quarrels once and for all. It is not a coincidence that the entire world's focus has shifted to this rugged region, a part of the world that would draw scant notice did it not provide most of the black gold that powers the world's economy. It has only been during my lifetime that Americans have even noticed the Islamic world, apart from a few oil speculators who braved the heat and sand to shake hands with Saudi leaders sealing sweetheart deals in the 1930s.

Soon after the fall of the Soviet Union and the almost complete collapse of the Communist philosophy, fundamentalist Islam began to fill the power vacuum and jump onto the world stage. As one British intelligence officer put it: "In 1914, 1939, or 1970 it did not much matter what was thought in the bazaars of Persia or Algeria— let alone Yemen or Kuwait. Today it is crucial."[88] There was nothing like waiting in the interminable gas lines of the late 1970s to teach the American public what the initials OPEC stood for and how our enormous economic machine was energized in large part by the resource spewing out of an almost purely Islamic region. Our presidents have been making peace with turbaned sheikhs ever since. It is not a stretch to say that the oil beneath Islamic lands determines the entire trajectory of the world economy. Instability in the Middle East causes traders many a sleepless night because they know that more chaos equals less production equals global recession. For this reason, fear of terrorist attacks in the Middle East already adds eight to ten dollars to each barrel's price tag, according to one OPEC member.[89] In addition, international economists link growth forecasts directly to the price of oil, according to the World Bank. Such growth will slow in 2005 and 2006 because of the rise in oil prices in 2004.[90] It is no stretch to say that God, in His sovereignty, has inextricably tied the whole world to the Middle East, a distant region that historically has drawn few American tourists and merited almost no attention in the U.S. until the past 30 years.

Muslims understand this worldwide dependency on a fuel of which they possess the lion's share of reserves. They definitely see

Allah's hand in vast supplies under his holy land as a reward for their submission to him. As Saudi Prince Turki al Faisal told British journalist Robert Lacey: "Arabia is rich today as it has never been before and many simple people in this country believe that this is for one reason and for one reason only—because we have been good Muslims."[91]

It's fascinating, is it not, how hundreds of peoples of the world believe they have divine benediction and are the apple of God's eye. Americans have certainly reasoned thusly, but now we need to stop searching Scripture for references to bears and eagles and capitalist democracies and simply allow verses to speak for themselves. We can construct a reasonable eschatology on far more solid ground that way, even though the new Beast might not be as familiar or inferior as previous antagonists. The early twenty-first century does not feature an arms race against a doomed economic system, as the Cold War did. It does witness, however, a grueling fight against a nebulous enemy who continues to be recast, first as terrorism, now as radical Islam, tomorrow as freedom-haters.

Jerusalem: Islam's Third Holiest City

Whatever your interpretation of Scripture, it cannot be argued that the land of Israel and the city of Jerusalem will be the stage for the final combat before the Lord's return. Jerusalem is not the biggest city, nor the brightest, nor the host of the Grammys or the capital of the free world. This moderately sized ancient municipality will be the 50-yard line for Armageddon, for it has played an important part in the development of the world's three most influential faiths. Zechariah previewed the starring role for the city of David:

> "Behold, a day is coming for the Lord when the spoil taken from you will be divided among you. For I will gather all the nations against Jerusalem to battle, and the city will be captured, the houses plundered, the women ravished, and half of the city exiled, but the rest of the people will not be cut off from the city. Then the Lord will go forth and fight against those nations, as when he fights on a day of battle...And people will live in it, and there will be no more curse, for Jerusalem will dwell in security." —Zechariah 14:1-3,11

Why, for hundreds of years, did Western Christians not conclude that Muslims would comprise the nations seeking the conquest of Jerusalem? Muslims surround Israel and are most adverse to her existence, and they are the ones most often shot and killed by Israelis, fomenting support for Islam worldwide and unifying Islamic nations and armies. Muslims cohabit the Holy City and guard undisputed control of certain sections of it. Muslims have been fascinated with Jerusalem since Muhammad's miraculous night journey, the *al-miraj*, which took place in 621. According to Islamic tradition, Allah supernaturally transported Muhammad from Mecca to Jerusalem, then lifted him to the heavens for a glimpse of Allah's plan and purposes in the world. Considering the importance of this event and its fantastic quality, the Koran has comparatively little to say about it. Chapter 17, verse 1, recounts: "Glory to God who did take his servant for a journey by night from the sacred mosque to the farthest mosque, whose precinct we did bless—in order that we might show him some of our signs: for he is the one who heareth and seeth all things." The importance of *al-miraj* has expanded over the years, for the location of that "far-thest mosque" (*masjid-ul-Aqsa*) was Mount Moriah in Jerusalem. A militia carries the name to this day, the Al-Aqsa Brigade, respon-sible for many attacks in Israel, absolutely committed to preserv-ing this holy ground for Islam, "to the last drop of blood."[92] The hadiths of Muhammad fill in the details of *al-miraj*. Taking off on a white, winged horse, Muhammad rose from the Wailing Wall in Jerusalem to the highest heaven. Despite this adventure, Aisha reported that her husband seemed to have slept quite soundly until morning.

Whatever the validity of this vision, human history would be changed forever. Sixteen years later, Muhammad's father-in-law would walk across the Temple Mount and, as the Holy City's con-queror, choose a site for a mosque. Within another 100 years, the spectacular Dome of the Rock shone as a permanent symbol of Islam's foothold in Jerusalem. The stunning beauty of this mosque did not arise by accident. It stands close to the Christian Church of the Holy Sepulcher which, after being rebuilt in 628, amazed the Muslim conquerors who arrived a few years later. According to the eyewitness account of a relative, the caliph had such a strong reaction to the Christian edifice that he took immediate action.

"When he saw the immense and dominating dome of the Church of the Resurrection (Holy Sepulcher), he feared that it would dominate the hearts of the Muslims, and he therefore erected the Dome which we see on the Rock."[93] To this day, the artfully engraved Koranic verses broadcast a warning to other residents of the city: "The religion before God is Islam (submission to His will)...If any deny the signs of God, God is swift in calling to account" (Koran 3:19).[94] Some sources believe this mosque represents the very abomination of desolation on the ancient Jewish temple's site that was predicted in several verses. The Al-Aqsa mosque will have to be removed or built around if the Temple is indeed to be rebuilt, as Scripture indicates. Well-equipped legions defend the mosque, to underscore the importance of it to Islam. The ferocity of the conflict over possession of this plot points to a much larger issue: Which faith will broadcast its message for all time from that spot? In other words, whose god is God? I believe that, for a time, most of the world will be convinced of Islam's supremacy, as they maintain control of this site. Yet, the Word of God stands sure:

> "And it will come about in the last days that the mountain of the house of the Lord will be established as the chief of the mountains, it will be raised above the hills, and the peoples will stream to it, and many nations will come and say, 'Come and let us go up to the mountain of the Lord and to the house of the God of Jacob, that He may teach us about His ways and that we may walk in His path.' For from Zion will go forth the law, even the word of the Lord from Jerusalem." —Micah 4:1,2

When we consider the primacy of Israel and its neighbors in the final drama, we must conclude on the basis of simple geography that Islam will play a key role in the fulfillment of Matthew 24 and other like passages. And, it follows that the primary players in this final act will be Muslims and Jews. The Pope will have no influence whatsoever on the rebuilding of the Temple in the Muslim strongholds in Jerusalem. Ted Kennedy has never lead the *infitadah*. Muslims will never trust an infidel organization like the European Union to resolve the complex issues in the Palestinian conflict.

Will the Islamic Curtain Be Rolled Back?

This theory of Islam playing a principal part in the End Times does have one hole in it: it is certainly possible that the Islamic "curtain" could be rolled back as the Iron Curtain was 15 years ago. Some Christian columnists have even indicated that this is likely, given God's penchant for withering world powers in an instant when He so chooses. Having lived among these people for the past 10 years and seen the missionary zeal of its preachers, I do not think that Islam will curl up and die anytime soon. Anything is conceivable with God, no question, but I think the idea that Islam will shrivel is based more on a fear of this faith than on a discernible trend. Islam continues to grow dramatically around the world due to a high birth rate among Muslim peoples, and its teachings enjoy an unprecedented worldwide hearing. The hypothesis that Islam represents another temporary roadblock to Christ's eventual dominion over all the Earth reflects a triumphalist philosophy that God (and America) will always reign supreme on planet Earth, that our country is an agent to spread Christ's kingdom, and our status as superpower is both eternal and divinely ordained. I think if you questioned evangelical Christians at length about this, you would find that, deep down, they believe such deception. The millions of "God Bless America" bumper stickers and prayers reflect fright and a corresponding reaffirmation that God will defeat all His enemies, and America will be His instrument for doing so. The idea that Islam will dry up into historical obscurity is included in this stream of thought. Unfortunately, this dangerous lie ignores scores of Scripture passages that tell of brutal warfare, intense persecution, and the temporary reign of a hideous Beast. In short, we read what we want to read in the Bible, many times, and we often interpret prophecy in a way that will ensure our country's dominance and the least amount of suffering for us. Let me go on record as saying that Islam will not go away, no matter how hard we wish it to or how many troops we send out to kill its adherents. Given America's invisibility in End Times prophecy, the U.S., not Islam, will be the kingdom that withers before Christ's return.

The simple process of Muslim children being born and raised in Islamic households will ensure the sustenance of this faith for years to come, especially in light of the damning punishments for conversion from Islam and the severe actions taken against anyone who renounces his faith. The twin concepts of children representing a blessing from

Allah and polygamy permitted in his law will expand the Islamic world well into this century on nearly every continent. Demographers predict nearly 2 billion people will call themselves Muslims by 2020.[95]

Thus, any preview of the Last Days, based on the biblical record and population facts, must include one-third of the world calling Allah "god" and Islamic nations at war with Israel. Given these truths, the identity of the "stern-faced king" of Daniel 8:23 comes into clearer focus. Could he be a Romanian, as *Left Behind* presents? I think we would all prefer this type of villain. He would be Caucasian, like many of us, able speak English fairly well, and he would use a relatively Westernized thought process. In short, he would be an antichrist we could understand and relate to, an anti-hero we have seen in a Bond movie, and we all know that Eastern Europeans are eventually outsmarted and outfought by Americans! Dear reader, rest assured, the Muslims fighting for a Palestinian homeland, planning another war on Israel, and rioting when Jewish leaders visit the site of the Al-Aqsa mosque will never, ever, ever trust a Romanian to negotiate the agreements needed to preserve Islamic gains in the Middle East. A "Christian" European will never be counted on by the Islamic bloc to destroy Israel. Muslims put their full confidence solely in other Muslims, brothers in the *ummah* (community). Sorry, Messrs. Jenkins and Lahaye.

No, one clear line of demarcation has been drawn by both protagonists in today's world: the West vs. Islam. Muslims feel attacked and thus justify jihad to defend their lands and faith. Presidents make speeches about an axis of evil that has a conspicuously Islamic flavor. Islamic terrorism swings elections, rocks entire nations, affects the world economy and continues to form political policy from Washington to Moscow. If indeed these are the Last Days, then the number one candidate for the birthplace of the Beast would have to be an Islamic nation, and there is far more evidence for this notion than today's headlines. God's Word should be read in a new, more global light and thus gain renewed respect as it centers on long-neglected lands that lay almost silent until recent history. The Bible, after decades of higher criticism that have reduced it in many quarters to a patched-together tool of a religious and political hierarchy, will prove its trustworthiness again, its veracity despite the many attacks on it. The Word of God has sat scorned and abused as the time to Christ's return has shortened. Now, she is ready to be plumbed again for clues to the future of our world. She was right all along: the ancient enemies of Israel will indeed play prominent roles in World ·War III, the antichrist will arise out of an overwhelmingly Muslim part of the world, Jerusalem will be the epicenter of the conflict.

Muslims eagerly accept a starring role in this final drama. They, too, have been patiently preparing for centuries and look forward to the triumph of their faith with an eerie confidence. Any reading of Islamic newspapers and books will quickly reveal variations on the theme of the West having its chance to lead the world but forfeiting that role due to its corrupting immorality. Allah will pluck the "Christian" rulers of the world and replace them with God-fearing Muslim monarchs. One Islamic caliph will oversee the Earth's complete submission to Allah in the Last Days. Islam has always been the only faith sufficiently holy and righteous enough to properly lead mankind, its proponents have asserted for centuries.[96] Khomeni, for instance, did not limit his vision of a theocracy to Iran, and his words continue to inspire thousands of jihadists roaming from one conflict to the next on our planet:

> "With a population of almost one billion and with infinite sources of wealth, you can defeat all powers. Aid God's cause so that He may aid you. Great ocean of Muslims, arise and defeat the enemies of humanity. If you turn to God and follow the heavenly teachings, God Almighty and His vast hosts will be with you."[97]

That speech to Iranians resonated with Muslims around the world, and the events of the 25 years since then have further convinced them that their time has come to give the world moral direction. Each time a traditionally Islamic land liberates itself from Western occupation or secular rule, Muslims notice and nod their heads. The revolution is coming, they say, one country at a time. When bin Laden and his army expulsed the Soviets from Afghanistan, a videotape was quickly produced and sent around the world. The narration over gruesome photos of dead Russian soldiers emphasized the theme of "if Allah be for us, who can be against us?" When the coalition forces leave Iraq, that same mantra will be repeated, as it will be in Chechnya and parts of the Philippines, I believe, for starters. After the 9/11 attacks, bin Laden quoted a well-known hadith cited by the son of Muhammed's friend

Umar: "I was ordered to fight the people until they say there is no god but Allah."[98] Citations such as this reflect twin motivations in the fundamentalist surge of the past 25 years: 1) they are doing Allah's will, and, 2) Allah will always fulfill his will. Thus, triumph is certain. Perhaps now you can see why I recoil when some State Department spokesperson says on C-SPAN that bin Laden and the like wage this war for political power, not religion. As politically incorrect as it might sound, we must understand that this final push at worldwide influence is all about religion.

In conclusion, several factors have thrust Muslim people to center stage in 2005: the geographical scope of biblical prophecy that seems ever nearer to realization, the leverage that oil-producing nations have on the world economy, and the military victories won by Islamic forces. This era could certainly signify another passing phase of world history, or it could be the prelude to Armageddon. I remind you again that Jerusalem and the Holy Land will be sites of that epic battle. Whose rage fuels the clashes today in that land? Who has claimed a part of that land for 1400 years, to the consternation of Israelis? Some scabs never heal.

In order to discern how the Last Days will unfold on earth, and if Islam will truly play a leading part in that time, we need to determine which version of Islam will emerge in the next decade: the religion of peace that President Bush famously referred to, or the faith that "loves death," to which both Khomeni and bin Laden call the faithful. In determining which form of Islam will rock our world, one key player merits close consideration, and he's not the PLO president or the head of OPEC. No, someone else will establish the form of Islam that will be held up to the world as the final revelation from God. You will not find him in a palace or in a parliament; she will not be a president or a prime minister. Just walk out the street next time you are in Cairo or Istanbul or even Paris. You see, the average Muslim will mold the movement. He or she will either rally behind bin Laden or spurn the call to jihad, respecting the right of all faiths to exist and the legitimate sovereignty of Israel. How does this man think? What are his concerns? How could he possibly applaud what occurred on 9/11? Were *Time* magazine to name a "Man of the Decade," this person would win my vote easily. Which way will he turn? The course of world history hangs in the balance.

Chapter Four

What Are Muslims Really Like?

Before I demonize an entire faith as the incubator for the most evil man to ever walk on the face of the Earth, let me first separate a group from a despot. This book has not been penned to arouse a renewed hatred for Islamic people—quite the opposite, actually. The fact that Stalin was a murderous dictator does not mean Russians are diabolic. Hitler did not embody the German soul, either. Although I do believe that the religion of Islam has endemic elements that will lead to a direct conflict with Jesus Christ in the Last Days, I do not believe that the faith is absent any truth or beauty, or that its followers willfully rebel against the true God. Muslims cannot help that they were born into their faith, and many of them are sincere, God-seeking people who have been fine personal friends. What I desire to convey in this chapter is that an enormous group of Muslims are susceptible to the influence of charismatic Islamists, and even the ordinary, non-suicidal believer can and will be swayed to a less tolerant, more violent version of his faith. If Islam is to conquer the world, then it will need numbers, foot soldiers, masses of people ready to do just about anything for the glory of Allah. How will a sufficient number of zealots be gathered? Probing the angry mind-set of the typical Muslim will give clues regarding the ripeness of time for worldwide revolution.

One reaction to the immediate suspicion cast on all Muslims after 9/11 was to claim that Islam is a religion of peace and that its true followers do not mean harm to anyone, that Islam is more about a personal journey of the soul, not murdering infidels. This certainly was a welcome perspective at the time, quite necessary to balance the zeal of the U.S. law enforcement agencies that hauled thousands of Muslims in for questioning in the fall of 2001 and held many for days in jail in scenes straight out of *The Siege*. Others from Islamic families earned swift deportation on sometimes scant evidence and technicalities, and all who had swarthy skin and Arab family names felt the wary glares from freshly wounded Americans. I was one of those Americans who desired lock-tight security in those tense days about four years ago. I took a Paris-Washington flight a few weeks after the tragedy, and I remember looking long and hard at the Muslim men and women on the plane with me, alert for any unusual movements. I confess that I did not feel much love in my heart for them that day. Muslims sensed this anger directed against them. A host of them left the U.S. of their own accord in late 2001, sensing prejudice and fearing attack. I recently spoke with a friend in North Africa who shared about a Moroccan family he met that had lived in the States for 20 years but left when they sensed the sea change in the national mood after 9/11. They were not alone in their anxiety.

Having been a resident alien in two countries, I can empathize with Muslims who live in the U.S. and face hostility on a personal and, at times, governmental level. However, before we classify fundamentalism as an aberration, not a trend, we need to paint a portrait of the truly typical Muslim person. Let's get right to it: does he or doesn't he wish harm on the United States? Does she or doesn't she dream of a worldwide theocracy with a caliph calling the shots?

Dissecting the average Muslim is a bit like answering "What are Italians like?" or "What are Hindus like?" It can be both difficult and dangerous to make generalizations. Nonetheless, I have spent enough time with Islamic people to identify some common characteristics, and more importantly, recognize sociological factors that propel the rise of fundamentalism.

Let us begin by casting aside the stereotype of Muslims as wild-eyed suicide bombers all. The middling Muslim, whom I am constantly asked to describe as I speak in churches, does not continually plan terrorist missions or have a closet full of bomb-ready chemicals and small arms. Yet, the conditions that compel a fraction of Islamic people to commit dastardly deeds do indeed predominate in the Muslim world, and they create an atmosphere that will continue to lead to an upsurge in terrorist activity and the anger that drives it. It is absolutely inaccurate to compare Islamic fundamentalists to the

Ku Klux Klan, each subset representing a tiny, fierce anomaly of the true faith. Unlike the KKK, Islamists make far sounder, far more convincing arguments for their cause to the bulk of their religion's followers, and their numbers are growing, not declining, because they call for transformation in parts of the world where conditions remain barely livable.

This chapter focuses on Muslims who live abroad, the 99.7 percent who do not live within America's borders. Those hundreds of millions differ greatly from the micro-thin layer of super-elite who attend college and graduate school and work in the United States as doctors and engineers. The average Muslim, in short, bears little resemblance to your cardiologist. Americans' attempts at understanding the Islamic mind-set must not be biased by their interactions with their secularized, well-fed Muslim coworkers. That would be like reading Salman Rushdie to discern how Muslims think. Yet, as I delve into the mind and soul of the average Muslim, I would caution that even the educated slice of Islamic society both here and abroad show a troubling tendency to support the fundamentalist cause. The new U.S. doctrine of preemptive war has alienated many formerly pro-American backers in the worldwide *ummah*. Many Islamic leaders see the Iraqi invasion as a rebirth of a colonialism thought to be dead for decades. As one former World Bank worker and longtime American admirer moaned shortly after the coalition troops rolled into Iraq: "I feel we have been deceived about the nature and character of the United States of America."[99] He speaks for a large, influential group of moderates, I believe, who will eventually throw their hats into the ring with the Islamists, defending their change of heart by saying that they were forced to radicalize in the face of obvious U.S. aggression. Scores of news stories have been written about these English-speaking people of influence who feel betrayed by a former friend called America.

A level below these influential leaders who have spent time in the West lie the throngs of regular Muslims, the grassroots movement that will eventually decide the course of Islam and, ultimately, the world. I base this unscientific analysis of Mainstream Muhammad (can we ever be entirely scientific when describing human beings?) on my thousands of hours of conversations with Islamic people, from interactions over sweet tea under mango trees in West Africa to cups of espresso in Parisian cafés. As a former journalist, I have retained the habit of posing cartloads of questions. Consequently, I have amassed an authoritative amount of data to depict the standard Muslim.

Were you to join me for a few hours of liquid refreshment and exposure to Islamic culture, I can predict without any doubt that the following issues would arise during our discussion with Muslim contacts. Despite the fact that Muslims are often famously hospitable, they will not begrudge you their opinion on a variety of topics. You will get a healthy dose of their views along with your tea and delectable pastries. Those perspectives will help us to understand the attraction of the fundamentalist movement today.

Their theses blend a mixture of truth and lies, with a couple of cups of urban legend added to the mélange. The common Muslim wrestles with his lot in life, trying to harmonize Allah's sovereignty with his poverty, and Islam's virtue with the corruption he sees in his country's leaders. The result is a frustrated man or woman whose confusion inevitably spills out all over you, his guest, as hotly as an overturned tea glass. This hypothetical experience of listening to this litany of complaints would prove to be somewhat unpleasant at times, but absolutely essential for decoding Islam today. I often ask acquaintances who work for the State Department, for instance, how many Muslims they have actually shared a coffee with in a café overseas. I can quickly tell who has and who hasn't, and I can just as easily divide the talking heads on C-SPAN into those few who have their ears to the ground in the Muslim world and those who read books and briefings but have never taken the time for tea with an Algerian or Saudi or Palestinian. Some foreign service employees talk to their cab drivers in Cairo, others avoid all contact with the teeming mobs and order hamburgers through room service between high-level meetings at the Hyatt. Our foreign policy would be far more prescient, I would wager, if such policymakers spent more time in dialogue with the donkey salesmen and less time with the Western-educated diplomats who skim illegal profit off the business deals transacted with their American visitors.

Real Muslims, the dominant Muslims (in numbers), draw on a surprisingly broad awareness of world events, and the resulting analysis by Islamic mullahs, to discern the root causes of their poverty and powerlessness. Believing the world to be a once idyllic place when Muslims ruled a vast empire that has become a morass of desperation, they finger the infidel powers of the past several centuries for their predicament. The most recent despised hyper-power is, of course, the United States, and because this self-centered giant seems to be treading on much of the rest of the world at the expense of the poor and suffering, your Muslim interlocutor undoubtedly will prove to be anti-American. Recent polls document the dismal approval ratings of the U.S. in the Arab world, numbers which have dipped even more dramatically since the Iraqi invasion. For example, nearly 100 percent of the people in Egypt, a key U.S. ally, hold an unfavorable opinion of our country. In Morocco, a favored trade partner, that negativity index has leaped from 61 percent to 88 percent in the past two years.[100] Thus, the most obvious difference between the Abdel Kader who lives in Amman and one who lives in Atlanta centers on the place of the United States in their hearts. Few Boston or Chicago residents hate the United States. Most are happy to be here and able to earn a decent living. I find far fewer barriers in talking to Muslims stateside than I do overseas. However, those who live in other lands evince a mounting antagonism toward a country that used to be admired in the Islamic world. For instance, poll takers last year asked Middle Easterners: "What is the first thought when you hear 'America'?" Respondents "overwhelmingly said: 'Unfair foreign policy.'"[101] The sliver of approval that we had long enjoyed from the Islamic elite has been shaved to microscopic proportions. As one Saudi radio show hostess analyzed:

> "If you continue on your present path, you will have no partners in the Middle East. In my generation there are thousands of people who studied and lived in America, who know America, love it, and understand that you can make mistakes. We explain America to our people. But in this next generation, you are creating so much bitterness. They don't understand you, and they don't *want* to understand you. What will come of that?"[102]

Added Hani Shukrallah, the editor of the English-language *Al-Ahram* weekly in Cairo:

> "To see the shift in 30 years, it is really quite amazing. It isn't just a matter of intensity. Before the second intifada and all

that followed, there was an ambivalence in people's sense of
the U.S. It's arrogant, yes, and it's imperial, but it's a
democracy. Now, anything from the U.S. is seen as part of
a design to bring us down, to humiliate us."[103]

This recent antipathy arises from a long list of grievances among
Muslims. From Casablanca to Cairo, from Kano to Karachi, from
Jakarta to Mecca, Muslims would repeat to any interested listener
some or all of the following charges against the United States, and
more generally, the West:

Islamic Perspective #1: The Crusades Have Re-Started

The demonic spirit that launched the Crusades remains alive and
well, and President Bush serves as the most current standard-bearer
in this quest to rid the world of Muslim people and reclaim all of
Israel for the non-Islamic world.

Muslims practice a religion that looks wistfully to the past, longing to re-create either the "era of right guidance" under the first four
caliphs or the age of the Ottoman Empire, when Islam almost conquered Europe. This emphasis on precedent produces followers who
often talk and think about ancient history, and they have been well-
schooled on the lasting effects of events long ago. In brief, the distance between 2005 and 1005 represents a far smaller leap in the
Muslim mind than for the average American, whose own nation
dates only a couple of hundred years. No recapitulation of Islamic
history would be complete without a thorough analysis of the
Crusades. In many parts of the Middle East, after-dinner entertainment in a local restaurant features an orator sitting on a stool
recounting both great Islamic victories and ruthless slaughters
inflicted by "Christians" during this hideous period. I dare say
Americans don't spend more than a few minutes, if any, considering
this time period after leaving high school history class. For Muslims,
it serves as a trustworthy guide to today's world, an evidence of the
evil lurking in the Western heart. Even a minor gaffe like the use of
the word "crusade" by President Bush to describe the U.S. military
response to 9/11 was interpreted as a Freudian slip by Muslims
worldwide. As one foreign correspondent in Cairo observed: "Bush's
word choice is a political footnote in the United States; here, though,
it remains a blazing point of contention."[104]

Muslims see the "Christian" West's ultimate goal to be the same as those of the Crusaders commissioned by the Pope: the domination, humiliation and eventual extermination of Muslim peoples. They trace a long parabola from the Crusades to the Iraqi conflict as evidence of a thinly-veiled Western aversion towards them. The composition of President Bush's "Axis of Evil" (majority Muslim) only proves their point, they say. A pamphlet I came across that had been distributed by an Islamic group in Britain summarizes this perspective well. Titled "The Campaign to Subvert Islam As An Ideology and A System," the leaflet announced that America has declared a "Crusade against Islam and Muslims" as she:

> "mocks and scorns Islam at every opportunity, humiliates her sincere sons, corrupts her societies, plunders her treasures, kills the innocent and challenges the Muslim day and night in their belief. While the Crusades of the past were aimed at occupying parts of the Islamic lands, today's Crusade launched against Islam and Muslims aims to subvert Islam by making Muslims reject their creed and embrace the creed of secularism."[105]

As President Bush reveals more about his personal faith in God and his relationship with Christ, Muslims become more convinced that war, especially of the preemptive variety, contains a religious element on the American side as well. High-ranking military officers who speak of demonic activity revealed from aerial photos of Islamic lands do not escape the scrutiny of the Arab press, either. Muslims know that many Americans see them as the enemy, and a monstrous one at that. Their reaction, predictably, tends to be aggressive and defensive at the same time.

Demonizing the enemy is as old as warfare itself, but given the history of the Crusades, this psychological tactic adds a particularly combustible component to the clash between Islam and the West. Many Muslims believe that deep in the hearts of all "Christians" lies an intense hatred of Muhammad's followers, and this loathing has risen to the surface in modern times. Perplexed Muslims ask how someone who claims to follow Jesus, as President Bush does, would bomb innocent people on a routine basis. The Jesus they know from the Koran was a peaceful prophet who performed many miracles for the poor and sick. The carnage of those same needy people today, ordered by political and military leaders who proudly wear Christ's name and regularly address prayer breakfasts, leaves a sour taste in the Muslim mouth.

Again, Muslims draw on a far greater wealth of information about President Bush than we have of Hosni Mubarak, for instance. They have heard far more of the president's speeches, watched many more of his interviews, and read more articles about him than you have of Egypt's president. They have compiled all this information to create an image of George Bush as the uber-Christian, a sort of Bible-toting Terminator whose religious zeal threatens the world. Is that caricature fair? No, but it mirrors reality in the Muslim mind. Every time President Bush or another American leader invokes God and Jesus when talking about the war on terrorism, Muslims hear echoes of Popes and kings of an earlier age who whipped mobs into a frenzy over the prospect of regaining the Middle East for Christendom. I would go further to say that such religious rhetoric pushes millions of Muslims toward the fundamentalist camp, the only group that they believe can counterpunch the "religious fanatics" in American government. To Muslims, holy warriors on the offensive with abundant nuclear weapons give cause for panic and reaction. Even the non-Muslim world, for that matter, fears President Bush more, not less, when he discusses his faith in the context of policymaking.

Islamic Perspective #2: The West De-Values Islamic Souls

Related to the topic of war and Islam, Muslims find further proof of the West's disdain for them in the late entry of American firepower into the Bosnian conflict. Only after tens of thousands of Muslims were slaughtered did the Clinton administration choose to counteract Serbian forces. Your Muslim contact concluded after delayed intervention that Americans believe Islamic souls to have less value than other peoples'; Bosnia was the confirmation.

As you debate your Muslim acquaintance, be prepared to bat around a long, long list of topics generated by recent international news. I advise you to do your homework and arrive at an opinion! The frightening ignorance of worldwide events among Americans lends weight to the Islamic argument that our country is no longer fit to lead the world. We know far too little about global issues to make wise decisions that will affect its future, they argue. I have often been stunned by the amount of exposure to international news that the common Muslim has. I think much of what they process has already been interpreted by clerics, who address current events far more at the mosque than the average pastor does in his pulpit. The everyday Muslim would surprise you, too, I predict, with how well-informed he or she is about world news and concerns.

Islamic Perspective #3: The U.S. Supports Oppression of Muslims

A similar failure to intercede for suffering Muslims continues today as Washington props up Islamic dictators around the world who starve their people and kill or imprison their opponents. The current administration's emphasis on freedom is a sham, skewed by American interests. The U.S. exports capitalistic, secular democracy only to certain nations in order to control the world's oil supply and continue to grow its economy, which exploits the world's poor, many of whom are Muslim.

The recent accent on liberty in presidential speeches would produce incredulous reactions from almost any average Muslim in the world today. He would rapidly tick down an inventory of recent international milestones to demonstrate that American support of free will has proven to be highly selective. While endorsing the overthrow of Saddam Hussein, a reviled figure to all but the Baathist party Sunnis who benefited from his ruthless rule, the typical Muslim would ask: why stop there? He would then orally race around the globe to highlight Islamic countries where dictators who are often Saddam's equal in cruelty remain in power, thanks to either American backing or disinterest. When passion for emancipation converges with American interests, Washington takes action, Muslims believe. Yet, when freedom fighters are butchered and jailed in other nations, the U.S. shrugs its shoulders and continues to welcome autocrats into the Rose Garden. Peasants seethe worldwide as their presidents stand next to ours and talk about how benevolent their kingdoms are. The fact that photo ops with our leaders produce smiles and handshakes lends a tacit approval to the monstrous regimes of these tyrants.

Examples of countries blessed by the U.S. despite their cruel, repressive rule include Egypt, Pakistan, Syria, Algeria and Tunisia.

Having received an earful from, particularly, numerous Algerian and Tunisian friends, I can vouch for the escalating anger among Muslims who resent Uncle Sam's pick-and-choose interventions based on selfish interest. Muslims prove to be startlingly aware of the suffering of their brothers in oppressed countries commanded by secular, authoritarian regimes. Consequently, when "freedom" becomes an evolving definition that morphs based on the benefit America can gain—invade the Iraqi oil fields, let the Tunisians suffocate—rage rumbles worldwide as surely as pressure on layers of rock produces an earthquake.

The lineup of our allies in the war on terror, for instance, reveals a dubious collection of countries with dismal records on human rights issues. Pakistan makes a good case study. Two leaders of the International Crisis Group pinpointed the hypocrisy of "freedom" fighting in Iraq while winking at other nearby dictatorships, such as Pakistan: "While the Bush administration repeatedly holds up Iraq as a nation that could serve as a shining example of Islamic democracy in action, it continues to offer a blank checks to a Pakistani government in which all power resides in the military. Curbs on democratic freedoms in Pakistan remain draconian."[106] This repression ballooned the vote totals of Islamist politicians in Pakistan's late 2001 elections. One political science professor in that country analyzed the reasons: "There is a deep sense of betrayal among all Muslim people that their elites, their governments, their institutions have all failed them. People have moved away from the mainstream parties hoping that the religious political parties will provide them with a better alternative."[107]

The above paragraph might be one of the most crucial that you read in this book. Desperate Muslims stream into the fundamentalist camp in search of hope and answers, and they will continue to do so. Being labeled "freedom haters" by the West puzzles such downtrodden Muslims. Most of them would be eager to fight and to die in the spirit of George Washington to ensure free and fair elections in their homelands. In fact, in at least one of the rare instances when such transparent balloting has been permitted in Islamic countries, the results have been overturned by the West. The entire Muslim world watched disbelievingly as the Islamic Salvation Front won 80 percent of the votes in Algeria's 1991-92 elections, only to have that outcome annulled by the army and a puppet president installed soon thereafter with the backing of French forces. The consequent reign of terror in Algeria, with hundreds of thousands assassinated on both sides of the political divide, remains a sore spot to Muslims and a prime example of the U.S., in fact, being enemies of freedom.

With every passing day that the U.S. seeks to please Hosni Mubarak or Perez Musharaf, the desperate citizens of Egypt and Pakistan grow more enraged. Despite extensive intelligence that has uncovered widespread corruption in both governments, at the expense of starving millions, the U.S. holds its nose and slings its arm around these men who imprison and kill their political opponents and potential enemies. The fact that such dictators bear a secular sheen only buttresses the argument that the U.S. favors freedom fighters of all but one stripe: devout Muslims. Why are they the sole political entity not allowed to flex its muscle at the ballot box? This extremely fair question, when pondered long enough by Muslim people, generates an inflammatory response: because the Christian West still desires the eradication of Islam. As long as the man sipping tea from a glass opposite you believes this, Islamist rolls will fatten and Wahhabite rallies will attract hundreds of thousands, with the accompanying shouts of "Death to the Great Satan."

Islamic Perspective #4: The U.S. Oppresses Muslims Through Its Support of Israel

Added to the infuriating defense of Muslim dictators, America's persistent backing of Israel draws Islamic ire across the *ummah*. Given the choice, again, of aiding the "right" side in a conflict between Muslims and "oppressors," U.S. foreign policymakers have blown their 50/50 chance of earning favor in the Islamic world and provided a rallying cry throughout the community. Connected to the belief that the Crusader spirit lives on, the notion that a Zionist conspiracy seeks to rule the world prevails throughout Islamic society.

The prominence of the Palestinian plight cannot be overemphasized when describing the common Muslim. He grows scarily emotional about Palestine because he has been inundated with one-sided coverage of the conflict in Israel by the media he watches and reads. On Arab TV, "blood-drenched images. Dead children, wound up tightly in sheets that show only the ashen skin of their faces, are a recurrent image."[108] Such coverage magnifies the suffering of the

Palestinians and justifies all terrorist responses. Muslims from Marseille to Mombassa die a little each day as they see on the news their brothers and sisters searched, arrested and shot by Hebrew authorities. If you have not had the opportunity to spend much time overseas, please take my word for it when I tell you that both Arab and European news sources heavily tilt the reportage of this fight.

This compassion for the underdog does not stop in the media. During my last four years in France, the city council of my Parisian suburb invited Palestinians on several occasions to address our town's residents at open meetings. The city went on to sign pacts with the Palestinians, pledging assistance in their struggle. Such exchanges only exacerbate the anti-Israeli, anti-American strain of ideology that runs throughout Europe and the Middle East. The extensive publicity that these forums generated also swelled Islamic fury at a time when France seeks to integrate and pacify its largest minority population. The distorted picture of what occurs in Israel was accepted as truth by city residents young and old, including many schoolchildren who heard presentations. I never witnessed an Israeli asked to give his side of the story in my five years in Europe.

I refuse to take up much space with my opinions on this matter. Obviously, both sides in this confrontation have done much wrong. The Jews have not welcomed the stranger as God commanded, nor have they always been measured in their responses to terrorism; the Palestinians have spent more energy tormenting Israelis than building a society, and they have not convinced anyone that they would be happy with a homeland alone. It certainly seems that they will not stop short of the destruction of the Jewish state. Whatever your or my opinion may be, the important consequence for this study is the anti-American ardor among Muslims that is stoked by the *infitada*, which they see as extremely justified in light of the brutal (in their minds) displacement of Palestinians from their lands and continual murder of their people. Muslims point to this debacle as further proof of the anti-Islamic bent of the U.S. If, in fact, Americans supported lovers of liberty, surely they would sponsor a people group that was callously expelled from a land that had been rightfully theirs for centuries. Yet the U.S. not only does not champion the Palestinian cause, it bolsters their opponents through arms sales, intelligence exchange, and all the other benefits of a rock-solid, enduring friendship.

I have never been so vain as to believe that I'm the only American who has had café chats with Islamic people. Chris Toensing, the editor of *Middle East Report*, testifies about the monologue he endured from his Egyptian waiter one day in Suez in 1998. The man's primary question: "Why do you Americans hate us so much?" (Sound familiar?)

He went on:

> "Numerous United Nations resolutions clearly define Israel's occupation of the West Bank, Gaza Strip, and East Jerusalem as illegal. Yet Israel receives 40 percent of all U.S. foreign aid....Israel uses all of this aid money to build new settlements on Palestinian land and to buy U.S.-made warplanes and helicopter gunships. Why do Americans support Israel when Israel represses Arabs?...The United States stands by Israel when it has flouted UN Resolution 242 (which urges Israel to withdraw from land occupied in the 1967 War) for over 30 years....The only logic this young Egyptian could see was that America was pursuing a worldwide war against Islam, in which the victims were overwhelmingly Muslim....America is a democracy, he concluded, so Americans must hate Muslims to endorse this war."[109]

Do you think your waiter at Ruby Tuesday's could expound on this topic, given the chance? Muslims at all levels of the economic and educational ladder display passionate emotions over this issue. Adds a journalist in Egypt, in response to the American inquiry of "Why do they hate us?":

> "Ask that question in Egypt, and you don't get long, complex derivations about clashes of civilizations or income disparity or the strangulation of civil society under repressive regimes. For the most part, you get one answer, over and over again, and with little variation. They hate us because of our policy towards Israel and the Palestinian."[110]

Another Middle Eastern journalist weighed in with an American colleague on how to improve relationships with the Muslim world:

"It's very simple," he said, "why don't you change your policy?
Enforce one U.N. resolution against Israel, and you would gain trust.
It would give people hope."[111]

Follow the road of twisted Islamic logic far enough, and one could
see how Muslims claim that Jews run the world and set the agenda for
the world's only superpower. Perhaps no reality could infuriate a person more than the awareness that a rich, successful cousin could
squash your own family at will, and has shown the requisite heartless-
ness to do so. Welcome to the Palestinian mentality. Their overachiev-
ing cousins have swept into the land, disposed of their rivals and made
ultra-powerful friends who can intercede if anyone objects.

Muslims weep, then scream as they see their brothers confined to
settlements that have limited economic potential and miserable living conditions, then are exterminated should they object to the
arrangement. The land's bounty produces riches for Jewish wallets,
while Allah's servants swelter in ruin. What kind of religion affirms
this, Muslims wonder, some strange hybrid of Judaism and evangelical Christianity that pledges unconditional loyalty to whichever
prime minister comes into power and orders the leveling of entire
Islamic neighborhoods? Scripture talks about a wicked ten-horned
beast. Muslims confront a fearsome two-headed monster every day:
the American-Israeli dragon.

True freedom lovers, Muslims reason, would fight more urgently
for a Palestinian state, for the Palestinian right to liberty and the pursuit of happiness. With every day that Washington remains low-key
or even mum on this white-hot topic, Muslims interpret passivity as
implicit approval, and the resulting rage feeds the fundamentalist
faction, the only bloc with the courage and firepower to slay the
dragon. I guarantee you that the most isolated, uneducated Muslim
person you could find, whether in the hinterlands of China or the
two-camel oases of Mauritania, will know about Palestine and have a
potent opinion on the matter. The issue serves as a flashpoint for all
1.4 billion members of the *ummah*.

Islamic Perspective #5: American Culture
Threatens Islamic Morality

Beyond the American-Israeli alliance that sparks revulsion in the
Muslim world, Uncle Sam's cultural and philosophical exports also
anger Muslims worldwide. Khomeni called the U.S. "the Great Satan"

not just because he saw us as thoroughly evil, but because he knew that American culture would prove to be an alluring temptress to Islamic youth.

Muslims struggle to raise their children in a godly manner much like we do. Their youth, like ours, tend to gobble up whatever Hollywood and music producers serve up as our entertainment world stretches its tentacles into more corners of the world than you might imagine. American pop culture sprouts in the most unlikely places, even in rigid Islamic communities. I will never forget walking under a brilliantly starry sky in the stillness of a night during Ramadan in northern Kenya years ago, only to hear the clear sounds of Kool and the Gang wafting over the breeze long after bedtime. I think of the teenage members of an English club I ran in France for junior high school students. Every participant issued from a Muslim family, and as they got to know me, the one question it took them some time to muster the courage to ask was: could they borrow my daughter's Britney Spears CD in order to copy it?

Unfortunately, many Muslims brush up against only the most crass elements of our culture, which gives them a terribly distorted view of our values. As a result, they see themselves as the future guardians of morality while we drown in our own filth. You and I know that decent entertainment does exist; it just doesn't get the press coverage—or distribution—that Hollywood blockbusters and syndicated television shows do. In short, the very elements of pop culture that we would like to hide out of shame have become what the Islamic world sees most easily.

Imagine the manager of a movie theater in Algeria who receives *American Pie* in his latest shipment of films. How would you feel when previewing it to determine its appropriateness for your city? What thoughts would go through your mind regarding America as you watched the sex-crazed actors and actresses dance on your screen?

The nausea induced by American pop culture doesn't stop at music or movies. Reportedly, the most watched television show in the world is *Baywatch*, and I doubt that the distributors of that series promote the lifesaving scenes as the primary attraction. If this program were the only one that you saw to represent a given nation, what would you believe about that people as a result? Muslims overseas have little if any contact with upstanding church youth choirs and Bible quiz teams, respectful, service-oriented, Christian college students, or kind, compassionate young adults. They get *American Pie* and *Baywatch* instead, and the ensuing skewed picture of American youth both scares and antagonizes them. How can they raise morally pure daughters when both girls and boys are watching MTV, renting *Showgirls* and listening to Ludacris? Because their family honor rests largely on the virginity of their daughters, any Muslim man who ends up with a deflowered daughter will often finger America as the ultimate culprit.

When the U.S. obsession with the sexual area intersects with Muslim people, as in the corridors of the Abu Ghraib prison, more petrol is rained on the flame. Perhaps the worst action that the U.S. Army could have taken in Iraq would have been to torment prison captives in a sexual manner. The photos that sped around the world in minutes, courtesy of the Internet, merely reinforced what Muslims have long believed about the U.S.: it is a society filled with perverted people. The resonance of those images cannot be overestimated. Those who have said that our relations with the Middle East will be affected for the next 40 to 50 years might not be far off in their calculations. Voluminous articles have been written about the scandal, but I do appreciate the insight of Richard Mouw, president of Fuller Theological Seminary, who pointed out:

> "This kind of sexual humiliation, it's bad enough to any human being. But when it violates deep convictions Muslims have about nudity and having their private parts exposed in front of other men and acting out homosexual things and being humiliated by women in your nakedness, it's deeply violating."

He added:

> "I think the overlay on this is a very strong tendency in our culture to demonize Muslims...that goes beyond what we did ideologically in our definition of Germans and Koreans in past wars. It's all tied up with a very strong religious warfare kind of mentality—that they're on a jihad against us and we need to respond in kind."[112]

American pop culture taints more than sexual mores, of course. Other insidious facets of our culture are transmitted to the world as well. As one UNESCO expert who has traveled the world notes: "The American media…transmits a constant and perpetual message of uncontrolled wealth, power, violence, crime and aggressiveness. The pop music does the same. That's a helluva thing to export as our image."[113] Quite true! Perhaps this is why a 2002 poll in Egypt found that a whopping 84 percent of the respondents thought it was a "bad thing that American ideas and customs are spreading."[114]

In addition to the questionable values communicated by American cultural exports, one should not discount the erosion of traditional culture as Western shows and movies bump ancient arts off the stage. Backed by significant financial resources that make it lucrative for foreign television stations and cinemas to show American fare, such exports have contributed to the decline in local productions of time-honored spectacles, chipping away at long-standing cultures until nothing is left but a few ceremonial dances and a handful of raconteurs.[115] Muslims mourn this Americanization of culture, and they do not see it as progress. As they watch the way of life taught by their ancestors take a back seat to the latest Janet Jackson CD or network prime-time soap opera, a certain weariness leads to yet more disdain for America.

I'll pause here and ask: have you had enough yet? As we sit in this imaginary living room of our Muslim host, does the date in your mouth taste almost sour after this blanket condemnation of your culture and country? You're actually getting a taste of ministry among Muslims overseas.

When I share these concepts with American audiences in the form of a Mr. Average Muslim monologue, my listeners sometimes forget that I am acting, and they shout back at me while I calmly list the faults of our nation, both real and imagined. Other audiences sit quietly and nod their heads, offering quiet, ashamed admissions. "He's right."

Pretend that you've finished the first two rounds of tea with your new Muslim friend. Now the time has come for the final batch: stronger, more bitter, the bottom of the pot. Mainstream Muhammad has much more to say.

Islamic Perspective #6: American Materialism Corrupts Islamic Society

Yet another American value menaces Muslim youth worldwide, to the consternation of their parents: good, old-fashioned material-ism. We can argue that *Baywatch* does not portray mainstream American culture, but who would dare state that materialism has not soaked our country's fabric through and through?

Muslim young people have not been immune to the siren song of Air Jordans, expensive cars and designer jeans, either. It pains Muslim parents that their children often seem far more interested in having an iPod than in developing their religious life. The constant encouragement to own the latest and most expensive version of any product, coupled with the stupendous birth rate in the Third World, could prove to be a marketer's dream, but a godly middle- or lower-class parent's nightmare. In conversation with me, many fathers have bemoaned the modern struggle to provide for their children in an increasingly materialistic world that continues to ratchet up the stakes. In Africa, the prized possession was blue jeans; in France, scandalously expensive sneakers.

As children come of age and no longer rely on their parents, they need gainful employment to earn the money to buy what they "must" have, yet economies across the Muslim world stagnate, and this aggravates the strain of poverty. Think of the explosive amalga-mation of high-priced goods that are publicized continually with sky-high unemployment rates, especially among young men. "How much is that sneaker in the window? I've got to have it. I also want a ride like I saw on MTV. Working at McDonald's won't provide this kind of lifestyle. I need some quick cash." The result? Endless strate-gies for making a quick euro that might include drug dealing or petty theft. Materialism might prove to be more morally corrupting in the long run than even sexual lewdness. French journalists who follow Muslim youth in the housing projects discover bands of non-working men unwilling to sweat in a factory as their fathers did for meager wages. They want pit bulls, stereo systems for home and car, and sleek outfits accented by Nike's latest model. It's no wonder that many in this group become bandits who steal everything from cell phones to automobiles and sell everything from pot to heroin. The new ways of life are to blame, Muslims believe, and the current emphasis on possessing ever-greater amounts of goods does not come from Islam. America is to blame, with its rampant capitalism and global marketing.

The upshot of this arrangement is that U.S. businesses enrich themselves while the Islamic social order is ruined. Sneaker companies rake in billions while Muslim parents helplessly watch their unemployed 20-year-old sons go out the door to scrounge up the $150 necessary for the latest model. He will obtain that three days' salary somehow, but not usually by working in a plant or by tilling the land. Many times he can't, even if he wanted to; there are no jobs. Who came up with this scheme of the richest nation in history impoverishing the poorest people in the world by convincing them that they must have the latest goods from the land of plenty?

Many Muslims lament the U.S. dominance of organizations like the World Bank and International Monetary Fund, which have produced a world of haves and have-nots, with many in the latter category living in Muslim countries. Every time the U.S. signs a trade agreement intended to further enrich the American way of life, Muslim people notice and resolve to bring justice. Americans who have little or no knowledge of the IMF, for instance, will always have a hard time understanding the "billion or so inhabitants of the planet who blame the IMF's 'structural adjustment' programmes (and hence America) for going to bed hungry every night."[116]

Islamic Perspective #7: The U.S. Could Solve All of the World's Problems If It So Desired

Finally, and perhaps most damaging to our reputation among middling Muslims, lurks the myth that the most powerful nation in the world can and should solve the world's problems by using its might for benevolent causes. If I had one dollar for every time a Muslim person has said, "You, the U.S., could solve my country's political and economic problems with the snap of a finger," I'd be a wealthy man.

Muslims are often dogmatic, but they're not ignorant or stupid. They see the firepower that rolled through Iraq. They see the preeminence of American culture across the globe. They read the business section, which can usually be summarized: As goes America, so goes the world. The failure to act to halt terrorism in Algeria or cure unemployment in Morocco or cede power in world trade agreements proves the U.S.'s indifference and shifts the blame from Islamic governments to "The Great Satan." What has been created in the average person's mind overseas is far more than a country of 260 million grappling with its own problems, but a legendary, omnipotent force that could probably stop the Earth from spinning on its axis if NASA determined to. Inaccurate as this might be, Muslims believe it, and it roils them perpetually. It's maddening enough that an infidel people controls the world and makes the rules; worse yet that this giant hates Islam and does very little to alleviate suffering.

Thus meanders the Muslim mind. Again, I generalize reluctantly, but hours and hours of conversation with Muslims from several dozen countries have given me a thorough read on the grievances of this bloc. "Happy" and "content" are two words I would not choose to describe Islamic people. Most live quite dissatisfied with their standing, and many feel pushed to take action to correct economic and cultural imbalances.

Yet, after overwhelming you with assertions about the blameworthiness of the U.S. and the West, your Muslim friend would halt the debate and probably invite you to stay for dinner. Over a heaping mound of couscous, he would reveal a more personal side, and this, too, needs to be understood as we evaluate the common Muslim, and, at the same time, the future of Islam. Common ground might quickly emerge as the two of you talk about raising children with moral standards and character. Perhaps your friend would mention the theme of last week's message at the mosque, when the imam preached about marital fidelity, modesty or honoring God with one's life. Beneath his angry exterior lies a complicated man who cherishes his family but is lost in his quest to obtain Allah's forgiveness. If you have an open ear and have gained some trust, eventually your friend might confess his worries about the judgment to come and the afterlife, the daily challenge of leading a submissive life to Allah, the frustration of seeking to grow in a faith that reveals itself primarily through the hard-to-grasp classical Arabic of the Koran.

It is foolhardy and incorrect to discard all Islamic teaching. Islam offers sound moral objectives, but it does not provide the spiritual resources to reach those objectives, and the resulting disappointment on a personal and societal level comprises the real source of rage in many Muslim hearts, I believe.

Another aspect of Muslim life is the centrality of extended family. They often maintain close clan ties no matter where they go in the world. It was fascinating to watch North African immigrants connect with distant uncles, aunts and cousins upon their arrival in France. This pro-family ethic does not necessarily yield harmonious families, but it does foster a pro-life sentiment and a far less individualistic mind-set than in the Western world. Children's births are fervently celebrated, and the practice of polygamy in some societies multiplies the rate of regeneration. Muslims are flexing their muscles world-wide in part because they see children as a blessing, not a cramping, of their lifestyle. While abortions continue in Western countries and many families choose to raise only one child, Muslims more than double the occidental birth rate, and will jump from a 20 percent current slice of the world's population to 30 percent by 2025.[117] I think that figure, even, falls on the conservative side.

This growing population needs room to live in. Harvard's Samuel Huntington noted in his powerful book *The Clash of Civilizations and the Remaking of the New World Order* that such dense people groups "tend to push outward, occupy territory and exert pressure on other less demographically dynamic peoples. Islamic population growth is thus a major contributing factor to the conflicts along the borders of the Islamic world between Muslims and other peoples."[118] He goes on to add that the Islamic "threat" will diminish as their reproductive rate slows between 2010 and 2030.[119] The obvious question, of course, is: will human history last that long?

The way a Muslim man cherishes his family connects with other core values in Islamic societies, including the key concepts of honor and revenge. Muslims desire to have functional marriages, peace at home, well-behaved children who honor God, and, most of all, the preservation of the family honor. This value must be understood if you are to unlock the Muslim mind. It is not only the immorality of a daughter that can stain a family name, but also a slight from a friend or enemy.

I will never forget a Tunisian friend changing his whole counte-nance as he discussed this topic. A smiling, gentle, wise man nor-mally, he narrowed his eyes as he insisted on the right to avenge any person who would touch his family's honor, adding that such retri-bution would be inflicted on me, if necessary. I can't remember the context of this conversation, but my friend's entire tone of voice changed and I left his apartment shaken, trying to comprehend this sudden metamorphosis. I knew I had touched a nerve when asking about this idea. Our friendship remained solid, but I had the feeling that I had seen a dark side of my friend that had never been disclosed before, an ugly, violent side. This commitment to family honor and revenge when necessary, multiplied by 1.3 billion, might help to explain why Iraqis don't want an occupying army and why Palestinians will not sit idle while their leaders are assassinated. When you come face to face with the primacy of honor and revenge in Islamic culture, you never forget it.

Perhaps now we can all better understand what happens when any part of the *ummah* experiences shame and humiliation. I repeat: do not *ever* discount this cultural feature of Islam, nor its repercussions. A few examples of the effects of the Iraqi invasion might prove helpful.

Abu Ghraib, for instance, will never be forgiven or forgotten, cleansed by a truth commission or a worldwide court. The swift capture of Baghdad, too, by American troops injured Muslims everywhere. As one correspondent noted, after scores of interviews with Muslims throughout the Middle East, "Humiliation is the word being used across the Arab world these days to describe the war in Iraq, in particular the dramatic collapse of Baghdad's defenses."[120] Those Muslims who interacted with this correspondent and other reporters did not mention Hussein's legitimacy to power as the reason for their discouragement regarding the war. Rather, these "Arabs were desperate to be masters of their own history."[121]

That same analysis of the "Shock and Awe" campaign by the U.S. military revealed the stunning revelation that Arab television stations focused on the capture of a single U.S. tank during the first weeks of the invasion, almost completely ignoring the overwhelming coalition victory (hardly impeded by the loss of one armored vehicle, I dare say!). One Jordanian political commentator observed: "People fed themselves spontaneously on that resistance. It was a kind of catharsis for the humiliation of setbacks over the last 50 years."[122]

Chew on that last quote for awhile. Imagine living in a country that was being overrun by a foreign army and, rather than seeing reports of that trouncing, the media spends precious minutes of broadcast time zeroing in on the destruction of a single enemy tank.

Now, imagine your entire neighborhood talking about that minis-cule victory for days afterward. How would you feel when the dreaded word arrived that Goliath had, in fact, squashed his enemies and was now in control of your nation? Now you have a small win-dow into the psychological state of the Islamic mind.

How Average Muslims Become Terrorists

I close this chapter with a plea for a more gracious understand-ing of "the average Muslim," a more nuanced knowledge of him and the application of his faith to his daily life. When all Joe Six-pack in the States sees are bearded leaders preaching hate to an answering chorus of enraged fist-pumpers, he can forget that those nameless people in the mob have hopes and dreams similar to his. The screaming crowd he sees has merely grown tired of waiting for those aspirations to be realized, and the charismatic speaker before them promises action. Voila, precisely how and why the fundamentalist movement will continue to attract adherents.

As an example, I introduce another gentle friend of mine, a funny, hard-working Algerian who had a Muslim makeover from deejay to terrorist. Sick and tired of the rampant unemployment and poverty around him, perpetuated by an inept and corrupt gov-ernment, he sought answers at his local mosque for the first time. The sight of soldiers playing soccer with the head of one of his slain neighbors lit a fire in my friend, he said, that would not be extin-guished. He would do whatever was necessary to seek liberation from the pitiless, dysfunctional military state in which he lived. One Friday, a zealous imam spoke of justice based on collective submis-sion to Allah brought about by holy war. Enraptured by the vision of a holy and just society, my friend joined the movement at that mosque, convinced of its righteousness and confident that it would achieve the national regeneration it sought.

Soon after, he discovered that this company of Muslims indeed used all means necessary to spread the insurrection, slashing the throats of those who opposed them, including members of the local police, for whom his father-in-law worked. Such cold-blooded killing only seemed to perpetuate the misery in his city, my friend thought, and he soon sought to distance himself from the rebels. As he tried to opt out of the faction, threatening notes appeared on his door and car windshield. Furthermore, as this group gained control in his neighborhood, his attractive, liberated wife was forced to cover herself from head to toe in black. This couple, which had met in a bar decades earlier, was being squeezed into a fundamentalist mold, and they resented the fit. Bullets ricocheted off their apartment balcony as the police fought back to regain jurisdiction in the community. Weary of the violence and intimidation, as well as the enforced devotion that muted his family's personality, my friend began to ponder a flight from his beloved homeland.

One day, a car bomb incinerated the vehicle in front of him as he sat in traffic. Remembering the death threats that he, too, had received, my friend concocted an elaborate scheme to escape the terror. Using his position as a travel agent, he organized a group trip to Portugal. Telling only his wife about his intentions, he ordered his family of four to pack two suitcases, being sure to include any precious items. En route to Lisbon, the jet had a layover in Marseille. There, the family disembarked. In the airport terminal, he broke the news to his shocked children: the family would remain in France. They would perhaps never again see their cherished cousins, aunts, uncles and grandparents.

I met this man several months after his arrival in France, subsequent to his wife's enrollment in an English course that my wife taught. Ill at ease in the impersonal West (he called French people "robots"), my friend restarted his life from scratch in an attempt to give his family a future. Rejecting the call to terrorism but not releasing the dream of a just world, my friend fervently prayed on his rug at home five times a day for the first time in his life. His attempts to read the Koran resulted in discouragement, due to the antiquated Arabic that remained unintelligible to him. Freed from the Islamic Salvation Front yet retaining a portion of the anger that led him to a radical mosque in Algiers, he continued his search for truth and justice in the world. He taught me much about the Muslim mindset, and I have attempted to reproduce many of his opinions in this chapter. He served as an eloquent example to me of the average Muslim, a mix of contradictions: the peace-loving jihadist, the Beatles-loving traditionalist, a man teetering on a balance beam who could fall either way. There are hundreds of millions more Muslims like this friend, people who are warm, funny, intelligent and informed, yet angry over the condition of the world, the Islamic portion in particular. They sometimes turn to those who speak the loudest and most eloquently, those who seem to follow Allah most closely. Some discover the underside of these groups and seek to exit. Others stay on board as they watch these groups gain strength and restore honor and pride to the brotherhood.

Fundamentalists do in fact make up a minority of the Islamic world, but they represent a very vocal and persuasive subset that will labor night and day to bring the large center of Islam along with it. I would guess that 80 percent of Muslims are like my friend, the typical Muslim. The combination of religious devotion with unceasing impoverishment yields a flammable faith that, as it grows increasingly militant, will no longer be described as a "radical" version of a religion of peace, but simply a pure form of a religion that has long talked about world conquest. The 10 percent who preach revolt occupy far more key positions in the *ummah* than the 10 percent who halfheartedly keep Ramadan each year, then pay little attention to their faith. The enormous, rambunctious assembly in the middle will have to turn to one or the other extremes as economic, political and spiritual change moves along at a glacial pace. Don't bet on the Oxford-educated doctors! As one writer has commented on the future of Islam: "In the Arab-Muslim world, where the moderate center was always a fragile flower, the political moderates are on the defensive everywhere, and moderate Muslim spiritual leaders seem almost nonexistent."[123]

Mainstream Muhammad will be the building block of the next great enemy of the West, and particularly the United States. The fundamentalist movement will progress from a grassroots level to political legitimacy, if the history of other terrorist movements proves to be a helpful guide. As one security expert has written: "the movement will grow from the bottom up by recruiting first disaffected individuals, then organizations and finally nations, in the Middle East and elsewhere."[124] If you think I'm overly pessimistic, know that Islamic journalists who have an intimate knowledge of the fundamentalist wave take an even dimmer view of its impact on the regular Muslim. Mohamed Sifaoui, an Algerian writer who spent months in a jihadist cell in France, says starkly that the very notion of a moderate Islam is a "wishful construct of naïve Westerners." He points to the French effort, in particular, to "define a moderate brand of Islam compatible with its secular liberalism."[125] Again, we often see Islam through our own cultural lens, and we end up with a toned-down, calmer version than the one that really exists, one reason I was compelled to write this book.

Another cultural value that affects our understanding of fundamentalism is the importance we place on personal choice and freedom, assuming that everyone in the world will opt for the best course for themselves alone and make decisions in a vacuum. However, one reason why mass movements flourish in the Two-Thirds World is the worldview that places society and family ahead of the individual. Thus, when common Muslims sense that one political philosophy is best for their nation, they often will override personal convictions for the betterment of their extended clans. The booming call of fundamentalists sounds extremely enticing to someone who wants his nation to advance, even if he personally would hesitate to call himself a jihadist. For this reason, a movement with fewer than 10 percent of the population can quickly mushroom to a majority.

The average Muslim, finally, is a human being formed in the image of God. He relates to God in the only way that he knows how, in the way that his family has taught its members for more than a thousand years, in many cases. The confession of faith serves as his bedrock: "There is no god but Allah"…whispered into his ear at birth…"and Muhammad is His prophet"…spoken as a reminder during the burial. From cradle to grave, Islam has been the only version of truth that he has known, in most cases.

In a final entreaty for grace when considering our Muslim cohabitants on planet Earth, I would proffer the radical proposition that, given the same background and context, we, too, in the U.S. would react similarly to current conditions as described in this chapter. We, too, would shriek for radical change through obedience to God. Actually, some of us already do! The intellectual distance between righteous anger over the world's injustices and the belief that religious fervor is the answer does not prove large. True Christians pray "Thy kingdom come" and live as Jesus did, introducing that dominion by one kind act, one healing word, one church planted at a time.

Muslims are often more inclined to reach for a weapon to extend Allah's reign, as their founder did. Their number grows as three formidable trends shape modern Islam, all of which both evidence and influence the change in Mainstream Muhammad's heart.

Chapter Five

Trends in the Islamic World

As the average Muslim tries to figure out how to improve his lot in life and best submit to Allah, the world waits expectantly. The much-heralded battle for the soul of Islam is waged day after day in villages and cities a galaxy away from American suburbia. As Muslims decide what their faith consists of and who they want to be, the pace of change in all cultures reaches new speeds. Islam, too, reconfigures every year, in ways that should cause concern to those outside the *ummah*.

From my reading and experience, I detect three prominent trends in the Islamic world that have particular bearing on the End Times.

The Rise of Fundamentalism

The first sea change one notices in surveying the Muslim world is the rise of fundamentalism. Entire books have been written about this development, which has caught most of the world by surprise, especially those Western philosophers who saw modern man moving away from such quaint notions as God and faith as he continued his intellectual evolution. The assumption was that as people became better educated and processed the evidence for the naturalistic worldview, they would lay aside a fervent practice of religion that simply divided the world anyway. The arguments for such "progress" fell on deaf ears in the Muslim world, however, issuing as they did from secularized infidel minds. The death of God was under-reported in Iran and Indonesia, in Pakistan and Mauritania. The common man in Islam never succumbed to the ballyhooed secularization of the world. Islam has catapulted in the opposite direction in recent decades, to the astonishment of even many of its own practitioners. What has powered this transformation of the second largest religion in the world? I focus on two primary causes: the desperation of the poor and the military success of Islamic armies.

The 2004 United Nations' Human Development Report found that half of the least developed countries in the world come from the Islamic world. More than 50 percent of the citizens of these countries live at or below the absolute poverty line of $1/day.[126] The numerous dictatorships in these countries have done a skillful job of squandering the income from natural resources such as oil and gas to fatten their family fortunes. Many of the countries listed in the UN's misery index also feature large Islamic minorities and, having lived in two such nations, I can verify that the poorest areas had the most mosques and the fewest infidels. The fault of this cannot be placed on Islam, but the correlation stands true. Muslims would argue that discrimination limits their economic opportunity in such nations, and their claim would contain much truth. That reason carries less weight, however, when Muslim-majority countries rich in natural assets make the roll of distressed nations.

Those of us who have lived in the Third World were amused by the American public's reactions to the unveiling of Saddam Hussein's fortune as coalition troops conquered successive cities in Iraq, and soon after publicized the lifestyles of the rich and not-so-famous from his family and inner circle. Such inequities can be found in dozens of countries, many ruled by secular Muslims like Hussein. Government service has never been sought for altruistic reasons in such countries; being appointed to any post in civil service equals access to state-run businesses whose coffers fill and then are quickly emptied before the general population is even aware of the transaction. Political office has long served as a means to enrich oneself. That is why elections often turn bloody in many societies—the winner gains much more than a title and influence, he or she hits the lottery!

Betrayed by rulers like Hussein, none of whom can be called "good" Muslims who practice a faith of simplicity and sharing, a growing number of desperate people are calling for change. High birthrates prevail throughout the Islamic world (the median age is often about 15) and large families with hungry mouths grow impatient with the relentless inequalities around them. Again, I would submit that you and I would be motivated to seek change as well, and we might not always choose peaceful methods were our bellies empty for a long enough period. Hunger and poverty cause people to do things that they might not normally do. I lived next door to an upstanding couple in Africa that passively watched two of their daughters turn to prostitution to make a living. My wife and I were delighted to help one of those women out of that lifestyle. She was a cheerful, gracious, generous woman who certainly didn't aspire to sell her body for money, but she went too many meals without food. I have never forgotten that drama as I think about poor people pushed to extremes.

In most Muslim countries, economic growth has not kept pace with the rise in population. A gigantic combustible segment of the younger generation can be seen throughout the developing world: unemployed men with lots of time and energy wandering the streets. When this portion of a population grows to a significant percentage, unrest will surely follow, Muslim or non-Muslim context. The fact that Islamic nations are often poorer and have more youthful men than most renders them most vulnerable to the call of the fundamentalist. One recent example would be the militia of Moqtada Sadr in Iraq. Despite suffering hundreds of casualties in battles with U.S. forces, the Mehdi Army's ranks continue to swell, primarily because the men who take up their weapons to defend Islam and possibly die a martyr's death have nothing else to do. One senior U.N. advisor to the interim Iraqi government stated it succinctly:

> "You cannot expect these young men to distance them-
> selves from the militia unless there is a program that will
> give them a chance to earn a decent living and improve
> their living conditions. They're a group of people with no
> jobs and no future. The same reasons that led them to join
> this movement still exist."[127]

Several books have been written on this phenomenon, among the most helpful a tome by a former CIA agent who worked undercover in Afghanistan. He opines that poverty, religious belief and political frustration are three of the primary ingredients in the cocktail that turns young men into terrorists, but argues that the desire to be in an intimate gang should not be discounted. When that small group is indoctrinated in fundamentalism, the author concludes, the target of its collective testosterone moves from fans of the opposing soccer team (as would be the case in England) or rival gang members sporting different colors (as in American inner cities) to infidels, and, most frequently, the U.S.[128]

Adds one former national security advisor to the president of the Philippines, a country that has battled Islamists for years, stated in a speech to a regional security conference in Honolulu: "At bottom, Islamism is a rebellion of the excluded, a rebellion that feeds on the unfulfilled longings and desires of impoverished peoples living on the margins of an unattainable consumerist world."[129] Well said!

And, that rebellion has gathered an ever deeper army, thanks to the colossal financial apparatus in Saudi Arabia that funds Wahhabite teaching around the world, printing Korans, tracts and pamphlets, subsidizing the recording of radical lectures, constructing Koranic schools and mosques in towns big and small around the globe. It is a curious experience to stumble upon a gleaming mosque in a largely impoverished African city, for instance. The combined incomes of all the surrounding residents could not possibly bankroll the erection of such a structure. When one asks the locals where the money came from, the answer is almost always Saudi Arabia.

The roots of this missionary effort can be traced to the 1979 Iranian revolution, which reverberated worldwide. Fundamentalists realized that with enough organization and zeal, they could overthrow the secular governments in their lands as well, spreading what Khomeni called "the first day of God's government" on April 1, 1979.[130] His vision whipped Muslims into a fever pitch:

> "With a population of almost one billion and with infinite sources of wealth, you can defeat all the powers. Aid God's cause so that He may aid you. Great ocean of Muslims, arise and defeat the enemies of humanity. If you turn to God and follow the heavenly teachings, God Almighty and His vast hosts will be with you."

Ed Hotaling, a longtime correspondent in the Middle East, rightly noted that Muslims learned several vital lessons from the overthrow of the Shah, among them that Islam could indeed battle the status quo and that terrorism is justified. Soon after Iran's revolution, religiously inspired guerillas took up arms with renewed vigor in Palestine and Lebanon, and zealots plotted the successful assassination of Anwar Sadat in Egypt, the initial ripples in what is now a stormy sea.[131] Islamists in Cairo captured this new boldness and vigor in Islam with banners that read: "The Muslims are coming. We are going to change the face of the world by Islam, and rule by the Koran."[132]

In that same year, the conflict between the new guard and entrenched authorities spread to Saudi Arabia. During two weeks of fierce combat, 127 Saudi troops and 117 Saudi insurgents died after Wahhabites seized the Grand Mosque at Mecca. King Khalid immediately pledged $25 billion to expand and modernize the shrines at Mecca and Medina, and billions more flowed into new universities that would graduate Islamic scholars by the thousands. The royal family had cut a deal with the Wahhabi clerics: allow us to remain in power and you can control the school system and thus spread your brand of Islam around the world. Ironically, one of the prime beneficiaries of this newfound fervor was the bin Laden family, which reaped billions in construction projects, including the most important one—the restoration of the two holiest cities in Islam.

It is unfortunate, but no accident in God's greater plan, that the strain of Islam most propagated around the globe is of the fundamentalist variety. Petrodollars have powered the brainwashing of a generation and flung indefatigable missionaries to the four corners of the Earth. I've met these preachers. When they arrive in a city, the entire population begins to buzz, as revolutionaries have electrified people for centuries in other times and places. Their call to military and spiritual jihad falls on the particularly open ears of the young and destitute. Huntington, in *The Clash of Civilizations and the Remaking of the World Order*, correctly observed that the disproportionately young Islamic population worldwide had significant ramifications: "First, young people are the protagonists of protest, instability, reform and revolution," and, youth "provide the recruits for Islamist organizations and political movements," citing Iran and Algeria as prime examples, as well as Saudi Arabia, where as far back as 1988 Crown Prince Abdullah said the greatest threat to his country was the rise of Islamic fundamentalism among its youth.[133]

According to eyewitnesses, the unemployed in Abdullah's kingdom do little else but sit around the mosque and watch Al-Jazeera, the blatantly pro-Islamic worldwide cable channel that does much to intensify unrest.[134] Can you imagine the impact of a entire class of such indoctrinated young men? We will soon see more of their faces in our newspapers and on our television screens as they strike for Allah.

We Americans should never underestimate the potential power of an unemployed age bracket. I can remember being among the scores of unemployed in West Africa, wondering what they did each day to pass the time. They led a miserable existence, and they searched for political philosophies that could promise a new day and give them a cause.

Just because a young person cannot find a job does not mean that they have to turn to jihad, but the loudest voices on the street corners in the Islamic world are currently those of the fundamentalist faction. Ironically, you and I have helped their cause. Every time we fill up our ever-larger vehicles with gasoline, we make it possible for another teacher of Islamic domination to earn a living or another set of books to be printed that call for a fierce upheaval of the world order in the name of Allah. As ex-CIA agent Robert Baer says in his book *Sleeping With the Devil*: "We buy oil from Saudi Arabia, refine it, and put it into our automobiles, and a certain small percentage of what we pay for it ends up funding terrorist acts against America and American institutions at home and abroad." I will return to this paradoxical arrangement in a later chapter.

Coupled with abundant cash to spread jihad has been a growing military capability to spread pure Islam. A faith founded by the sword still believes in its stricter sectors that military conquest equals the understood approval and encouragement of Allah. When the *muhajeedin* ran the Soviets out of Afghanistan, the validity of Wahhabite arguments gained much ground. Muslims concluded all over the world that Allah had awarded the victory because the warriors had purified themselves before him, following the detailed prescriptions for daily life that conservatives had urged for decades. The 35,000 warriors from 43 countries returned home with a passion to continue their efforts to decontaminate Islam, and their influence continues to this day.

Of course, this ragtag group would have never been able to expel a superpower without the backing of the U.S., which miscalculated on this particularly shortsighted Cold War strategy. The largest covert operation in the history of the CIA—$3 billion in aid dispensed—was part of a U.S. policy to pump up fundamentalism as a counterbalance to Soviet influence. Other authors explore this tragic tactic in great detail, among them a Columbia University professor who links today's war on terror far more closely to the Reagan era than previously thought.[135]

As Islamic rebels attempt to seize power in republics like Chechnya, parts of the Philippines, and now Iraq, the message of Allah's will being expressed in glorious victory shall repeat itself. You should note that every time an Islamic force gains a victory, it reinforces two foundational beliefs: that Allah has big muscles, and that he lends those muscles to holy and pure warriors, even as he did in the day of Muhammad. As one defense expert put it:

> "In Al-Qaeda's battle traditions, Saladin's long-ago victories over the Crusaders have merged with victorious battles against the Soviets and the heroics of suicide bombers and action groups against Jews and Americans—including the 1983 bombings of a U.S. marine barracks in Beirut, the near-sinking of the USS Cole in 2000, and actions in Afghanistan, including the successful standoff against American and local forces at Tora Bora. Finally, resistance to the American-led invasion of Iraq, starting with the suicidal resistance of Saddam's Fedayeen and continuing through the current uprising, have created for Al-Qaeda and like-minded Muslims a strong martial tradition that, until recently, was wholly absent from modern times."[136]

An objective observer could read that last paragraph and rightfully wonder, "What victories?" However, fundamentalism feeds more on emotion and passion than reason, and jihadists take irrational pride in even moral victories. As the same observer continued:

> "In the Middle East, perception is often more important than reality, and legends can be born overnight....
> Popular Islamic opinion in the Middle East perceives a string of jihad 'victories' over Western arms...facts are immaterial; whether or not American wins a battle or even a series of battles, the belief that Muslims successfully stood up to foreign soldiers has galvanized and will

continue to galvanize Islamic pride and support for anti-Western agendas."[137]

Jihadists see Iraq as the latest proving ground for their movement and Allah's corresponding blessing, and they evince confidence in that divine benediction. Abu Musab al-Zarqawi, the Jordanian terrorist now seen as the head of Al-Qaeda's "Mesopotamian" branch (newly opened by him), adds: "There is no doubt that the Americans' losses are very heavy because they are deployed across a wide area and among the people and because it is easy to procure weapons. All of which makes them easy and mouthwatering targets for the believers."[138]

The catch-22 in Iraq and future fields of battle is that Islamic enthusiasm for jihad will not rise and fall based on wins and losses. Simply staging battles in Allah's name is sufficient to lure a continuing stream of recruits. As one U.S. Army colonel summarized: "Regardless of the eventual success or failure of the new Iraqi Government, resistance to the United States and our allies will become the stuff of heroic history throughout the Middle East to those who agree, secretly or openly, with Al-Qaeda's agenda."[139] And that history, being made as you read, will steer in the fundamentalist direction for years to come, if past terrorist organizations bear any clue. The colonel continued:

> "If, as I expect, Al-Qaeda makes the transition in the coming
> decade from a deadly, popular but rootless terrorist group-
> ing to the sitting government of a number of countries, this
> heroic theme will inspire their governing institutions,
> including regular military and paramilitary forces, and will
> become part of the pan-Arab, anti-Crusader tradition."[140]

This revival of "anti-Crusader" tradition has given Muslims a renewed sense of pride. They stand up straight now, no longer hunch their shoulders, projecting the assurance of a people who believe their time has come. The era of Western domination has come and gone, they believe, and Allah has been moved, in his good time, to judge the morally corrupt Occidental powers, thereby granting an unstoppable momentum to his choice for global governance: Islam.

Arabia magazine summarized this view as it covered the first successful strikes made by fundamentalist terrorists in the 1990s: "We
are witnessing the upsurge of anti-Western, radical Islam. It is perhaps too late for the West to do anything about it, except sit tight
and brace itself for the tidal wave that will soon hit the ship."[141] That
wave looms perilously close in European countries with large
Muslim minorities. As a disenfranchised generation of Islamic
youths grows more frustrated with its lack of advancement in
French society, for instance, the call to overthrow the infidel government gains support. A political system built on the rock of absolute
secularism clashes continually with its Islamic population over
everything from *Halal* meat (prepared by a Muslim butcher) in
preschools to headscarves on schoolgirls, from the proper celebration of Islamic holidays to mixed-sex school gym classes. French
authorities have made calculated accommodations; on other
statutes they refuse to bend, like the prohibition of veiled schoolgirls. A growing group of Muslims has realized that the only way for
them to express their faith without restraint will be to change the
supreme authority, from Chirac to cleric. Confirming the germina-
tion of this idea, French police report military-style Al-Qaeda units
of 35,000-45,000 men in their country.[142] These recruits draw their
inspiration from the preaching of imams who, in two cities about 30
minutes from my former residence, recently called their congregations to holy war against all infidels and an attack of U.S. interests
both in France and worldwide.[143]

In a delicate effort to soothe its restless Muslim population,
France has gone so far as to allow the legalization of The Muslim
Brotherhood, an outlaw organization in most other countries, as
well as to coordinate the election of an Islamic council that regularly
meets with government representatives to air its grievances. To the
shock of then-Interior minister Nicholas Sarkozy, the most fundamentalist party garnered 40 percent of the vote, the highest percentage of all competing factions. The president of this delegation
asserted "our constitution is the Koran," telling words that summarized this contemporary mind-set and surely vexed those in the halls
of power in Paris.[144]

France's neighbor to the north has also struggled with an outbreak of this latest incarnation of Islam. As weekly busts reveal an
infestation of terrorist cells, British authorities scratch their heads in

confusion over how a generation that grew up on "soccer, pop music and cricket" has fallen prey to "the strong pull of fundamentalist clerics who preach the glories of struggle against Western convention and of the ecstasy of martyrdom."[145] One doesn't have to travel to Iraq or Saudi Arabia to verify fundamentalism's surge, just book a flight to London or Paris.

This Islamist renewal shows no signs of abating, and the Iraqi conflict has perpetuated the upsurge. More and more of the dead in Falluja and Baghdad carry European citizenship cards, having been recruited through mosques, Muslim centers and militant Web sites, and those fortunate enough to return to Hamburg and Marseille will have become full-fledged jihadists. As one French intelligence official said, "We consider these people dangerous because those who go will come back once their mission is accomplished. They can use the knowledge gained there in France, Europe or the United States. It's the same as those who went to Afghanistan or Chechnya." The Iraqi conflict provides a "galvanizing cause that sends idealistic young men abroad, trains them, and puts them in touch with a more radical global network of terrorists."[146] To prove their fears, security officers note that almost all of the major terrorists arrested in Europe in the past three years spent time in Bosnia, Afghanistan or Chechnya. The sophisticated conscription networks provide forged documents, financing, training and information about infiltration routes into Iraq.

A Growing Anger and Hopelessness

A second trend in Islam that lays the groundwork for fundamentalism's comeback is a growing anger and hopelessness among Muslims. As their secular, crooked governments have betrayed them and gobbled up national resources, their patience runs thin, especially because Islamic rulers are expected to be just, simple men, like the founders of the faith. When those who claim to be submitted to Allah comport themselves more like the prince of Monaco than Muhammad, the wound pierces deeper among their trampled citizens. Corruption in the name of God crushes the spirit; hypocrisy fuels an especially intense antagonism.

It would be difficult for Americans to fathom living under a government where the president appears to be even more religious than President Bush, with a constitution claiming to be submitted to divinely inspired scriptures, then have freedom of expression suppressed and state treasuries filled while unemployment soars and scandals remain unexposed. Any normal human being with even a trace of political awareness would be furious with such an arrangement. A like separation between ruling elite and peasant has provoked revolution on every continent. When a phony layer of religious devotion protects the powerful in the name of divine order, the backlash can be ferocious. Just ask the French. How similar rage expresses itself in Islamic countries concerns all of us now. Their revolutions rock the world, too.

Sociologists and political scientists have long predicted a revolt of the impoverished "South" when clean water and food ran low and the destitute began to demand their piece of the world pie. As *National Geographic*'s explorer-in-residence prophesied: "The voices of the poor, who deal each moment with the consequences of environmental degradation, political corruption, overpopulation, the gross distortion in the distribution of wealth and the consumption of resources who share few of the material benefits of modernity, will no longer be silent."[147] Many hundreds of millions of those poor live in the Islamic world. The latest Arab Human Development Report issued by the United Nations Development Program details the woeful numbers: the least politically free region of the world has one in five citizens living on less than $2 a day, even amidst the oil riches. Sixty-five million adults are illiterate, nearly two-thirds of them women, producing a populace that can be easily swayed by fanatical, illogical arguments.[148] The majority of Muslims form an indigent, undereducated bloc ripe for the picking by fundamentalist fury. They do not have the schooling to read and process contrary arguments in favor of a more personal, moderate adaptation of Islam. As someone who has lived among the poorest of the poor, believe me when I tell you that 95 percent of Muslims will never give full hearing to both sides of the debate over the form of Islam that will dominate the twenty-first century. These people do not lack intelligence, but they have never been taught critical thinking skills, and it's hard to be judicious on an empty stomach. When a bearded, seemingly righteous man stands up in the mosque and promises a lamb in every pot, the needy will follow him. You and I would, too, in their shoes. The Muslim in the suit running the government in the capital has let these people down for too long. They are hungry and incensed.

One reason they are more irate than in previous generations generates little discussion, but obviously has played a prominent role in the past 30 years: the boob tube. Television has shown the poor just how underprivileged they are, and they now have a window into how the other 10 percent lives. Unrest is inevitable. As one foreign policy leader stated: "Arabs are increasingly exposed to the world through the electronic media, and likely to become more angry and frustrated about their degraded status in a globalizing world economy. You don't have to strain to see such forces at play in the blind rage of Islamic radicals."[149]

I've seen, up close, the effects of this exposure to the wider, richer world. I remember passing busy courtyards in Africa that would suddenly become quiet at 4 P.M. as everyone gathered around the sole television set hooked up to a generator placed on a flimsy table in the middle of the common area, next to the mango tree. The reason for the halt in activity? J.R. Ewing and the gang of *Dallas* entranced the Ivorian audience. At the show's conclusion, the questions flew at me in short order: "Does every American live in a huge house/have two cars/swim in backyard pools?" No matter how much I tried to dispel such notions, many Africans believed that I was just trying to hide the wealth of America and, consequently, my own riches. I would wager that one of the most durable urban legends in the world is the bounty of the United States, where the streets are thought to be paved in gold and everyone lives on spacious, multi-million dollar ranches. Programs like *Dallas* scrape at a scab among the world's poor, whose brutally hard lives seem even more miserable when they realize that others, especially the infidels, have unlimited access to an all-you-can-eat buffet. Even David wondered how the wicked could be so prosperous in many of his psalms. That sentiment abides among the deprived today, and those in the Islamic world pray to Allah for a correction of such inequities. When a traveling Wahhabite preacher urges such disadvantaged people to take action and join the revolution, he faces a receptive audience. Moderate Muslims realize the fight they are up against in the battle for the Islamic soul in such conditions. They acknowledge that the defection of huge numbers of people from a purely religious Islam to a violent, politicized version has arisen "because of the oppression, illiteracy, dictatorships, poverty, human rights abuses and hopelessness into which millions of Muslims are born."[150]

Another verifiable evidence of this relationship between poverty and fundamentalism is the appeal of Koranic schools in dozens of nations. Such schools do not graduate students ready to compete in a sophisticated global marketplace. They are quite skilled, however, in producing young people who have memorized large portions of the Koran and know just enough Arabic to spread Islam. Most of the teachers hail from Saudi Arabia and Egypt, and they spread the Wahhabite doctrine that insists on the fundamentalist version of Islam. What balloons the rolls at these schools? The promise of something as simple as a free lunch, in many cases. Hundreds of thousands of Muslim parents face a choice every fall: should they send young Kareem to the state-supported school or to the *madrassa*? They often opt for the free lunch, and another generation of zealots bent on world conquest is formed. The impact of these schools should never be underestimated. Even Secretary of Defense Donald Rumsfeld questions whether it is possible to kill militants faster than radical clerics and religious schools can create them.[151] Koranic schools around the world churn out millions of graduates who have no employment possibilities at the end of their studies; they often turn to jihad. Coalition forces would have to bomb every Koranic school in the world to snuff out this lifeline of fundamentalism, an untenable option.

Regrettably, not even our allies in the war on terrorism are doing all they can to staunch the flow of hate-filled graduates. As two veteran observers of Pakistan, for instance, noted:

> "U.S. officials are rightly beginning to grumble that they are not getting what they are paying for with billions of dollars of economic and military aid. In high-profile pledges two years ago, Musharraf vowed to crack down on *madrassas*, the religious schools where many Pakistani children receive their education and which have often been a wellspring of extremism. Pakistan has failed to deliver on those pledges; most *madrassas* remain unregistered, their finances unregulated, and the government has yet to remove the jihadist and sectarian content in their curricula."[152]

In addition to free lunches, Islamic social services often do a better job at caring for the poor than the government agencies in their

countries, another means of winning the vulnerable to the fundamentalist side. I applaud such care for the destitute, but it comes
with a price tag. Aid groups often extract commitments from those
who seek help, and Muslim societies become further radicalized.

This struggle with the realities of poverty, and particularly
unemployment—a maddening condition for any man—reaches its
nadir when a martyr's death becomes an attractive option in many
societies. It chilled me to see, for instance, a recent televised report
on Palestinian youth affirm that 70 to 80 percent of them confessed
a desire to die as martyrs. Children who see older brothers and sisters, cousins and neighbors complete school, find jobs and become
contributing members of a functioning society do not dream of
becoming martyrs! They choose life, not death. The tongue-in-
cheek statements about terrorism as a career path contain more
truth than we realize. Perhaps the reason why killing Americans
seems like such an appealing career option in Iraq is its estimated 60
percent unemployment rate.[153]

Rather than focusing our full anger on the religious teachers who
glorify such death, we should never forget that it is Satan himself who
created this booby trap in Islam. In a religion where no one knows if
they have done enough to enter Paradise, the Devil offers one "sure"
way to lounge among virgins for all eternity. He whispers into the ears
of an entire generation that has little or no future: "Kill yourself." If
any Western military analyst believes that suicide bombings will eventually cease due to a lack of volunteers, he should consider this: every
unemployed person in the Islamic world is a prime candidate for such
a dead-end role. As long as there are young men (and sometimes
women) with too much time on their hands and no prospects for the
future, locked in a religion with no assurance of salvation, the queue
for glory in martyrdom will never end. Paradise sounds far more
appealing than living as an unemployed failure in a tiny apartment in
Palestine or as a frustrated job-seeker dwelling in a filthy high-rise in
France. Enraged Muslims who want to make a statement to the world,
who desire to have an impact in this life despite their insignificance,
find a voice in terrorism. As one writer explained, "A disenfranchised
minority cannot sack Rome, rape Nanking, burn Atlanta or firebomb
Dresden.... A disenfranchised people...will use the means at their
disposal. Amoral though it may be, terrorism succeeds in focusing
attention on whatever cause its practitioners espouse."[154]

This hopelessness and resentment appeared vividly to me one July 15th. Walking down a wide avenue in the Parisian suburb of Colombes, I witnessed what looked like a war zone: shattered glass spread over a half-mile length of street, bus stops blown up, telephone booths in shards. It looked as if a huge bomb had been dropped on the street, but the perpetrators were actually young Muslims who had gone on a rampage the entire previous night. When one journalist asked local residents why such destruction had been wrought, one boy answered for his entourage: "This is what we think of France's Independence Day. This is how we celebrate here."

In summary, a combination of economic and religious factors contribute to the rising tide of rage in the Islamic world. Quick fixes and large donations alone will not cure the disease; part of the problem lies in Islam itself. Sadly, unemployment is rising, not decreasing, in most Islamic countries. The resulting despair has a symbiotic relationship with fundamentalism, both feeding it and growing from it.

A Renewed Hatred of Jews

Throughout history, a convenient scapegoat for a country's woes has often been the Jews, and Islam has them in their crosshairs as never before, the third trend I would highlight for this study. An abundance of evidence worldwide points to a renewed contempt for this people group by Muslims. Numerous Web sites, textbooks and even public discourses describe a world where Jewish people seek to rule supreme and therefore must be destroyed. This contempt finds its apex, of course, in the Middle East, where Muslims have sought to obliterate Israel since its birth. As one veteran observer of the region succinctly noted: "For over a half century, the majority of Arabs have persisted in seeing the state of Israel as a temporary condition, an enemy they eventually expect to dispense with, permitting Israelis to, at best, live as a subject people in 'Palestine.' At worse, who knows?"[155] Long-time observers sense a new level of intensity in this furious fight between cousins. Current technology speeds the transmission of explosive rhetoric and images from both sides of the conflict, and an entire generation grows up marked by this mutual abhorrence.

I have a friend who has a special love for Jewish people and keeps a close eye on their treatment in the media. She occasionally e-mails me Web links that might interest me. One of her messages did not come with a warning about explicit content, but it should have. Before my eyes, after my mouse click connected to the site, a horrible illustration filled the screen: two bearded men stood with skulls in their hands, appearing to bang on large green doors. The caption? We Muslims will knock on the doors of Paradise with the skulls of Jewish people.

The explosive issues surrounding Palestinians in the Holy Land have served as a focal point and excuse for this demonic hatred. Without question, Israel has not welcomed the stranger as Yahweh commanded, as I previously mentioned, but as the suffering of Palestinian people is amplified worldwide, one important fact seems to escape mention time and again. The 1998 Camp David talks between former President Clinton, Yassar Arafat and then-Israeli Prime Minister Ehud Barak proved the existence of an Arab agenda that left many mystified. Why would Arafat reject the most generous terms ever for a Palestinian state and partial control of Jerusalem? Simple: Muslims want more than a state for the Palestinians; they want Israel destroyed.

Space does not allow me to cite all of the anti-Semitic rhetoric pouring out across the Islamic world. I leave *U.S. News and World Report* to summarize this expansion of Jew-hating:

> "In the Muslim world, a culture of hatred of Jews perme-
> ates all forms of public communications—newspapers,
> videocassettes, sermons, books, the Internet, television and
> radio. The intensity of the anti-Jewish invective equals or
> surpasses that of Nazi Germany in its heyday…Throughout
> the Islamic world, one finds slanderous quotations about
> Jews as the sons of apes and donkeys."[156]

This increased anti-Semitism has infected the young as well, and will continue to until the end of Time, I believe. Koranic school text-books reinforce the popular Muslim myth that Allah turned Jews into apes for seven days as punishment for their disobedience in Old Testament times. These textbooks also teach that Judgment Day will not come "until the Muslims fight the Jews and kill them."

This detestation will have implications for the U.S., of course, which stands as one of the sole unflinching supporters of the Jewish state. The book *Preachers of Hate* makes the connection:

"Americans will be stunned to discover the depth and
extent of anti-Semitic hatred in today's Middle East and
that Arab leaders from Saudi Arabia to Egypt are not just
encouraging it, but spending a great deal of money to
spread the kinds of ideas inherent in…anti-Semitic tracts,
even as they declare their support for peace in the Middle
East. It is vitally important that Americans of all back-
grounds understand that much of today's anti-Semitism,
while aimed at Jews, stems from a belief system that equally
rejects America and indeed Western civilization as a whole.
Jews get attacked first, when the enemies of America can't
attack Americans. But make no mistake: we're next. It
begins with the Jews, but it never ends with the Jews."[157]

Digest that last sentence for a few moments and think about its
truth. Calculate the place of that truth in God's divine plan as you see
it revealed in His Book. Add it all together and you will realize that this
inferno of hatred for Jews comes straight from the pages of Revelation,
and several Muslim leaders take the prize for this End Times charac-
teristic. Can you see where this is headed? Can you see why I submit
that Muslims will play a central role in the Last Days in which we live?

Muslims often do not even attempt to hide their revulsion with
Jewish people, and a suspicious silence has muted coverage of the very
public expressions of their heart attitudes toward the children of
Abraham. For example, every newshound in the world should have
screamed in protest after the comments of Malaysian Prime Minister
Mahathir Mohamad at a summit of Islamic leaders in October 2003.
This supposedly progressive, moderate leader with 22 years in office
floated commonly held ideas about Jewish people that earned him a
standing ovation at the conference, which should have disgusted us all.
He stated: "The Europeans killed six million Jews out of 12 million,
but today the Jews rule the world by proxy. They get others to fight and
die for them…Jews have now gained control of the most powerful
countries and they, this tiny community, have become a world power."
Fortunately, he refrained from a call to arms against Jews worldwide,
but his statements fanned the flames of this historical hatred. Leaders
of countries allied with the U.S., such as Saudi Arabia, Afghanistan,
Pakistan and even Russia, said afterward that they had heard "nothing
untoward" in Mahathir's remarks.[158] Really?

Anti-Jewish venom flows more abundantly from such leaders, in part, due to the Arabs' inability to destroy Israel thus far. Jewish people must be smarter and/or more diabolical than Muslims in order to withstand the military and political opposition of one billion persons, they reason. The anger also arises out of a frustration with inept Islamic leaders who are unable to fairly govern their countries or annihilate Zion.[159] This loathing cannot be confined to verbal attacks alone; it inevitably erupts in violence. As columnist Richard Cohen states in his commentary on the Mahathir address:

> "The use of such language, the support of such ideas, is too often a precursor to violence....it does transform the opposition to Israel from a political-nationalistic dispute into a kind of vast pogrom in which compromise becomes increasingly impossible. In the end, such language could justify the use of the so-called Islamic bomb, an atomic weapon such as the one Iran is now developing and Pakistan already has."[160]

I believe the antichrist will capitalize on the popularity of these ideas and this history of frustration to justify such an attack right out of the apostle John's vision. Keep your ears open for greater doses of anti-Jewish slander in years to come. It will be a sure sign to lift up your head!

One doesn't have to travel to Islamic conferences or the West Bank to witness this growth in anti-Semitism. Violence against Jews has reached problematic proportion in many European countries, including France. Starting in the year 2000 following the *infitada* uprising, six synagogues were burned down in less than three weeks. By 2002, France was experiencing 12 anti-Semitic incidents daily.[161] *Le Parisien* newspaper reported 40 serious anti-Semitic acts warranting police investigation between January and May 2004 alone,[162] and France's Ministry of the Interior reported 135 acts of physical violence against Jews in little more than six months during 2004, most of them Muslim on Jew.[163] As synagogues continue to be torched at a record rate, rabbis are being beaten in the streets and Jewish schoolboys are staying home to avoid bullying by Muslim classmates. The entire country wrestles with this new phenomenon, a touchy issue for a nation that turned vast numbers of Jews over to the Nazis just 60 years ago.

This anti-Jewish bent should not surprise anyone who knows the history of Islam. Muhammad had a problematic relationship with the Jews in Medina as he tried to take full control of the city by persuading them that he was a prophet in the line of Abraham. After a time of peace in which he hoped to win them over to his new faith, he realized that conflict was unavoidable if the Jews rejected his message. Three tribes that lived in Medina suffered diverse fates as Muhammad sought to consolidate his power.

The first tribe was defeated in battle and the survivors fled north into Syria. The second tribe earned expulsion from Medina for their non-conformity a year later. The third, most obstinate tribe, the Qurayzah, tried a more creative strategy to survive. Initially, this group joined Muhammad's enemies in the Battle of the Confederates. "Filled with terror and dismay" after the battle, these Jews "shut themselves up in their castles" outside the city. After a 25-day siege they surrendered, and their sentence was announced: beheading for the 500-900 men, the sale of the women and their property divided among holy warriors. Muhammad memorialized this significant event in Islamic history: "And those of the people of the book who aided them (the pagans), god did take them down from their strongholds and cast terror into their hearts, (so that) some ye slew, and some ye made prisoners." (Koran 33:26)[164]

And so the millennia-old tension between the lines of Ishmael and Isaac flared up anew as Islam sought to establish a foothold in the Middle East. I believe that deep in his heart, Muhammad desired a monotheistic religion and more civilized culture for the Arab peoples, perhaps after observing the more advanced state of both Jewish and Christian peoples as he traveled abroad in trader caravans as a young man. To his credit, he initially tried to persuade the Jews around him that he was the last in the prophetic line of Abraham, Moses and David. When the Jews rejected his claims, he turned to the sword, and the Islamic impatience with them has continued to this day. It should be noted, in fairness, that Jews have lived peacefully in certain Islamic kingdoms. I think of the long history of Jews in Morocco as an example of tranquil co-existence for centuries. Other countries have also seen a minimal amount of conflict between these two leading religions. However, the fact that the founder of Islam brutally murdered Jewish people when they stood in his way rarely earns mention in today's discussions of tensions in the Middle East.

That spirit lives on in Islam, I believe, as does Judaism's refusal to acknowledge Muhammad as a prophet from God.[165]

The animosity between Sarah and Hagar and their offspring endures to this day. In recent years, Muslims seem less hesitant to vilify Jewish people, or beat and kill them if they so desire. This enmity bears watching as we consider the stage for the Time of Jacob's Trouble. Our country increasingly will be caught in the crossfire, and some observers believe a massive anti-Jewish and anti-American movement gains momentum by the day. For example, a "60 Minutes" reporter recently conveyed that American troops in Iraq are called Jews in Iraqi slang, reflecting the distrust that they have of our military. This lumping of America with the Jewish people, and resulting scorn, has intensified since 9/11, observers of the Arab world report. The great enemy of Islam has been labeled JIA: Jews, Israel and America.[166]

What a clear line drawn for the early twenty-first century! Whether or not the United States wants to cast the war on terrorism as Christianity versus Islam, Muslims have already seen the conflict in religious terms, as they see all clashes, given the lens of Islamic history. For now, the battle rages, but even the most optimistic jihadist must agree that the primary goals of his holy war remain elusive: Islam ruling the world, Israel destroyed, America overthrown. As disparate militias battle infidels the world over, Muslims realize anew that their united forces will accomplish much more than a patchwork deployment of armies. They also recognize that one voice must arise to rally the troops, bring them together as never before, and be wise and just enough to lead the world back to the enlightened age of Islam's first decades. This calls for no mere man. This calls for a superman. And when that man arises, Jesus himself will assist him in the forced submission of humanity to Allah, Islamic eschatology teaches. The time is ripe. Muslims are waiting and watching. You should be, too.

Chapter Six

The Men All Muslims Await

The Islamic world resembles a bubbling cauldron of angry people bobbing around, looking for opportunities to snatch food, water, territory and power in the modern world. The object of their desires depends on their place in the economic pecking order. As I have demonstrated, many have a legitimate need for adequate nourishment, and they often believe that a change to a fundamentalist government will ensure enough to eat and drink for all citizens. Others who have those basic needs met yearn for greater Islamic influence in the world. Still others desire to establish breakaway republics ruled by *sharia* law.

Every now and then, this boiling pot splashes over its brim and the world takes notice, as a Muslim leader arises and grabs an infidel by the throat, expelling him from holy ground and increasing the brotherhood's profile around the world. Terrorists strike and elicit intense media coverage, renewing the debate over the essence of Islam and its application in the modern world. These isolated "victories" on the part of fundamentalists do not layer upon one another to the point of Islamic domination. Muslims realize that, were they to challenge directly the American war machine for global supremacy, they would sustain heavy losses and perhaps be blasted into historical obscurity. Jihadists know that rocks and smuggled arms will not defeat U.S. firepower anytime soon. So, they nip at the giant's heel from time to time, consolidate their informal army, intensify the call to martyrdom and seek to amass increased weaponry for a final clash. The hardening of both sides in this conflict has left many anxious, including moderate Muslims, such as the Egyptian newspaper editor who stated recently, "The situation has become very scary. There's a real sense of doom. What's interesting to me is that no one has any kind of scenario on how this disaster will unfold."[167]

Ah, but such scenarios do exist. Scripture tells us about a final global showdown. What might surprise you are the parallels in the Islamic version of the end of time. Muslims use much of the same language, similar portents and a corresponding time frame in discussions about the end of this age. Amazingly, they, too, await the return of Jesus, and another messiah-like figure who will supersede Christ to bring the world under the sway of Allah.

The time seems to be right for these two men. Global tension will continue to mount as Iran joins the Nuclear Club, the Islamist majority in Pakistan gains control of the launch switch linked to warheads, and Saudi Arabia teeters on the brink of disarray. Soon, a clarion call will sound for a mediator, a deal broker, someone to stand in the East-West gap. Muslims have a clear picture of the man who can fill this bill, and his appearance will signal the final wave of Islamic expansion to the ends of the earth. This Islamic superman will need an assistant to convince the world of the truth of Islam. Who better than the one cited by two billion Christians as the chief rival to the religion of Muhammad? The emergence of these two men will set into motion Allah's plan for the ages: his name worshipped by all peoples.

Any Islamic book or teacher who treats the Last Days mentions these men and their ministries. The fact that few in the West know about them represents another odd secret of Islam, especially considering that these men will one day battle Western powers. One possible explanation of this ignorance is that Westerners have never bothered to consider the likelihood of such conquerors. Now, as we watch Islam gain strength, momentum and access to nuclear weapons in increasingly great numbers, we need to take seriously the many references in Islamic literature to this messiah and his right-hand man.

Muslims watch for signs of the End Times as eagerly as Christians do, at the urging of their founder, who also commanded a state of alert for his spiritual descendants. According to one hadith, Muhammad held up his thumb and forefinger with a tiny space between them and said, "I and the Last Hour are like this."[168] He and his companions had great interest in the Last Days, and many of his sayings referred to this nebulous period. The Koran also discusses the Day of Judgment and the days preceding it, and as is the case with many Koranic passages, the verses dealing with the end of the world sound quite biblical and seem to be describing the same final events of history.

The primary mission of Islam's leading two men will be to prepare the world for a final reckoning before Allah. The Koran explains this day of judgment as "a day" that might last 50,000 years (70:4), a day that could come at any time, because "One day with your Lord is as a thousand of your counting" (22:47). Only Allah knows for sure when "the Hour" will come: "The people will question thee concerning the Hour. Say: 'The knowledge of it is only with God.' What shall make thee know? Perhaps the Hour is near" (33:63). The Koran goes on to describe a terrifying doomsday, when mountains will "pass by like clouds" (27:88), the sun will be enfolded and the stars darkened. This terrible day will not arrive as long as even one Muslim dwells on planet Earth, "as long as there is someone on the earth saying, 'Allah, Allah,' " one hadith states.

Other similarities to the Bible's vision of the Apocalypse abound. The Koran, too, mentions a "beast" that will seek to discredit Islam (27:82), and the mysterious nations of Gog and Magog appear in sura 21: "When Gog and Magog are unloosed, and they slide down out of every slope, and the true promise draw near—then the eyes of the truth-concealers will stare: 'Woe to us, we were heedless of this! No, we were wrongdoers' " (vv. 96,97). In addition, much disruption of the social order and family relationships will occur, echoing Scriptural statements of a crumbling society.[169]

The preceding paragraphs should caution everyone to beware of the similarity of these Koranic verses and hadiths to biblical truth. Satan has created an incredibly close counterfeit that will deceive many in the Last Days, as it has already. Were I to paraphrase many of the above references, you would guess 1 Thessalonians or Revelation as the sources. The parallels to Christianity's version of the End Times don't stop there, as we will discover in a moment.

To prepare the world for judgment, Allah must first spread his religion from sea to sea to give everyone a chance to accept or reject his name. Islam burst out of Saudi Arabia soon after Muhammad began his ministry. It later stretched across several continents as it expanded through both missionary efforts and military conquest. Today, almost every country in the world has at least a small community of Muslims. However, large portions of the world, especially in those regions that dominate world events, have only a scant Islamic presence, and the leaders and cultures of those nations, primarily in the Western world, dishonor Allah daily. They have even gone so far as to send their infidel troops to the sacred ground of Islam. Surely they have overstepped their bounds, Muslims believe. Courageous heroes such as bin Laden have declared, "Enough!" and waged war on the infidel powers. These attacks represent a commencement of the overturning of the world system and the global adoption of Islam. The test run that was the Iranian revolution marked another important step in this process as the first modern theocracy was inaugurated. The sky-high Islamic birthrate generates additional momentum as the Islamic percentage of the world population continues to rise.

Al-Mahdi

Indeed, Muslims are almost giddy as they look for the man who will revive the Islamic empire. He will be called Al-Mahdi (also spelled Mehdi and Maadi), whose full name in Arabic translates to "The Awaited Savior" or "The Guided One."[170] According to Islamic teaching, Mahdi will be the first of the final "clear" signs of the Last Days, emerging just as mankind reaches a stage of great suffering.[171] Mahdi will grow up in an Islamic country, and through his leadership and holiness, attract the devotion of Muslims yearning for a righteous caliph to succeed the upright men of yesteryear. His coming was predicted soon after Islam began. Ali, the last of the "rightly guided ones," said (according to a reliable hadith), that Islam would "prevail over all religions...when the Messiah of this *ummah* makes his appearance."[172] Mahdi will be the super-caliph, not only a leader in the military and the commander of the faithful, but also the number one imam, the spiritual leader of the Islamic brotherhood.[173] He will be a general-priest-descendant of the prophet, a power-packed package of divine and physical power. No wonder Muslims can't wait until he shows up!

This final caliph will facilitate Muslims in achieving the dreams they've guarded for centuries, not only of worldwide domination, but, at least as importantly, a return to complete submission on the part of the faithful. The first four caliphs demonstrated the connection between these two strands in Islam. Their reign was marked not only by righteous living but, not without cause, rapid and far-reaching military triumph. The two have a symbiotic relationship in Islam. Persecuted, occupied and disadvantaged Muslims have been waiting nearly 1400 years for this double-edged flaming sword to slice through human history again. As Jason Burke, author of *Al Qaeda: Casting a Shadow of Terror*, defines: "Precisely how the utopian caliphate would function is vague. The militants believe that if all Muslims act according to a literal interpretation of the Islamic holy texts, an almost mystical transformation to a just and perfect society will follow."[174]

Some Muslims believe that Mahdi has already come. A sizeable sect originated in Pakistan after the ministry of one particular imam in the nineteenth century. Hazrat Mirza Ghulam Ahmad proclaimed himself to be Mahdi in January 1889 and wrote a powerful book explaining his ideas about the proper practice of Islam that convinced many of his authenticity.[175] The resulting Al-Amadiyya movement is regarded as a cult in the wider world of Islam, but the devoted followers of this group fervently preach a message of repentance and faith in their founder, refusing to compromise their distinctives or give up their trust in their legendary teacher. The more than a half-million devotes evangelize primarily in Pakistan.

Other eager Muslims thought Khomeni to be Al-Mahdi, but his death and limited influence eliminated his candidacy. He certainly had the charisma for the part, and I believe his revolution paved the way for the true Mahdi. Perhaps the bitter disappointment of that revolution not spreading to all countries and ushering in Paradise on Earth helps to explain why millions trampled each other to touch his casket. Not only was there a blessing to be gained in contact with the ayatollah, partially explaining the fervor, but those pilgrims knew that they were bidding adieu to the most likely aspirant for the title of Mahdi that the Muslim world had seen in centuries.

Still other Muslims look to bin Laden to lead the brotherhood in an hour of power, he being the warrior with the guts to stand up to the evil West. His image has been a rallying point for oppressed Muslims worldwide, and it's not hard to find his photo on apartment walls in Africa or T-shirts in Europe. Rather than a "Wanted: Dead or Alive" caption underneath his mug, one finds phrases like "Hero of Islam" and "Blessed Warrior" written around his face. However, Osama's age and the limited strength of Islam globally disqualify him as well, although, again, I believe he has helped to set the table for the real Mahdi. So, the wait continues.

Mahdi's profile has long been established, and Muslims are confident that they will know him when he appears on the scene. He will be of Muhammad's family, from the line of Fatimah, his first wife. Certain Islamic traditions pinpoint his center of operation in Iraq, near Karbala. Internet chat rooms now buzz with speculation that the conflict in Iraq has paved the way for his return, because, as one legend has it: when he comes, "The people will be chided for their acts of disobedience by a fire that will appear in the sky and a redness that will cover the sky. It will swallow up Baghdad."[176]

The idea that Mahdi will direct his campaign from Iraq dates to the assassination of Hussein, Muhammad's grandson, in the fateful battle near Karbala, when those who believed the caliphate should remain in the line of Muhammad were crushed by the Umayyad majority. The son of Ali, the last of the rightly guided leaders, was slaughtered, along with his family, in a tragic end still violently mourned by Shiite Muslims. How remarkable that our world reads news stories from these very areas every day now! Could the Muslim Messiah be lurking in the shadows of a bombed-out mosque in Iraq as I write? Could the global focus on Iraq be God's way of resurrecting these ancient cities to play a prominent role in the End Times? Why was President Bush so obsessed with invading this land? Could there have been reasons beyond his finite comprehension for this focus on a holy and historic land of Islam?

Such speculation could continue for years, but the portrait of Mahdi grows sharper still as we read of how he will lead Muslim people during his dominion. One teaching predicts that "every believer will be obliged to support him."[177] He will engender such loyalty through his miracle-working power. As one prediction clarifies: "In the last days of my ummah, the Mahdi will appear. Allah will give him power over the wind and the rain and the earth will bring forth its foliage." This supernatural power will not launch a torrent of wealth to fill his own storehouses in the manner of so many Muslim rulers today. No, Mahdi "will give away wealth profusely, flocks will be in abundance, and the ummah will be large and honored.[178] Allah will honor such generosity by opening up the storehouses of Heaven: "In those years my community will enjoy a time of happiness such as they have never experienced before. Heaven will send rain upon them in torrents, the earth will not withhold any of its plants, and wealth will be available to all. A man will stand and say, " 'Give to me, Mahdi!' and he will say, 'Take.' "[179] How appealing would this vision be to the hungry masses I've described in this book? No wonder "Allah will sow love of him in the hearts of all people."[180]

Mahdi's influence will spread far beyond the Islamic community. His rule will be over all the world, accomplished through military conquest. Fascinatingly, the duration of his reign in many accounts matches the biblical time frame of the seven-year tribulation before Christ's judgment. Most Islamic traditions refer to a seven-year peace agreement between the "Arabs and the Romans," which, given the time frame of the hadiths, could be understood as accords reached between Muslims and the West. One hadith that refers to this time of peace contains this extraordinary reference to Mahdi: "The people asked, 'O Prophet Muhammad, who will be the imam of the people at that time?' The Prophet said: 'He will be from my progeny and will be exactly 40 years of age. His face will shine like a star.' "[181]

Are you noticing the mounting evidence for the notion that the antichrist will be a Muslim person? Granted, this conjecture could be entirely false, but the number of parallels between Islamic and biblical prophecy should cause even the most ardent skeptic to reflect. Many of these similarities can be attributed to the same reason that the Koran sounds much like the Bible in many chapters: Muhammad had interacted extensively with Jews and Christians during his life as a trader, and he liberally borrowed from both traditions in his recapitulation of God's dealings with mankind. Even with this in mind, Mahdi sounds like a man we have read about in the Bible. That biographical description, coupled with our daily newspaper, yields an uncanny portrait of the Beast—a seven-year reign, possibly centered in Iraq, with great wealth at his disposal? Wait, it gets better.

Mahdi will inspire the Islamic community to take up arms for Allah. One writer predicts: "The Mahdi will establish right and justice in the world and eliminate evil and corruption. He will fight against the enemies of the Muslims who would be victorious."[182] Another adds: "He will reappear on the appointed day, and then he will fight against the forces of evil, lead a world revolution and set up a new world order based on justice, righteousness and virtue...ultimately the righteous will take the world administration in their hands and Islam will be victorious over all the religions."[183] This "new world order" will taste deliciously sweet to those who have suffered under dictators: "He is the precursor of the victory of the Truth and the fall of all tyrants. He heralds the end of injustice and oppression and the beginning of the final rising of the sun of Islam which will never again set and which will ensure happiness and the elevation of mankind...The Mahdi is one of Allah's clear signs which will soon be made evident to everyone."[184]

The clerics who wrote those last lines have engaged in the same sort of exercise that I have in the research of this book. Rather than finding biblical figures in Islamic literature, as I have attempted, they have done the contrary, supposedly unearthing Mahdi in certain portions of Scripture. Again, this typifies the Islamic desire to legitimize the faith of Muhammad as a continuation of Judaism and Christianity, an improvement on each, the last, best interpretation of God's will for man. This revisionist history has produced the doctrine of Muhammad as the coming counselor predicted in John 14, not the Holy Spirit, for instance. Likewise, Muslims believe the warrior for God in Revelation will be Mahdi, not Jesus: "It is clear that this man is the Mahdi who will ride the white horse and judge by the Qur'an, and with whom will be men with marks of prostration on their foreheads."[185]

The military campaign led by Mahdi sounds like a scene out of *Lawrence of Arabia*. He will lead a wave of black flag-bearing soldiers from Central Asia, probably Iran, across the Middle East in search of the final prize: Jerusalem. One hadith reports: "The Messenger of Allah said: 'The black banners will come from the East and their hearts will be as firm as iron. Whoever hears of them should join them and give allegiance, even if it means crawling across snow.'"[186] Black flags have historically been used by Islamic troops on jihad. That holy war will proceed into the holy city, where Mahdi will crown his reign. Muhammad reportedly said, "Black flags will come from Khurasan (Iran). No power will be able to stop them and they will finally reach Eela (Dome of the Rock in Jerusalem), where they will erect their flags."[187] Another hadith fills out the picture:

"Jerusalem will be the location of the rightly guided caliphate and the center of Islamic rule, which will be headed by Imam al-Mahdi...that will abolish the leadership of the Jews...and put an end to the domination of the Satans who spit evil into people and cause corruption in the earth, making them slaves of false idols and ruling the world by laws other than the sharia of the Lord of the worlds."[188]

That hadith also promises that Mahdi will eradicate "those pigs and dogs," referring to Jews and Christians. Does this sound like a person who could fit the profile of the antichrist? Do you feel as I do as I research this Islamic messiah, that as I learn more about him, the more he appears to be the last great enemy of the true and living God? The deeper I delve into his legend, the more I feel like I'm looking at a Polaroid picture. With each hadith I read, he becomes clearer and clearer, and he increasingly resembles the fearsome figure found in Daniel, Revelation and Ezekiel.

Isa, the Islamic Jesus

The correspondence with biblical prophecy in Islamic tradition doesn't stop at the description of Mahdi, it also offers a profile of the supernatural assistant who will bolster Mahdi's movement and discredit Christianity once and for all. Who better to refute the arguments of the Crusaders than Jesus himself?

Isa, the Islamic name of Jesus, will return to serve as Mahdi's vice president because Muslims do not believe that Easter weekend ever took place. Muhammad could not fathom a prophet of God hanging crucified on a cross, in such a position of weakness, so he invented the doctrine of substitutionary death, but not the one that Christians understand. No, the replacement was an imposter who was crucified on Golgatha, fooling the assembled masses as Allah performed another miracle and spared the life of Jesus. As Sura 4:157 claims: "That they (the Jews) said, 'We killed Christ Jesus the son of Mary, the Messenger of Allah'; but they killed him not, nor crucified him, but so it was made to appear to them, and those who differ therein are full of doubts, with no knowledge, but only conjecture to follow, for of a surety they killed him not." Jesus later ascended to Allah, Muslims believe, and he relaxes in Paradise while waiting to return to Earth and fulfill a normal course of life. When he does return, it will not be with trumpets blaring and judgment at hand. Rather, a weary, sweating Jesus will descend without much fanfare near Damascus, Syria. As one common tradition predicts: "At this very time Allah would send Christ, son of Mary, and he will descend at the white minaret in the eastern side of Damascus…and placing his hands on the wings of two angels. When he would lower his head, there would fall beads of perspiration from his head, and when he would raise it up, beads like pearls would scatter from it."[189]

Jesus will descend at Damascus because Mahdi's army will be assembled there, and he will immediately assume a secondary role to the Muslim Messiah. "Muslims will still be preparing themselves for the battle drawing up the ranks. Certainly, the time of prayer shall come and then Jesus, son of Mary, would descend."[190] Mahdi will ask Jesus to lead the soldiers in prayer, but Jesus will decline, deferring to Mahdi. This important event will establish the rank of these two men as they go on to lead the *ummah.* "Jesus will be following the Mahdi, the master of the time, and that is why he will be offering his prayers behind him."[191] After participating in the Islamic pilgrimage to Mecca to complete his résumé as a Muslim leader, Jesus will concentrate on evangelism and discipleship in *sharia* law. "Mahdi will lead the Muslims in prayer," one tradition states, "and Jesus will rule the Muslims according to the Divine Law."[192]

He will be particularly aggressive in spreading Islamic truth to Christians, to whom he will offer a stinging rebuke for their centuries of improper worship. One Islamic teacher expresses it this way: "Jesus will testify against those who had called him son of God, the Christians, and those who had belied him, the Jews."[193] Another adds: "When Jesus returns he will personally correct the misrepresentations and misinterpretations about himself…. He will affirm the true message that he brought in his time as a prophet, and that he never claimed to be the Son of God. In his second coming many non-Muslims will accept Jesus as a servant of Allah Almighty, as a Muslim and a member of the community of Muhammad."[194] I can imagine that Jesus would be accepted as a Muslim if he forgoes his claims to divinity. His first go-round on Earth would have proceeded far more smoothly had he adopted such a strategy!

Jesus will demonstrate his disgust with Christianity by "breaking the cross," according to Islamic prophecy. He will also kill pigs to correct Christian liberty in dietary matters, as well as abolish the Islamic tax on non-Muslims, not out of kindness, but rather to symbolize the end of peaceful cohabitation with non-Muslims. Infidels will no longer be able to pay a tax for the right to live in Islamic lands. They now will have to convert in order to prepare for the imminent judgment of

Allah. Jesus' ministry will prepare mankind for a time when "Allah will perish all religions except Islam," and his life's work will be dedicated towards Islam's worldwide supremacy.[195] "Jesus, the son of Mary will soon descend among the Muslims as a just judge," one teacher predicts, "all people will be required to embrace Islam and there will be no other alternative."[196] In a footnote of a Saudi translation of the Koranic verse that says that Islam will be "victorious over all other religions" (61:9), the translators cite the key person in this worldwide triumph: Jesus. "Isa (Jesus) the son of Maryam (Mary) will descend as a leader of the Muslims and it is a severe warning to the Christians who claim to be followers of Isa and he will break the Cross and kill the pigs, and he will abolish the *jizyah* (tax); and all mankind will be required to embrace Islam with no other alternative."[197]

It fascinates me that Islamic prophecy links the return of Jesus so definitively with Islam claiming complete allegiance among all nations, as if Allah has patiently allowed human beings to practice other faiths until the return of Jesus, who will come back not to set men free, but to enslave them in Islam. Jesus will also be a Jew-killer, reportedly, slaughtering the 70,000 followers of an antichrist-type figure named Dajjal, who will find a following among Jewish people.[198] After this exhausting work, Jesus will slow down a bit, marry and have children, living to age 40, according to some traditions,[199] 19 years after his marriage, others prophecy.[200] After battling the enemies of Islam with doctrine, miracles and military genius when necessary, the Islamic Jesus will then serve as the "spiritual head of a transnational government of peace. Everyone in the Middle East will willingly convert to Islam, and there will be no more war."[201]

Should we be surprised if and when such an imposter makes an appearance? Jesus said that many, I repeat, many, would come saying, "I am He." He told us to ignore such charlatans, but unfortunately, I can foresee millions of "Christians" falling for this Islamic imposter, duped by his supernatural powers and the logic of his words. Tens of millions of untaught Christians could be convinced by a charismatic teacher that Christianity was a cult grown out of Islam, which has been the only true religion since the beginning of time. This successful deception would fulfill the predictions of Jesus in Matthew 24, where he said, "For false Christs and false prophets will arise and will show great signs and wonders, so as to mislead, if possible, even the elect. Behold, I have told you in advance" (vv. 23, 24). He goes on to contrast His return with the lives of His imitators. Rather than having a 40-year life complete with wife and children, Jesus says, "For just as the lightning comes from the east, and flashes even to the west, so shall the coming of the Son of Man be" (Matthew 24:27). These will be important words to remember in a few years, I believe.

Reading over a wide variety of Islamic End Times literature, I find my mind edging toward one chapter in Scripture, a chapter that describes two men who will hold the world in the palms of their hands just before God's final judgment. Mahdi and Jesus sound disturbingly like the two figures described in Revelation 13. Some writers, such as Livingston in *The Final Clash*, believe that the Islamic Jesus will be the antichrist, the primary beast in this chapter, but Islamic prophecy seems to point to Jesus having a subordinate role, as I have demonstrated. Also, the Jesus of the Koran elicits high praise for his miraculous powers, which will be a feature of the primary beast's assistant in Revelation 13.

Let's dig deeper: verse 3 tells of the beast gaining a worldwide following due to his recovery from a fatal wound. Verse 14 details that the wound was caused by a sword. This sounds like a gash suffered by an Islamic war hero. Muslims have long favored the sword in battle, and even in a nuclear age, this instrument will figure somehow in Armageddon, apparently. Verse 5 records a three-and-a-half-year period of authority, arrogance and blasphemy on the part of the beast. Mahdi will certainly promote Islamic belief during his reign, mocking the Jewish and Christian god as he consolidates his power, which will "prove" the divine approval of his cause. The antichrist will "make war on the saints" verse 7 relates, overcoming them and gaining sovereignty over all people groups, similar to Mahdi's influence in Muslim prophecy as Islam will stretch from sea to shining sea. It is no leap in logic to presume that war in verse 7 could be in the spirit of jihad, which arouses a passionate violence among all who engage in it, as we see even now. Everyone will worship this leader except for the truly born again, verse 8 says, echoing Islamic predictions of Mahdi's dominion. An allusion to Christ's words in Matthew 24 can be found here, where he predicted that the false prophets would be so persuasive that even the "elect" would almost fall into their camp. Thus, the only subset that Scripture tells us will not worship this beast will be those who follow Christ as Lord and Savior. I trust that you, reader, will be in that company, especially after reading the warnings in this book. As John pleaded in verse 9, "If any one has an ear, let him hear." Amen.

The second, assistant beast appears in verse 11. He will have all the authority of the first beast, but will defer to him, urging the world to worship him, even as Isa will refuse to lead the faithful in prayer, taking a back seat to Mahdi. This humility does not indicate any lack of firepower on beast 2's part. He will "perform great signs," according to verse 13, an attribute that Jesus was given even in the Koran, where he is the only prophet of Allah said to have worked miracles. These supernatural abilities will deceive many, verse 14 continues, and the call for an image made in the beast's honor will resound. This mysterious image will even speak, and those who do not worship it will earn a quick death sentence, verse 15 assures. The last three verses of the chapter unveil the famous requirements of a mark on the right hand or forehead in order to buy or sell. The number that has provoked centuries of speculation then appears in verse 18, the infamous 666. Curiously, some Arabic scholars count either 6666 verses in the Koran or 6616. If you have a good study Bible, you already know that some ancient manuscripts have the 616 figure in verse 18.

The beast in Revelation 13 could be Islam itself. It could be the Koran. It could be another system of thought, another influential book. Heck, it could even be a Romanian smoothie. I do not think that the inclusion of two supermen in Islamic prophecy is an accident, however, and that duo matches up quite well with Revelation 13, with one figure emerging as the leader and the other providing respectful, supernatural support. Crazier guesses have been hazarded. I will fill out my case from Scripture in chapter 9.

In the meantime, let us consider further the trajectory of Islam. As you have read this chapter, perhaps you had the same thought that many in my audiences have when hearing my description of Mahdi's power. How will the world, as presently configured, ever agree to follow a Muslim, no matter how polished, especially given the low esteem in which Islam is held in the dominant Western world? I respond by asking: are you sure that we will have a choice to follow or ignore such a man? To build the case for Mahdi's kingdom, we need to consider what type of crescendo could lead to him and Jesus in tandem calling the shots. What elements in Islam portend a global empire?

Chapter Seven

What Muslims Want

The two Islamic supermen, Al Mahdi and "Jesus," hopefully will bring to fruition everything that a sincere Muslim would want: a just kingdom ruled by *sharia* law, economic equity as greedy despots are replaced by simple-living holy men, and the end of oppression by Muslim enemies as the entire world sees the light of Islam. The goals of Islam have been public for a long time. Strangely, few sources of information in the Western world publicize them. I am not sure why this is, but it creates a stunning gap in our understanding of this faith. It is absolutely stupefying that one of the largest people groups in the world has an agenda that would overwhelmingly change the world's political and religious landscape, and yet few people know about it in the non-Islamic world.

I suppose that fear keeps many of us from critiquing their worldview and considering its implications. Perhaps our glued-on occidental lens does not allow us to analyze accurately a religion that plans political conquest. Surely, Muslims aim for a spiritual transformation alone of mankind, by peaceful means, not an enforced Islamic state! Whatever the reason, I find very few sources in the English language that discuss what Muslims envision for our world. The fact is, Muslims believe they have a God-given charge to make the world a better place, and submission to Allah is the key to the realization of that goal.

One source that discusses these plans can be found in your public library. *The Complete Idiot's Guide to Islam*, written by an American convert to the faith, offers a reasonable, easy-to-understand explanation of Islam. The chapters roll by without incident until the reader arrives at the chapter on the Islamic vision for the world.

Then, the words leap off the page when the author explains Islam's vision for tomorrow. I often wonder how many U.S. government officials have read these aspirations of Allah's followers:

> "In summary, Muslims are looking for: 1) redress for all the wrongs done against them by outsiders, 2) the right to revive Islamic civilization without interference from the West, 3) the unification of all Muslim territories into one federally organized Islamic caliphate, 4) the replacement of antireligious ruling elites with sincere Muslims who will rule according to the *shariah.*"[202]

Sounds like a straightforward enough list, but allow these demands to rumble around in your brain for a moment. What would the world look like were these longings to become reality? Better yet, ponder what Muslims might do to achieve these changes. How do these ultimatums intersect with Western interests in 2005? Is conflict over these objectives inevitable, or can the West grant these petitions and still maintain supremacy? Let's analyze each aim point by point and, consequently, gain insight into the present and future clash of civilizations.

Redress for All Wrongs

I am unsure how the first objective could be achieved exactly, how redress for all wrongs can be made, but I am sure that it involves some kind of compensation for attacks on the Islamic world dating from the Crusades to modern colonial occupation. As I stated in chapter 3, the injury and humiliation of the Crusades, as well as more recent colonization by infidel powers, remains far more fresh in Muslim minds than we Westerners can fathom. More recently, battles of the past 40 years have created a newly victimized and bitter generation. For instance, every Algerian I knew in France had a relative who had been killed by French troops during their homeland's struggle for independence in the late 1950s and early 1960s. These memories burn brightly each time an Algerian senses discrimination or racism in France. I am sure that the Algerians of France, for instance, would claim great loss at the hands of their former colonial masters, if given the chance, and they have confidence that any neutral court would agree. If plaintiffs can win millions of dollars in lawsuits against McDonald's for choking on a French fry and lifelong smokers can sue tobacco companies and win, then surely countries that massacre another people, import the survivors for exploitative cheap labor, nullify the elections in the former colony, then bar the immigrants from most political offices and positions of importance in business would owe something to the browbeaten. Wouldn't they? How would you arbitrate this case? Obviously, French courts will not be granting such compensation any time soon; neither will the European Union or the United Nations. True justice will have to come at the insistence of Islamic leaders. Is it any wonder that literature calling for an overthrow of the French government gains an increasingly wider audience?

Muslims in other countries also sport fresh wounds, or at a minimum various grudges that they nurse. Recall my earlier words about honor and revenge in Islamic culture. Both come into play when "redress for all wrongs committed" emerges as a goal of Muslim people. The bulk of the "outsiders" who have committed the aforementioned crimes are certainly Caucasian, and the lines of separation harden between Islam and the West when such ideas are repeated in the Islamic world. The form of reparation requested remains unclear, but it is not hard to picture Al-Mahdi seeking to settle old scores by changing the rules of the world's economy, for instance, to award damages to the "victims" of past crimes against Muslims. The oil card that he will hold will give him the means to make Goal #1 a reality.

Revival of Islamic Civilization

Goal #2 should also cause every American to scratch his head. How exactly will Islamic civilization be revived "without interference from the West"? Sensing a growing ability to impact world affairs, Muslims have been emboldened to argue for what they have long desired. This insistence on the freedom to govern themselves has been mentioned by bin Laden, who famously said after the March 11, 2004 train bombings in Madrid, "I offer a truce to them (Europe) with a commitment to stop operations against any state which vows to stop attacking Muslims or interfere in their affairs."[203] Anyone familiar with Muslim objectives in the early twenty-first century would not even raise an eyebrow over that statement, yet American pundits expressed a variety of reactions, from disbelief to mockery. Bin Laden's statements should not have been strange to our ears. Fundamentalist leaders frequently couple these two ideas in their speeches and writings: the "attack" on Islam led by the United States and Great Britain, and their "interference" in Islamic affairs, more specifically, in the Middle East. Muslims continue to see themselves under assault, and they do have substance for that charge, such as the Iraqi invasion and the threats of the U.S. and other powers to bomb any nuclear facilities in Iran, for example. Al-Zawahiri summarized this perspective in a recent audiotape that was quickly disseminated worldwide:

> "We shouldn't wait for the American, English, French, Jewish, Hungarian, Polish and South Korean forces to invade Egypt, the Arabian peninsula, Yemen and Algeria and then start the resistance after the occupier has already invaded us. We should start now. The interests of America, Britain, Australia, France, Norway, Poland, South Korea and Japan are everywhere. All of them participated in the invasion of Afghanistan, Iraq and Chechnya."[204]

Despite his intellectual capacity as a physician, al-Zawahiri should read his newspaper a bit more closely to understand who has done what in recent times (Japanese in Chechnya?). However, his message does show a shrewd understanding of the interests of Western countries and where they might invade next to secure ever-scarcer resources such as natural gas and oil. Muslims are sick and tired of being the marionettes jerked around by energy-hungry countries that overpower them time and again, then negotiate the terms of the deal for whatever fuel lies under the soil. I cannot argue with their desire to be free of outside influence as they seek self-rule, but such autonomy will inevitably endanger all countries.

It is no accident that a book written by a seemingly moderate Muslim of American origin shares the opinion of Public Enemy #1: bin Laden. If you retain any message from my work, let it be this: a common thread runs through all forms of Islam—that it stands supreme among world religions, and it will be best for all nations to adopt it. Any obstruction of that divine plan represents war on Islam and Allah, which justifies jihad as an act of self-defense. Our tendency to categorize Muslims as "radical," "moderate," "secular," "fundamentalist" or "peace-loving" obscures the point that Muslims desire to be left alone by more powerful nations in order to regroup before a final push for worldwide salvation. I do not have the space to document all the links between what bin Laden says and what Muslim leaders all over the globe assert. These connecting ideas prove the unity of Islam, its core, which is why I prefer the title "pure Muslims" for those who engage in jihad and devote their full energies to spreading Islam from pole to pole. Such "fanatics" understand true Islam best, as it is revealed in the Koran, and I give them credit for fully grasping the implications of their holy book's commands. Bin Laden is more "purist" than extremist. He thoroughly understands the destiny of Islam as relayed in Allah's incarnation, the Koran, and it has captured his soul. Oh, that we all would see the links between what we supposedly believe and how we are to bring revolution on planet Earth! The Church can learn from the fundamentalist movement about devotion to God's will, albeit through entirely different methods yielding a completely different outcome. I do not canonize bin Laden, far from it, but I do acknowledge that he understands his faith.

As to what Muslims would do if left alone, many observers foresee a disastrous infighting among sects that would nullify any collective power that the *ummah* could generate. Do not forget, however, the Arab proverb that the enemy of my enemy is my friend. When Muslims sense that Islam itself is under attack, they unify in the name of Allah. Sunnis and Shiites will definitely join forces against infidels, and other branches of Islam will, too. Given a choice between poverty, suffering and separate branches of Islam that preserve doctrinal purity, or power, prosperity and sovereignty in the modern world for Allah's glory, Muslims will opt for the latter every time. Doctrine does not count for as much in the trenches, and the basics of the faith that unify Muslims outweigh their differences when war is declared.

True, horrific battles have erupted between nations dominated by one wing of Islam or the other, as the Iran-Iraq debacle of 1980-88 demonstrated. Sunnis often still see Shiites as ill-informed half-heathen, and Sufis as misguided nutcases, but when an outside infidel power puts all three of their backs to the wall, they will combine for combat, I assure you. I think that if and when Muslims even sniff the opportunity to dominate the world, they will lay aside their differences for a time, especially as the charisma of al-Mahdi works its magic on them.

Unification of All Muslim Territories

The revival of "Islamic civilization," however we should understand that term, will result if the third goal is achieved. Muslims
know that strength lies in numbers, and a unification of "Muslim
territories" (again undefined) under the rule of one Islamic leader
would cap the realization of the deep-seated yearning in many
Muslim breasts for a step back in time, when Islam was united and
expanding under the leadership of godly men. This unification
would reverse the divisive measures of the colonial era in the Middle
East. Muslim schoolchildren are taught from an early age about the
Sykes-Picot Treaty of 1916, under which British and French diplomats redrew the map of the Middle East, carving up the region into
nation-states. This portion of history remains a sore spot for hundreds of millions of children, and remembrance of this pact stokes
Islamic anger. To illustrate how distant from that anger we are in the
United States, I wonder how many college-educated adults could
identify the significance of the aforementioned treaty. One in a
thousand? One in a million? Anyone other than Ken Jennings of
Jeopardy fame? Muslims recall that agreement so vividly that they
jokingly call the coalition's efforts to reshape the Middle East the
Powell-Straw treaty, named for Former Secretary of State Colin
Powell and British Foreign Secretary Jack Straw.[205]

The point is that Muslims remain painfully aware of their second-
tier status in the world, and they believe the world would be far
more egalitarian and just were a unified bloc of Allah-fearing societies to emerge. Before considering that possibility, we must unpack
a couple of the terms used by Islamic visionaries. "Civilization"
implies a unified culture and consequent influence that Muslim
nations do not currently enjoy. Followers of Islam long for the day
when they have a loud enough voice on the world stage to properly
herald the beauty and sophistication of Islamic culture and spread it
worldwide, as they did centuries ago. Any book on Islamic civilization by Muslim authors will feature a long section on the golden era
of the faith, when its followers led the world in math and the sciences, architecture and art, as academics founded huge universities
throughout the world. Non-Muslims appreciated these contributions to humanity's advancement, and many lived peacefully in
lands conquered by Islamic armies. Such interpretations of history
are open to question, as any history is, but one cannot deny that

Islam had a much wider influence 1,000 years ago, and Muslims made crucial contributions in the arts and sciences. Islam has not always meant terrorism and suicide bombers; it once brought to mind mathematical genius and breathtaking art. A familiarity with this history is important before we slander all Muslims past, present and future, which seems to be the knee-jerk reaction of many Western writers. The other extreme, of course, is believing that once Islam regains its former influence, it will usher in a second Renaissance. This, too, is doubtful.

For evidence, we need only look at what occurs in lands where modern fundamentalist clerics have gained control. In contrast to intellectual freedom and a blossoming of the arts, muftis have restricted educational opportunities and outlawed most artistic expressions. A religion that produced significant intellectual advances in the twelfth century seeks a retreat now as Muslims hark back to an earlier epoch. Koranic schools have not produced any Rhodes scholars or Nobel Prize winners, the last time I checked. They are quite effective, however, at graduating narrow-minded men and women who have memorized large portions of their holy book and can apply its law to modern life. The Islamic civilization of Afghanistan, circa 2000, does not match the progressive culture of the Ottoman Empire at its height.

Another term to reflect on among these goals of Islam is "Muslim territory." What criteria are used to slap this designation on a given country: a population that is majority Muslim, a significant Muslim minority, an Islamic republic? If such territories are to be unified , the definition used will be crucial, and the choice could generate all kinds of chaos in our world. It would be far easier to wish Muslims well in uniting their "territories" were such lands 100 percent Islamic, but they are not. Judging from the increasing call for revolt in a country like France, for instance, I would wager that Muslims consider any country containing a significant Islamic population as a Muslim "territory." If a magnetic caliph were to unite all such regions, a dangerous new superpower would be instantaneously inaugurated.

I do not want to criticize these goals too harshly or belittle legitimate Islamic yearnings for greater say in their affairs on both a personal and national level. I only desire to draw attention to these published aims of Islam and lead a critical discussion of them. Even if you agree that these objectives sound both reasonable and legitimate, they definitely will clash with any agenda being composed in

Washington or Brussels. A projection of these goals, if and when attained, creates a radically different world than the one in which we live, a giant Islamic empire under *sharia* law, newly wealthy due to long-overdue compensation for past injury. The only person capable of drawing together such a kingdom will be al-Mahdi, I believe, which is why Muslims eagerly anticipate his appearance.

An assessment of these goals should also cause Westerners to awaken from their slumber and realize: 1) that the Islamic world declared war several decades ago, and, 2) in any future discussions of the world's political map, we must turn from our traditional foci on Europe and Asia and factor in this burgeoning movement.

I recently had a conversation with a banker who spoke in grave tones of the euro's increasing value and the new strength of the European Union. Many Americans discuss this looming threat to U.S. economic dominance, and they might be correct in their concern if the world consisted solely of competing Gross National Products and economic output, as we so often perceive. Chinophiles, too, have urged me to keep a wary eye on the Asian tiger that will emerge and gobble up all smaller economies. I don't think I have ever heard a similar prediction about the economic and political force of a united Islamic republic, but it is time to have such talks! The enormous difference between such a republic and the European Union or China or any other great power is that this alliance would have a centuries-old agenda that brooks no compromise—to govern the world in the name and authority of Allah. In short, the possibility of this new union should cause us many more sleepless nights than the latest stock market or trade imbalance figures. Our refusal to acknowledge the potential of this confederacy reveals, again, our myopic Western perspective that has rarely acknowledged the Muslim world unless a bomb goes off somewhere.

Think of it! If France or China or Russia released official documents listing goals similar to those at the start of this chapter, it would instantly become front-page news and draw constant analysis, then forceful reaction, from the United States and its allies. Why the deafening silence over these Islamic ambitions (which, I would remind you, has a population behind them greater than Europe or China)? Will we always picture this people group as an uneducated mob of desert dwellers who should not be taken seriously? We do so at our peril.

The Replacement of Ruling Elites

The fourth point of this Islamic manifesto zeroes in on the more immediate plan being implemented by bin Laden and his comrades. This aim underlines the greatest source of Islamic anger, which surpasses even their hatred for the United States and Israel. Muslims can be most cruel when judging their own, as Christians have been at times through the centuries. What animates Islamists every morning is the dream that their countries will one day again be ruled by simple-living devout clerics, as earlier chapters have discussed. The enduring vision of an Islamic utopia ruled by men who are vessels of Allah lives on, despite the abysmal failures of such theocracies in Afghanistan and Iran.

The language used in the Islamic call for revolution from within sounds eerily similar to the rhetoric of the Christian right in an election year. Character counts most importantly in a leader, we are told, and God will honor and bless our country when men and women who serve Him are in power. We should be very slow to criticize Muslims who deliver the same exhortations to their public. The Islamic emphasis on law-and-order also resembles conservative calls for a return to Pleasantville. Muslims crave a trip back in time, too, when *sharia* law ordered society correctly through its emphasis on family values, the rights of the poor, economic justice and swift punishment. Such themes would play well to many Americans if couched in different terms, and will prove to be extremely alluring one day, I predict. This longing for a purer age, a true *jame towhidi* (society of believers) has animated Islam for the past 25 years, as fundamentalists have swept new governments into power in Iran, Afghanistan and Iraq. The hitch with this ideal, even when sought by a new vanguard of holy men, is that flawed human beings enforce and apply the law. No matter how noble the law's goals, sinful men will always botch a perfectly just application. *Jame towhidi,* in a word, is unachievable. No matter how simply dressed an ayatollah is, how lofty and inspiring his words, how earnest his demeanor, he cannot overcome his sin nature and become a perfect instrument of Allah. Theocracy is unattainable in a fallen world, as the Old Testament showed, and absolute power still corrupts absolutely.

Despite the failure of Islamic states, Muslims continue to cry out for more of the same, chasing an impossible dream. Any person who would be enraged by a tiny wealthy class hoarding the profits of an entire nation can understand their frustrations. Any traveler who has spent time in a country where the government exacts bribes, taxes and other payments in a random and sometimes terrifying manner can empathize with the bulk of Muslims in our world today. There is no more bitter feeling than to pay a policeman a day's salary at a roadblock, a tax collector a week's income to rent your market stall, etc., then see nothing come of it in proportional government services. The water supply remains iffy, the electrical current spotty, and the social safety net nonexistent. Muslims suffer such hardships across the globe. Their anger simmers as they wait for relief.

I have seen such legitimate anger with my own eyes, and it moved me forever. I will never forget the scene one day in the former market of the city of Bouaké, Côte d'Ivoire, the country's second largest metropolis. My Muslim trader friends were sweeping up the ashes of their incinerated wooden stalls, victims of a suspicious fire set ablaze early that morning. Their crime in this tragedy? They had refused to move into an adjacent state-built concrete market because the rental rates would double. After a fairly brief war of attrition between businessmen and government, which lasted a few months, one side took action. My powerless friends rushed to their burning buildings in the wee hours of one morning after witnesses saw a blaze ignited at the four corners of the immense complex. The African-style mall transformed into a tinderbox in minutes, and life savings went up in smoke. As tears filled their eyes, these heartbroken men repeated, "Allah sago lo," "It is God's will," prohibited from expressing grief by Islam's insistence on accepting Allah's predetermined bidding. I gathered funds from American supporters to help some of these men restart their businesses, and told them of a God who, rather than burn down markets, wept with them.

The nausea I felt that morning will remain with me for all time, as I pondered how these Muslim men would view Christians, given that the party in control of the government boasted many churchgoers among their leaders and had now devastated the entire Islamic community in my city. Some merchants had died while trying to rescue their savings accounts carefully buried in their market spaces; others committed suicide, knowing that they were financially ruined and shamed for life. Still others fled to Mali and Burkina Faso to escape their now-unconquerable debts. The fabric of the city's two-thirds Islamic population had been torn to shreds. Is it any wonder that civil war broke out little more than a year later?

It is easy for a person in prosperous, free America to denigrate the desire for justice on the part of Muslims. But if you have ever witnessed some of their suffering and understood their grievances, you would stop your tongue. How these issues are resolved is the key, but their legitimacy cannot be questioned. Muslims wait on Allah to save them through a theocracy headed by one anointed man.

Given these four goals of Islam, we can better understand why Muslims engage in terrorist acts, even if those acts are indeed inexcusable. The definition of a just war in Islam differs from St. Augustine's. One writer put it this way: a just war can be waged "to defend your community or nation from aggressors; to liberate people living under oppressive regimes; to remove any government that will not allow the free practice of Islam within its borders."[206] With such a broad definition, dozens of countries are vulnerable to attack. The United States becomes a target because fundamentalists believe that Islam is under siege by the coalition we lead. Other nations earn a bull's-eye because they continue as "oppressive regimes." Strife will continue to wrack these nations until the secularized governments are overthrown. Watch for constant action in Saudi Arabia, Turkey, Algeria, Tunisia, Syria and Pakistan. Leaders will be the targets of assassination, and as small victories pile up, the moderate middle will swing to the side they believe will emerge victorious. I believe the entire Islamic landscape will change in the next 10 years, setting the stage for events I will describe in the next chapter.

The third and final portion of the definition should provoke shudders from Paris to Lagos. Nations that attempt to integrate Muslims and allow them to practice their religion freely now wring their hands as they try to understand how far to bend. With each concession, and as their numbers grow, Muslims push for their culture to be recognized and legitimized by governments unaccustomed to such complete rule of life by religion. I have described the terrible plight of the French as they seek to keep the peace. Many other nations face their own challenges, such as Nigeria, which has allowed many northern cities to be ruled by Islamic law and battle frequent massacres of infidels in such territories. Muslims could say that 200 nations don't "allow the free practice of Islam" within their borders because they will not permit a minority to change the secular laws of the majority. In brief, the entire world will not be up to snuff with Muslims until all countries adopt the Koran as their constitution. I am not extrapolating a fantasy from these goals of Islam; I'm only using hard, cold logic, and I've talked to enough Muslims to know how they think any just society should look.

The intensity of the drive for the fourth pole of the Muslim wish list can be proven from a multitude of sources, among them Al-Qaeda's guidebook, entitled *Military Studies in the Jihad Against the Tyrants,* which reveals the "main mission" of the military arm in Muslim-majority countries to be "the overthrow of the godless regimes and their replacement with an Islamic regime."[207] For this reason, and others, I repeat my assertion that if democracy does indeed sweep through the Middle East, fundamentalist candidates will triumph almost across the board as furious commoners give phony Muslim tyrants the boot. Islamists worldwide resent the intervention of American military forces in sacred lands of Islam, but one day they will thank them, seeing the wisdom of Allah in allowing their temporary presence in order to refashion Islam through a new generation of holy leaders.

The four primary desires of Muslims, even in a tame tome by an American writer, should give us all pause as the twenty-first century proceeds. What would happen if a community of nearly a billion and a half people ever had the ability to realize these goals? How exactly will fundamentalist Islam's nerve center move from a cave somewhere in Pakistan or Afghanistan to the marble palaces of the West? "Flesh it out, man," you say. Wish granted.

Chapter Eight

A Possible Timeline

Given the confluence of events described in the preceding chapters, I humbly offer a possible timeline for The Time of Jacob's Trouble. Please do not stumble as some do when dates and times are ventured—no offense is intended. I do not claim to know the day and hour. I simply desire to paint a picture of what could occur so that no one will be caught unaware.

2010

Given the various proofs I have previously explored, along with the progression of world events, I begin in the year 2010. The first event to watch for is the change in government in Saudi Arabia. Repeated attempts to terrorize the reigning powers will continue. Bombs will go off, people will be killed, terrorists executed. As the number of young people who do not work and have majored in Wahhabism in school grows, the sheer numbers will favor a massive change in Saudi life. As we learn more about some of the next generation of leaders, we see that a few insiders also share fundamentalist sympathies. Thus, there is pressure on this government from within and without. Its reaction to 9/11 was instructive, as a handful of government leaders insisted that the terrorism was a Jewish invention and a hoax. Prince Nayef, for example, the powerful interior minister, publicly blamed Zionists, rather than his own citizens, for the attacks on Washington and New York. In addition, the Saudis only started to cooperate with the 9/11 investigation a year and a half after the attacks, and then only after Al-Qaeda had launched suicide attacks in Riyadh.[208]

The conditions for revolution in Saudi have existed for decades. As one author of a book on Al-Qaeda puts it: "The inequities of the Saudi system—in which most people are very poor and ruled by a super-rich clique—continue to create a sense of disenfranchisement that allows extremism to flourish. Many of the most militant preachers come from marginalized tribes and provinces."[209] Several elements have been percolating in Saudi society that will eventually produce a geyser of unrest, and then, change. Average annual income has plummeted from $20,000 to $8,000 in the past two decades as a stagnant welfare system seeks to keep pace with explosive population growth. Half of the population are teenagers, many of whom will graduate with degrees in religion and no job to occupy.[210] As one observer wrote: "Saudi Arabia is in the throes of a crisis. The economy cannot keep pace with population growth, the welfare state is rapidly deteriorating, and regional and sectarian resentments are rising to the fore."[211] A Western diplomat who had been stationed in Riyadh added: "Instead of a wonderful utopia, where young men were attracted to academia to learn about Islam, you get thousands of religious graduates who couldn't find jobs."[212]

The largest buyer of U.S. arms ($1 billion/year) fortifies itself against its own people, a stunning assemblage of armaments against a nation's own citizenry. This defense system will not go down easily, but the death of a few of the elder statesmen in the government, coupled with the ascension of ministers with fundamentalist philosophies, will pave the way for the leadership's surrender to the will of the people. When power does change hands, the new leaders will have a formidable armory at their disposal, and an old historical lesson will be relearned, as one CIA agent said: "As history has proved time and again, arms sales to unstable nations have a way of circling back and biting the seller in the ass."[213] Indeed.

A continuous civil war in Saudi Arabia will lead to a government leaning far more toward bin Laden and his ilk than Prince Bandar. The corps of radicals needed to wage this war on multiple fronts will have received much battle experience in Iraq. They will return home encouraged by their successes against the infidels and poised to duplicate their tactics in their homeland in order to root out the corrupt royal family. Even as Afghanistan proved to be a valuable country in which to do a terrorist internship in the 1980s, Iraq will have served as a hothouse for terrorism in 2003-05.[214] Loaded down with "tons of explosives and ammunition," according to Saudi border guards, these fresh-faced war vets will replace the older group of Al-Qaeda terrorists that had ties to bin Laden, an age group that has been whittled down by age, capture and execution. Other armed reinforcements will come from Sudan, where they have assisted the Arab militias that inflicted genocide on the Negro tribes of the South.[215]

One band of purists will eventually capture control of the country and its oil infrastructure. Those with intimate knowledge of the country marvel at the ease of this potential changeover. As one former CIA agent put it, "Taking down Saudi Arabia's oil infrastructure is like spearing fish in a barrel. It's not a question of opportunity; it's a question of how good your bang men are and what you give them to work with." One group of U.S. disaster planners opines, for instance, that if just five of the many sensitive points in the Saudi pipeline were struck, the country would be unable to produce oil for two years.[216]

The upsurge in terrorist attacks in Saudi Arabia that began in May 2003 pushed oil prices to record highs, primarily due to concern that rebels would target pipelines or refineries. Such shocks to the world economy served as a preview of what will occur when Islamists take power in Saudi Arabia.[217] Again, the question of this change in power is not if, but when. As Baer predicts: "The Al Sa'ud know one other thing as well: They are hanging on by a thread, presiding over a kingdom deeply torn between past and present, and dangerously at war with itself."[218] He continues: "What you need to bring down a regime like the Al Sa'ud is a readiness of its citizens to pick up those arms and use them, to fight and die for their beliefs, in this instance against a heavily armed, well-paid, and very extensive palace guard." He adds that 9/11 proves the supply of such martyrs in Saudi, noting, "Militant Islam has energized young Saudis like we never thought possible."[219]

As this coup approaches, some influential government leaders have begun to sound populist themes. Nayef, for instance, should be closely monitored as he tests anti-American themes with Saudi youth. Could he be preparing for a run at leadership with post 9/11 statements like: "the great power that controls the earth, now is an enemy of Arabs and Muslims."?[220] He would find a ready audience among the substantial numbers of seminary graduates who fill Saudi streets, thoroughly indoctrinated in Wahabbite philosophy. Two of three earned doctorates today in the kingdom are in Islamic studies.[221]

Others who observe Saudi politics quite closely note that several Wahhabite disciples have wormed their way into leadership and political positions.[222] In addition, the bin Laden family remains quite close to the rulers in the kingdom, a fact well illustrated by Osama's sister-in-law's recent autobiography. This book reveals not only the horrors of living as a married woman in Saudi Arabia, but the intertwined past, present and future of the bin Laden family and Saudi rulers. Whether or not Osama escapes the expensive manhunt of our military forces, his family will play a prominent role in Saudi for years to come.[223]

Another factor propelling the coming coup will be the escalating violence against foreign workers who make the ruling clan's prosperity possible as they oversee the petroleum industry. Such workers sense that their days are numbered in Saudi as attacks increase on neighborhoods inhabited by expatriates and society's resentment turns against them. One example of this change in reception was the fatwa quickly issued in May 2004 by a prominent Saudi cleric that justified the mutilation of an infidel corpse, soon after the disfigurement of several American bodies in Iraq, and at least one in Saudi Arabia. These sporadic rulings, which apply Islamic law to daily life in different contexts, might seem trivial to outsiders, but they carry great significance in Islam. As one veteran journalist explained: "Fatwas like this one help pave the way for bloody assaults against foreigners that have plagued Saudi Arabia for the past year, many Saudi intellectuals believe."[224]

In fact, many Saudi leaders believe that their country could descend into another Algeria, where the government battles an enormous army of rebels in an eternal conflict. If that does occur, and I think it will, foreign workers will flee to the airports and the kingdom will fall apart, precisely the goal of Islamists. One member of the Saudi diplomatic corps explained the fundamentalists' position: "They know many people support them, so they want to force them (Saudi security forces) into it (a war)."[225]

Like a home built of rotting wood, the house of Sa'ud will eventually collapse, sooner rather than later. A recent poll found that 95 percent of educated Saudis between 21 and 45 support bin Laden and his quest to replace the royal family, 95 percent! He has already said what he will do with the Saudi oil supply if in power. Even if he is captured and killed, others like him will be delighted to charge the $144 a barrel he gleefully announced as the going rate, or, more ominously, cut off the oil faucet, bringing the American economy to a screeching halt.[226] Our country's reluctance to change to alternative forms of energy will catch us with our pants down. As Baer pointed out: "But what if chaos in Saudi Arabia slopped over the border into the other

Arab sheikhdoms that collectively own 60 percent of the world's oil reserves? My contacts won't even touch that one, but my guess is that we'd see oil at $150 a barrel or a lot higher. It wouldn't take long for everything else to follow suit: economic collapse, world political instability, and a level of personal despair not seen since the Great Depression."[227] Even the possibility of a collapse of the house of Sa'ud has sent oil speculators scrambling. As Robert Mabro, the chairman of the Oxford Institute of Energy Studies has said, "People who trade oil futures in New York and London read 10 articles saying that the Saudi regime is going to collapse, then they bid up the price of oil. The fears may be exaggerated, but they are having a big effect on the oil price."[228]

Remembering the widespread effects of 9/11 on our economy, which has yet to recover fully, we should not pooh-pooh the impact of a Saudi oil embargo on our businesses. Gears would stop turning, transportation vehicles would be grounded, gas lines would stretch for miles and consumer dollars would go toward petroleum, not buying nonessential extras. Most economists believe even a steady price of $40 a barrel would eventually drag the entire world into a recession. What would $150 a barrel do?

The old unspoken agreement that OPEC will continue to produce enough oil to meet our needs and facilitate the luxurious lifestyle of its directors will be broken. As Robert Ebel, head of the energy program at the Center for Strategic and International Studies, a Washington think tank, notes, "We take it for granted that they (OPEC) will come forth with whatever volume of oil is needed to balance supply and demand."[229] Bin Laden couldn't care less about such arrangements that money-hungry royals made with infidel American companies in the 1930s.

Would our own supply of oil be sufficient to compensate for a pipeline run dry in Saudi Arabia? Unfortunately, if forced to rely on our own reserves, the well would run dry in just four years and three months or, as planners have calculated, enough to keep the economy going for a few months during an emergency, such as the outbreak of war that would cut the supply lines to the Middle East. That cache, regrettably, would not be nearly massive enough to keep gasoline prices low for a more extended period, despite what various politicians have suggested.[230] Simply put, we would be forced to take action to acquire oil as a thirsty, desperate nation backed into a corner, taking up arms to defend our way of life. Ideas about a plan of response to any disruption of the oil supply goes back to at least 1980, when then-President Carter declared in his State of the Union address: "Let our position be absolutely clear: an attempt by any outside force to gain control of the Persian Gulf region will be regarded as an assault on the vital interests of the United States of America, and such an assault will be repelled by any means necessary, including military force."[231] This Carter Doctrine has led to the flexing of American military muscle in the Middle East at several opportunities, most recently in Iraq. For this reason, "the very first military objective of Operation Iraqi Freedom was to secure control over the oil fields and refineries in southern Iraq," Michael Klare points out poignantly in his book *Blood and Oil.*[232]

We would not be the only nation brought to an economic standstill. As I travel and speak about End Times scenarios, many people ask me about China, it being the world's most populous and rapidly developing nation. What role will this huge nation play in the Last Days? We must remember that China's booming economy draws its sustenance from oil as well, and its recent increased demand (oil use has jumped 36 percent in just the past three years) has shaken the world market, sucking dry the surplus production and driving prices skyward.[233] A country that used to sip oil in moderation while riding bicycles to and from appointments is rapidly learning how to consume like its Western rivals. Two million cars were snapped up by the new professional class in 2003, a 70 percent increase over the year before, and China leapfrogged Japan as the second largest oil user in the world. Just 20 years after the first private vehicle appeared in Beijing, five concentric beltways surround the mushrooming metropolis.[234] China's need has caught even OPEC's analysts by surprise, playing a key role in driving global demand up 3.2 percent in 2004, an almost 50 percent increase over the increase from the previous year.[235] China's bubble would burst immediately were the oil industry in Saudi Arabia controlled by fundamentalists. China's recent enrollment in the oil addicts clinic will prove to be its downfall.

Back to the principal players in our imagined year 2010. After several months' negotiation to alleviate its brutal gas crisis, the U.S. would be left with the sole option of military intervention, and I think that this time even Democrats would see the need to invade. One of the frequent word choices that the current administration has chosen to galvanize us in the war on terrorism is the statement that

"American security is at risk." I think it would be far more precise to say "American interests" or "American lifestyles." When those are threatened, we spring into action.

Two or three quarters of economic collapse would allow enough time to amass troops for deployment and refine a strategy (already on the books) to invade Saudi oil fields. With a few tweaks, our soldiers would soon be jumping out of planes and seeking to neutralize the enemy, absent nuclear force. Saudi Arabia is not one of the seven nations on our nuclear hit list that is planned for attack if necessary.[236] This initial thrust would not, of course, be met by a meek surrender on the part of the newly emboldened Saudi government poised to revive a vast Islamic confederation. How exactly would this new regime respond militarily? Muslims have proven again and again that they do not feel compelled to fight in accordance with the Geneva Convention or any other agreed-upon restrictions. There is not a section for suicide bombing in such agreements! Muslims do not fight "fair," as we define it. Any form of striking to achieve victory for Allah is acceptable. The ends justify the means. For this reason, I think that the Islamic forces would drop a nuclear weapon on the heads of our troops without hesitation. Such weaponry will be readily available to them by 2010, if not sooner.

The volatile combination of nuclear technology and jihad has drawn more attention in recent days, and justifiably so. The proliferation of this know-how causes many sleepless nights for those who seek to restrict such activity today. "Rogue" nations, many of them Islamic, fund research to create such capacity and thus frustrate negotiators who seek to restrict membership in the Nuclear Club. Moreover, unemployed scientists in several countries provide a ready source of brainpower for nations eager to play with the big boys. The intersection of Islamic goals and available nuclear materials and technology rivals the power of The Bomb itself. As an example, an Iraqi scientist recently wrote in *The New York Times* that "hundreds" of his colleagues possess knowledge that could help other nations to build nuclear weapons, and it was up to the U.S. to assist these experts in finding well-paying jobs in post-war Iraq to reduce the risk of this happening![237]

One nation that already has this capacity is Pakistan, the second country to track in coming years. Perhaps no nation on earth hosts a higher percentage of fundamentalist believers. One expert on Islam calls it "the central point of mobilization of the Islamic radicals," given its generous supply of suicide bombers who gladly give of their lives to escape the oppressive poverty of their native land.[238] This fanatical atmosphere will eventually envelop President Musharaf, who will soon be killed or deposed. Repeated assassination attempts have failed to this point, but the law of averages dooms this counterbalance to radical Islam in Pakistan. As one Pakistani journalist observed last year: "The situation is very precipitous. Terrorists are not only going after Americans but now are also targeting anyone thought be to be close to the Americans."[239] That includes Musharaf, and investigations into the attacks against him reveal a systematic plan to change the regime in Pakistan.[240] When these murderers meet success, the world will confront a force unknown in history: a fundamentalist Islamic country with nuclear weapons. For this reason, the country has been called a "present and future nightmare," with its "nuclear arsenal, a firmly untrenched radical minority and porous borders," a worrisome trio for sure.[241]

In the meantime, Pakistan has emerged as a critical supply hub for other nations seeking to join the Nuclear Club.[242] Fundamentalists who have access to both the technology and required resources are eager to help their brothers acquire The Bomb and give jihad a huge boost around the world. As one writer summarized: "If a nuclear weapon destroys the U.S. Capitol in coming years, it will probably be based in part on Pakistani technology," citing the sale of nuclear technology by scientist Abdul Qadeer Khan (the founder of Pakistan's nuclear program) to Iran, North Korea, Libya and several other nations. The writer added: "It's impossible to overstate the risks if countries like Saudi Arabia or Syria develop nuclear weapons because of Dr. Khan's help."[243]

Nicknamed "Dr. Nuke," Khan "led a smuggling ring whose activities have proven difficult to unravel." The investigation of this network "has proven difficult and time-consuming," according to one senior Bush administration official. "We continue to look for, and expect to make, new discoveries. We don't think the story is fully revealed yet." Musharraf admits as much: "I can't say surely that we have unearthed everything that he's done, but I think we have unearthed most of what he's done."[244] U.S. and U.N. investigators confess that they have no idea how close fundamentalists are to building a nuclear bomb. The 9/11 Commission Report revealed that U.S. officials have worried about reports that Al-Qaeda "was intent on carrying out a 'Hiroshima'" since 1998.[245] One month after 9/11, aides told President Bush that a CIA source had reported a 10-kiloton nuclear weapon from Russia smuggled into New York City by Al-Qaeda. Regular reports in the intelligence community continue to warn of such deal-making.[246]

Another fresh nuclear trail appears to be even more certain. Intelligence agents believe that Al-Qaeda recently did negotiate a $1.5 million purchase of uranium from a retired Sudanese cabinet minister, and its envoys have indeed traveled repeatedly to Central Asia to buy weapons-grade nuclear materials. Bin Laden's top deputy might not be bluffing when he boasts, "We sent our people to Moscow, to Tashkent, to other Central Asian states, and they negotiated, and we purchased some suitcase nuclear bombs."[247] In light of the free-wheeling networks between Islamists and nuclear weapons vendors, former Secretary of Defense William Perry direly predicts a nuclear terror strike before the end of this decade. "We're racing toward unprecedented catastrophe. This is preventable, but we're not doing the things that could prevent it."[248]

Much of the newest literature on the U.S. reaction to 9/11 has urged a concentrated crackdown on "loose nuke" countries like Russia and Pakistan through a renewed monitoring of the technical capacities of these nations and their scientists.[249] In Russia, for instance, at least 80 nuclear "suitcase" weapons are missing from its arsenal, and 2 million pounds of weapons-usable fissionable material in nuclear reactors are "often an underpaid guard and a chain-link fence" from theft by Islamists.[250] The iron-strong ties in the Islamic world and the labyrinth that they have created stymies international authorities as they seek to decode the unregulated financial system that funds Al-Qaeda and the distribution of nuclear secrets. "It is taking longer than anyone expected," says David Albright, a nuclear expert and president of the Institute for Science and International Security. "But if we don't succeed, there's a real chance the network will reconstitute itself and spread again."[251]

As more research is done, troubling plots from as far back as 1995 emerge, such as Pakistan helping Iran with designs that would lead to the production of bomb-grade nuclear fuel.[252] This course of weapons development on the part of Iran has not been slowed since. Despite U.N. insistence that it halt its enrichment of uranium, which can lead to weapons development, Iran shoulders on. Surrounded by four nuclear powers—Russia, India, Pakistan and Israel—Iran seeks a higher profile in its neighborhood, as well as a counterweight to Jewish possession of The Bomb.[253] As I write, Iran has thus far refused to heed calls for a halt to its enrichment of uranium, even after skilled and sympathetic European negotiators made the pitch.[254] As one official involved in the talks sighed: "The Iranians are determined to continue until they know they can assemble a bomb within hours should they need it. No diplomacy will stop that." Iranian Foreign Minister Kamal Kharrazi confirmed this doggedness, adding that Iran "has to be recognized by the international community as a member of the Nuclear Club. This is an irreversible path." The most the diplomats had hoped to accomplish, anyway, was a delay until 2006 for Iran's entry into the exclusive group of nations with nuclear weapons.[255]

After Iran joins the club, Saudi Arabia and Egypt will soon follow, according to those who have served in Middle East peace negotiations in recent years; Saudi to counterbalance the Shiite government in Iran, Egypt to guard its image as the leader of the Arab world.[256]

Ironically, the Iraqi invasion also could have accelerated this progression of nuclear proliferation, as well as the spread of chemical weapons, according to Peter W. Galbraith, a former diplomat who at one time had cheered the argument for the war. Weapons looted from an arms site called Al Qaqaa, for instance, might have wound up in Iran, he said, which would assist its pursuit of nuclear weapons. To illustrate the troublesome uncertainty of what happened to weapons and toxic chemicals during the invasion, Galbraith relates this story. In April 2003 he told a young U.S. lieutenant that H.I.V. and black fever viruses had previously been looted from the site he was guarding. The stricken soldier replied, "I hope I'm not responsible for Armageddon."[257] As do we all!

Even without this possibility straight from a Bond movie, every citizen of the world must face the truth that fundamentalist Muslims will have nuclear weapons at their disposal in the near future, and with new members in the Nuclear Club comes an entirely new ethic. Truly, the restraint of use of nuclear weapons represents a modern miracle. Nuclear nations have maintained a shared understanding that the launch of even one nuclear missile could lead to mutual assured destruction, a term everyone in my generation grew up with. The 1968 Nuclear Non-Proliferation Treaty would not be worth the paper it's written on should one such bomb be detonated by an excitable member of Al-Qaeda, for instance, and the long-held principle of mutual self-restraint would vanish in the time it takes to press a button. Beware, nations with dissimilar values will not necessarily adhere to this unwritten agreement. As one writer put it: "Then, every nuclear danger would rise dramatically: miscalculation, preemptive attacks, theft, a global market in weapons technology, and use by terrorist groups....We will cross a threshold with unpredictable and frightening consequences."[258]

Those closest to the detailed intelligence reports available on such matters believe that the next large-scale terrorist attack will involve nuclear weapons. For example, the anonymous author of *Imperial Hubris: Why the West Is Losing the War on Terror* sees such an attack as the logical climax of what he calls "focused, principled hatred" for the United States that gains an ever-larger share of Muslims worldwide.[259] Many experts believe that nuclear terrorism has a better-than-even chance of occurring by 2014, and such an attack would kill a half-million people.[260]

2011

I wager for the year 2010, to continue my projected timeline. By 2011, one or multiple nuclear bombs will have been unleashed on American soldiers seeking to secure Saudi oil fields, the resulting damage to the petroleum industry be damned. Aroused Muslims, armed with their clearest proof yet of a Crusader invasion on sacred ground, would not have to justify such extreme measures to anyone in the *ummah*. I can guarantee you that Muslims would not hesitate to launch such weapons in this case. They would sleep well after such a drastic response, deaf to the rest of the world's outrage. They would see the very institution of Islam under seige, with infidel troops mere miles from controlling sacred sites. Such high stakes would provoke an equally extreme answer.

The West, I think, would be shocked by the universal approval among Islamic nations for such a ghastly counterattack. Remember who the enemy of my enemy is in Arab culture. The steady gain of fundamentalist parties in Islamic nations will produce a unified front by 2011, one that applauds any attempt by a fellow-Muslim nation to smash the "Crusaders." The American attempt to establish democracy in the Middle East will have completely backfired by 2011. An alliance of anti-American, democratically elected governments will reign across the Islamic world, creating an informal new empire to be reckoned with. One recent news analysis by a veteran Middle East reporter will be remembered as a faint cry in the wilderness. Highlighting elections in that year in Pakistan, Bahrain, Morocco and Turkey, Neil Macfarquhar interpreted them as "a sign that voters...want to assert pride in their faith to the outside world." Quoting a professor of political science in Morocco, he added, "Arab and Muslim populations think the war against terrorism is nothing but a war against Islam, the culture of Islam, the Arab culture. The Islamist parties have been able to exploit this." Elections held under the American news radar screen nonetheless planted seeds that would bloom less than a decade later. Balloting that "gave religiously oriented parties far larger than expected representation" should have awakened the many talking heads and politicians from their stupor who insisted that Islamists comprised a tiny minority of Muslims.[261]

The introduction of nuclear weapons onto the battlefield in 2011 would place U.S. strategists in a difficult position. Given the unpopularity of U.S. foreign policy and the weakening alliances between our country and others, it would not surprise me in the least to see a sharp division among other nations as this war escalates. In contrast to the famous *Le Monde* headline that proclaimed "We are all Americans" after 9/11, several Asian and European nations will defend Islamic sovereignty as a welcome check on U.S. supremacy. Undoubtedly, a coalition of First World nations will come down on the side of the fundamentalists, to the consternation of all Americans. The real or perceived desire of the U.S. to control the world economically, or at least establish the terms under which the world economy operates, would be in full view as our troops claimed Saudi oil as our own. This outbreak of modern "imperialism" will repulse the world and mute opposition to the sandy holocaust.

The world will not become a more tranquil place in light of this war, though, and all mankind will wait nervously for the American response. There would be no shortage of missiles or targets, but the troubling question would be: exactly which Islamic nation should be struck first? How would you like to be in the womb of the Pentagon at such a time? I do not envy those who will have to make such decisions.

I will not pretend to be qualified to map out the likely reprisal by U.S. forces, but I doubt that we would answer bomb for bomb for at least three reasons: 1) we are loathe to unlock our nuclear arsenal because we know it could incinerate the world, 2) we would not want to annihilate the very oil fields that power our economy, and, 3) we would not know which nation or nations to strike, given the Islamic unity at such a time.

When I present these doomsday scenarios to my audiences, especially in the Washington, D.C. area that I call home, there are inevitably a few Department of Defense or military listeners who seek to reassure my hearers by discrediting this vision. American military might would brush off any pesky Islamic flies, they say, and secure a bright future perpetually dominated by the U.S. Other insiders, however, have had the opposite reaction, telling me that I am overly optimistic regarding the time frame for Islamic nuclear capabilities. Whatever the future brings, I would remind my readers of the many insights given by veteran Middle East watchers who warn the West about overconfidence when faced with infuriated Muslims. Longtime journalist Ed Hotaling, whom I've cited often, alludes to numerous instances in his provocative book *Islam Without Illusions* when Muslims defeated infidel foes over the past 40 years, many of which he reported on. Two characteristics should never be forgotten in considering the fundamentalist movement's strength, he says, in envisioning a possible World War III: their patience and their zeal.

Like most other residents of the Third World, where Islamic fundamentalism flourishes, soldiers on jihad are not in a hurry. They do not live by a daily clock chock full of meetings and appointments. Rather, they wait patiently for the proper time to strike, and then do so with ferocity. Underlying this patience is a determination that even the most ardent Marine would have difficulty matching. Glimpses of that resolve could be found in the battle plans written by the 9/11 terrorists, which became public shortly after the attacks. One of the 15 duties listed for the perpetrators read thusly:

> "Remind your soul to listen and obey and remember that
> you will face decisive situations that might prevent you from
> 100 percent obedience, so tame your soul, purify it, con-
> vince it, make it understand, and incite it. God said: 'Obey
> God and his messenger, and do no fight amongst yourselves
> or else you will fail. And be patient, for God is with the
> patient.' "[262]

The guidelines go on to encourage the holy warriors to pray during the night and to remember God frequently, reading the Koran to keep the mind stayed on Him. One particular verse in the eighth chapter was to provide special reinforcement: "When you meet those who disbelieve in a battlefield, never turn your backs to them." To do so would earn the coward hell fire, the chapter goes on to say.[263]

Finally, thoughts of Paradise fill the mind of the soldier after fears of Hell. He recalls "the women of paradise are calling out, 'Come hither, friend of God.' "[264] The sexual frustration evident in many Islamic societies should never be discounted as a potent part of the jihadist's chemical mix. Finding a woman to marry can prove difficult enough for many Muslim young men; amassing the money to pull off a proper wedding often proves even more daunting. Jihad provides a shortcut to sexual bliss without the hassle.

2012

Frozen by this monumental stare-down between the United States and an Islamic confederacy, the rest of the world will plead as never before for a peacemaker who could bridge the gap between Islam and the West before the seven continents go up in smoke. By 2012, the world will be more than ready to meet al-Mahdi, a rigorous yet charming Muslim formed from youth to straddle the two worldviews in conflict. He will be a man fluent in several languages with the Koran in his heart, equally comfortable in a gown while dispensing justice in an Islamic court and in a business suit while shaking hands with international leaders at a global summit. He will be the anti-bin Laden, with a smoother appearance more palatable to Western tastes, an antichrist who will look as good in *People* magazine as on Al-Jazeera.

After filling the power vacuum in a world that endorses neither the U.S. nor Saudi Arabia completely, he will offer an alternative vision to the paralysis that will grip the world. Given the shocking devastation that just two nuclear devices will have produced, and the disabling uncertainty as to who can best chart the course for the political, military and economic worlds, Mahdi will be granted far-reaching powers. Drawing on endorsements from a heretofore neutral European Union and a United Nations bent on negating American hegemony, this dream candidate would then begin to implement a policy that would eventually reveal more and more of his pure Islamic beliefs. In chaotic times, a law-and-order candidate often does quite well in the polls. This *sharia* law-backer would be no different, riding a crest of public approval to: 1) force nations to cooperate, rather than annihilate one another, 2) empower those nations to corral the criminal elements let loose amidst the economic depression of the previous year. Have you ever seen the looting that takes place both during and after a riot? Imagine that on a global scale. The nations will beg for a take-charge leader with the moral basis and backbone to quench crime. The Koran, at your service.

In boardrooms and bars, in tearooms and cafés around the world, Mahdi's agenda would be debated and dissected, earning grudging approval and full-throated opposition, as all human chiefs have. The emergence of a seemingly divinely appointed assistant will act as the coup de grace, winning over the last holdouts to his administration. Who will be able to argue against a genuine prophet of God? What will happen when the question: "What would Jesus do?" becomes moot?

Returning to Earth after his ascension 2000 years ago, "Jesus" will burst onto the world scene to bolster the Mahdi government. His name and character already familiar to the world's two leading religions, this pretender will woo millions with his miracle-working and argue powerfully for acquiescence to the inevitable Islamic domination. Many American preachers, convinced of God's judgment on their own nation for sins ranging from abortion to homosexuality, will be happy to find a human enforcer of that divine sentence and urge obeisance to him. Neglecting to "test the spirits," these ministers will lead their flocks into an unwitting apostasy as they are persuaded by the raw supernatural power and dominance of the new government. Surely any power that can topple America must be from the Lord, they will reason, and just as surely, someone who can perform these miracles must come from Heaven. Cheered by the unapologetic morality of the new authority and sure of Jesus' credentials, the one institution capable of resisting the Mahdi-Jesus alliance will be split like a melon at a summer picnic.

The formidable ticket of Jesus and a seemingly moderate Muslim who embodies the term "law and order candidate" will gain impetus as a dazed global citizenry looks to its available options for prevention of mutual destruction. Pockets of opposition will become increasingly intolerable, among them the discriminating followers of the true Jesus

Christ, son of God. At some point in time before the post-Tribulation return of the real Jesus, large numbers of born-again people will be slaughtered for their faith, a development that Scripture has long predicted. Depending on your eschatological position, these believers will be either Christians who live through the Tribulation or those who come to Christ after the Rapture of His Church.

2014

As the second half of Mahdi's reign dawns in 2014, he will home in on renegade groups as he seeks to consolidate his power. He will turn to the one nation that refuses to bow to a Muslim or anyone named Jesus, the one nation that has never claimed allegiance to Allah or the Christ: Israel. The millennia-old dispute between the descendants of Ishmael and Isaac will come full circle in the Last Days. The chronic aggravation of Jewish resistance to Islamic domination of the Middle East will be have a final solution. Israel will be ripe for the picking by 2014. Having been pressured by every government in the world, including long-time friend America, to grant concession after concession to the Palestinians in a global quest for peace a decade earlier, Israel will have received scant benefit from its good faith negotiations. Rather than congratulating Israel for its generous conditions in repeated pacts and its surrender to the notion of a Palestinian state, the surrounding Arab nations will only interpret its enemy's new-found flexibility as weakness, and they will turn up the heat on Israel as the director of the Middle East Forum predicted 15 years earlier, "Diplomacy, in other words, unintentionally revived Arab dreams of obliterating the Jewish state."[265]

Zarqawi, the #2 man in Al-Qaeda, gives a hint of Islamists' plan for Israel. When asked recently about whether or not he possessed chemical weapons, he replied, "God knows that should we—and we ask God to shortly empower us to—possess that kind of bomb, we would not hesitate one second to use it on Israeli cities."[266] He also proclaims unashamedly his desire to overthrow the government in his native Jordan, and when fundamentalists win elections there as well, the stage will be perfectly set for their neighbor's defeat. Scripture often speaks of the rivalry of these two nations. Edom and Israel will clash again, and, as in former times, the Gentiles will have the patronage of an array of nations. This time, more than swords and shields will be aimed at Jerusalem.

This diabolical anti-Jewish spirit has existed for several thousand years, and the sons of Isaac have been victimized by it in a variety of settings, with the same message transmitted in different languages over time. As one adept writer put it, in the years before the Holocaust, European graffiti read: "Jews to Palestine." In recent years, it now reads: "Jews out of Palestine." The message? "Don't be here and don't be there. That is, don't be."[267] Much of the period between 2014-17 will be dominated by this offensive against Israel, with the eventual overrun of Jerusalem and its temple, to be further developed in the Scriptural analysis of the next chapter.

2015-2017

As Mahdi's stature grows, his Islamic heritage will emerge more plainly. The world will see once and for all the essential elements of Muhammad's faith: its intolerance for other religions, its tendency toward violence and its zealous belief that it is the agent for Allah's rule on earth. Nation after nation will submit to Islam rather than face nuclear attack and/or economic disaster due to a blockade on oil exports from Islam's heartland. Mahdi will hold the two cards necessary to bring the nations to their knees: military and money. He will be wise enough to allow vestiges of the former way of life to remain in Europe, Asia, America and elsewhere, yet he will quickly smash any dissent, especially when it's powered by religion. Upon much reflection and reading, I have gained a sense for the early years of the antichrist's regime and what course it will probably take. How it will unfold in the latter half of Mahdi's seven-year reign (predicted in Islamic tradition as well) remains murky. Other books on prophecy can be consumed for details regarding the last years of the Great Tribulation. However, one book can be scanned for further clues regarding a Muslim Beast. In fact, the description of the antichrist in that oeuvre contains a remarkable number of references to a man much like Mahdi. These hints stand like road signs pointing to a Muslim man, I believe. Their sheer quantity might surprise you. We continue on to other biblical proofs for Mahdi.

Chapter Nine

Other Biblical Evidences of an Islamic Antichrist

The danger of examining Biblical texts with the idea of assigning a certain nationality or ethnic identity to the antichrist is that we can justify just about any choice! Every single commentator on the relevant passages comes to the job with a lens through which he or she sees the prophecies.

In the 1970s and '80s, it seemed that every popular preacher identified the 10-horned monster in Daniel as the European Economic Community. Now that this organization has changed names and expanded to 25 member nations, I no longer hear those conjectures! Others make a case for the Roman Catholic Church heading up the one-world government, citing Rome's prominence in prophecy. What a surprise that no Catholics ever come up with this interpretation of Scripture. We definitely all wear a set of spectacles when we examine the Bible, even if we do not care to admit it or desire such distorted vision.

I will ante up and confess to a certain perspective before making my argument. I do believe that abundant evidence exists for an Islamic antichrist. I will extrapolate arguments based on that conclusion throughout this chapter. I also concede that I could be completely wrong about the religious background of the antichrist. If I am mistaken, my life will not have been in vain. I do not base my reason for existence on the arguments presented in this book. I can say, though, with deepest heart conviction, that I am absolutely persuaded that Muslims will play a key role in the End Times, and that those times are approaching. If the antichrist is not a Muslim, surely the titanic clash of Islam versus the West will set the stage for a world dictator who tries to bring a resolution to this tremendous battle of cultures and faiths.

I have briefly touched on a few Scriptures that seem to point to
an Islamic world leader such as al-Mahdi, whom Muslims await. As
I've demonstrated, several passages indicate an antichrist that bears
a peculiar resemblance to an Islamic caliph in the role of Beast.
Other books of the Bible explore the roots of the conflict between
Arabs and Jews, giving us a context for our search, while other chapters give more details about the Tribulation that can be used in the
argument for an Islamic Beast.

The Genesis Story

Genesis lays the foundation for many realities in our world today,
such as man's sinful condition and loss of fellowship with God, the
diversity of language and culture, and the beginning of the Jewish
people. It also provides an extremely brief history of other peoples
which could lend insight to the present Arab-Israeli tensions. I find it
fascinating that the "curse of Ham," for instance, affected the inhabitants of Canaan, not black Africans, as past racists have maintained.
Called "Canaan" by his father Noah as the curse was pronounced in
Genesis 9, Ham's destiny was predicted: "a servant of servants he shall
be to his brothers." Ham's descendants spread from modern-day Israel
both southward into Egypt and east, including Nimrod, whose kingdom began at Babylon. I wonder if this curse has been fulfilled as
Palestinians live in subjugation to the Israelis in the same area they
have inhabited for 6,000 years. Our future-facing American worldview
often discounts or ignores history and makes us uncomfortable with
talk of curses and destinies forged multiple millennia ago, yet I think
world events will soon make our Bibles come alive much like a fire-
cracker that was presumed to be a dud. Boom! The world situation
will all make sense as ancient sentences are carried out, forgotten predictions are fulfilled, historical enmities are culminated, and antedilu-
vian peoples with names like Edomites and Canaanites and Medes
re-emerge as key players. The Bible, as it has many times in history, will
prove itself to be true, in a fresh, relevant way. Stay close to this book.

Returning to the foundational book of the Bible, we learn that
one of Noah's other sons, Shem, went on to father a line that led to
Abram. Ham's progeny, meanwhile, constructed the Tower of Babel,
bringing divine punishment and the confusion of languages that has
hindered communication to this day. How did these two branches of
Noah's family come together? Not in the best of circumstances.

One of the first arguments you will have with a Muslim as you discuss spiritual matters will be over which of Abraham's sons was to be offered on Mount Moriah during God's great test of that man's trust. Muslims insist it was Ishmael, their forefather; Christians and Jews adhere to the biblical record and name Isaac as the imperiled teenager. Interestingly, I have never heard a Muslim comment on Ishmael's origin, and when I have quizzed them about it, they profess ignorance. Perhaps it is a lack of awareness borne of shame, for the birth of Ishmael represents one of the great failures of faith in the Bible, labeled "a carnal plan for children" in my New American Standard version. As Abram and Sarai grew famously impatient with the lapse of time between God's promise of descendants and the birth of a son, Sarai persuaded Abram to have sex with her Egyptian maid Hagar. (Before we grow too judgmental, we must remember that 10 years had dragged by between the Lord's promise and this immoral choice. How many of us wait even 10 months on the promises of God, let alone 10 years?) When her success at conceiving was immediate, Hagar faced Sarai's jealous wrath, and she soon fled the mistreatment of her mistress. What follows is a tender and captivating story.

God sends an angel to find the hiding Hagar and tells her to return to her mistress and submit to her authority. The angel then goes on to promise that Hagar's offspring will become a great nation, giving her son the name Ishmael, or, "God hears." Verse 12 of Genesis 16 has produced much speculation regarding the Arab peoples, some of which is legitimate, I believe. Ishmael would "be a wild donkey of a man" with "his hand...against everyone, and everyone's hand...against him." Having lived among Arabs for several years and heard them describe themselves as a big feuding family, I think even they would tend to agree on the truthfulness of this prophecy. More than one Arab friend has sighed to me about his people's inability to get along on a family, clan and national level. This could be said of many ethnic groups in our world, but Arabs mentioned it more to me than any other group that I've been around. I would, however, hesitate to construct a theology of Arabdom on this verse. The people most apt to do so when I interact with them demonstrate an anti-Arab prejudice to begin with, I find.

Apart from this ominous prophecy that has given many pause, we find evidence of a God who loves Arab and Muslim people. The angel tells of God seeing Hagar's affliction and taking action, promising to make her son the head of a great nation. He ordered the boy's name to be Ishmael as a testament to His vigilance in her case. Praise the Lord for His omniscience and omnipresence. Nothing escapes His watch, not even a pregnant servant girl about to give birth out of wedlock. Could this special love for Ishmael, evidenced by the visit of an angel, be the reason why God repeatedly uses dreams to communicate His Gospel to Islamic people? For those of us who have worked with Muslims and heard such testimonies of night visions prompting a seeker to search for more information about Jesus, it has become obvious that Muslims have a very special place in God's heart.

In chapter 17 of Genesis, God goes on to tell Abraham that Ishmael will receive His personal blessing and become exceedingly fruitful in response to Abraham's prayer for blessing on this young man. We should always keep in mind that both Abraham and God loved Ishmael dearly, and that love for Ishmael's descendants should remain in those of us who follow that same God now. Christians should be the greatest lovers of Muslims alive, despite the battles that ensue when our cultures collide.

Despite this fervent affection for Ishmael, God did not alter His original plan, even after Abraham's passionate intercession. Yahweh specifically stated that He would make His covenant with Isaac, not Ishmael (17:21). I think this rejection stung Muhammad thousands of years later. He realized his people lacked not only a monotheistic faith and unifying holy book, but an alliance with the one, true God. So, he formed one!

Abraham's love for Ishmael surfaced again when Sarah asked that the boy be expelled from their household after the birth of Isaac in chapter 21, some 15 years later. "Distressed" by Sarah's request, Abraham received divine approval for the exile, and he gave Hagar bread and a skin of water for a trip that led into the wilderness of Beersheba. The words of God surely rang in Abraham's ears as he watched the duo depart: "And of the son of the maid I will make a nation also, because he is your descendant" (21:13).

When the two travelers soon grow thirsty to the point of death, God again reveals His special, active love for Ishmael. "Do not fear," He tells Hagar, but "lift up the lad, and hold him by the hand; for I will make a great nation of him" (21:18). Soon after, Hagar saw a well, they were refreshed, and "God was with the lad, and he grew; and he lived in the wilderness, and became an archer" (like his forefather Nimrod), eventually marrying an Egyptian (vv. 20,21). The offering of Isaac on Mount Moriah follows years later in the next chapter, occurring long after Ishmael had departed to Paran. From this point the biblical record focuses, naturally, on the line of Isaac, tracing the story of God's formation of a people in preparation for His Son's coming.

I comment briefly on the Genesis record simply to set the context for a millennia-long battle between cousins: the Jews and the Arabs, which crashes into our headlines a hemisphere away to this day. This fracas did not begin in 1948 or 1967 or 2001. It has its roots in events that transpired within Abraham's family. Remember the clear and repeated choice by God to enter into covenant with Isaac, born after divine intervention in Sarah's womb, a miracle child according to His will. Do not forget that Ishmael, the acknowledged father of the Arab people, was born out of wedlock, not God's design. Despite this dubious arrival, Ishmael was loved and blessed by Jehovah, and he has become a great nation as well.

This matter of covenant came to a head in Medina several thousand years later as Muhammad strived for acceptance as a prophet. Most of the Jews in Medina rejected his claim, based on the choices of Jehovah in Genesis to work exclusively through the Jewish people. Muhammad later executed many of these Jewish holdouts, and al-Mahdi will do the same in a few years. Arab anger over this ancient agreement will rage until the world's end. This background also serves to solidify the geographic context in which the Last Days will be played out. To our chagrin, perhaps, this final act takes place in lands where we don't understand the language and can't properly pronounce the names.

The Ministry of Jeremiah

In addition to the prophecies noted in chapter 4, I find timely parallels to our day in the ministry of Jeremiah. Much of this weeping prophet's ministry to the kingdom of Judah involved a difficult and dangerous task: urging his countrymen to submit to the invading Babylonian armies. Open to charges as a traitor, Jeremiah knew that God was using a pagan kingdom to spiritually purify His chosen people. The people of Judah would never worship idols again after this conquest. God later, in His wisdom, punished the punishers for having chastised His people. A principle materializes in this story: God allows alien armies to triumph over His chosen people for a time, according to His purposes. He never allows cruelty against His own to go unrequited, however, "for the Lord is a God of recompense, He will fully repay," Jeremiah promises (51:56). That is what we must remember when Islam dominates our world for "a time, times and half a time."

In chapter 51, Jeremiah also writes of the Medes disciplining the Babylonians. Iran and Iraq fought perhaps the most vicious war of recent memory from 1980-88, with one million killed, a huge chunk of the countries' populations. This longstanding rivalry did not begin with Sunni-Shiite conflict instigated by Saddam Hussein, as any reader of Scripture knows; its staying power verifies the veracity of biblical prophecy. As I write, Iraqi Defense Minister Hazim Shalan charges in an interview that Iran has taken over Iraqi border posi-tions, sent spies into the country and infiltrated the new government, including his own ministry. He states that Iran remains "the first enemy of Iraq," adding that "Iran interferes in order to kill democ-racy." He concludes the interview with these ominous words: "We can send the death to Tehran's streets, like they do to us. But we can't do it if we are a democracy. But if my people say do it now, I will do it."[268]

Daniel Speaks of the Beast

Daniel stands as the Old Testament book most loaded with apoc-alyptic visions, and for that reason I return to it to delve more deeply into the descriptions he gives of the reign of the Beast. Chapter 7, chock full of prophecy, has spurred much debate. Some interpreters believe that Daniel's vision here merely supplemented the dream interpretation that he gave in chapter 2. In other words, the four beasts correspond to the Babylonian, Persian, Greek and Roman empires, all long gone. This stance has merit; one can find character-istics of all of these empires in both chapters, and analysts who build a case for the pre-End Times realization of this chapter have identified the ram as the former Medo-Persian empire and the goat as the long-passed Greek era, with Antiochus Epiphanes as the small horn of verse 9 and Alexander the Great as the large horn of verse 21.

Many other Bible teachers, however, view the "little horn" in chapters 7 and 8 as being the antichrist.[269] These scholars see the first three kingdoms as signifying Babylon, Medo-Persia and Greece, but believe the last reign awaits inauguration. They point to verses 21 and 22 for proof, noting that the fourth beast's persecution of believers will not cease until "the Ancient of Days" comes and passes judgment on him, then gives "the saints…possession of the kingdom." The description of this little horn also mirrors "the man of sin" in 2 Thessalonians 2, who will be revealed just before the day of the Lord. I join the commentators who see this fourth kingdom still to come, qualitatively different from the empires that preceded it. With this perspective, let us look at the frightening predictions about this fourth kingdom, which I believe signifies the rule of the antichrist.

Verse 25 reports that the Beast will "speak out against the Most High and wear down the saints of the Highest One." This verse strikes me as I consider the popular argument that the antichrist will be a Jew. I don't see how a blasphemous Jew will win the support of either Gentiles or Jews or Muslims. No, this man will offer a constant stream of anti-Semitic thought and be a habitual blasphemer of Jehovah. Such an attitude exists within Islam, not Judaism, as I have discussed.

The Beast will not stop with hot air. He will apply other forms of heat to the "saints" of God, the born-again believers who will live on Earth during his dominion. Whether or not you subscribe to a pre- or post-Tribulation stance on the End Times, it cannot be disputed that some Christians somewhere will suffer under the Beast. He will slaughter many and wear them down, Scripture tells us. Could this unrelenting persecution be in the spirit of jihad summarized in Sura 8:39 of the Koran: "Go on taking the fight to them until there is no more subversion and religion is wholly God's."? This verse was one of about a hundred where Muhammad needed to give his weary troops a pep talk and urge them to again pick up their swords in defense of the new faith.

Verse 25 continues by stating that the Beast will change "the times and the laws." Could this be a Muslim leader insisting on an Islamic lunar calendar dated from the time of Muhammad's flight to Medina (622 AD)? Any devout Islamic ruler will favor the calendar of his faith, as current leaders do. For evidence, read a newspaper in any one of several Islamic countries. Take a look at the date. You will not find 2005 inscribed on the masthead, but rather 1426. The changing of the "times" will not represent a simple cosmetic alteration but one replete with meaning. The measurement of time is foundational in a culture's worldview. How a society decides when history begins and ends says much about its people. Instituting an Islamic calendar would be a forceful move on the part of the Beast, in essence saying, "The traditional Western interpretation of time, which has prevailed for centuries, has become obsolete, replaced by a proper starting point, when Allah protected his prophet and Islam began to grow." Obviously, this change would also replace Jesus Christ as the man whose arrival began the modern calendar.

Muhammad's run from his home city of Mecca to the refuge of Medina would become the touchstone for world history, an enormous change of perspective indeed. Much of the world at present is completely ignorant of the year in which Muhammad galloped to Medina, if they even know that he did change residences to jump-start his career as a prophet. An overhaul of the world calendar would ensure that everyone would gain at least some knowledge of Islamic history, as the very reference to each day will echo with the beginning of the last major world religion.

Perhaps some versions of Scripture say the Beast will "intend" to make these alterations because the Western world will have an exceedingly difficult time reprogramming its computers and adapting other technologies. If this monumental shift resembles the preparation for Y2K, look out! Proclaiming time to be measured by Islamic culture and seeing the world's infrastructure reprogrammed will be two different processes. It could be that the time needed to change non-Muslim systems of time measurement will exceed the Beast's period of leadership! Time measurement and law distinguish Islam from all other faiths. It's curious, is it not, that Daniel mentions these changes?

Changing the law could foreshadow al-Mahdi's insistence on an application of *sharia* law based on the Koran and hadiths. Any true Islamic ruler will insist on the adoption of *sharia* because it represents Allah's perfect justice. The implementation of Koranic law, from Iraq to Nigeria, bears watching for a preview of the Beast's great change. If the antichrist were a typical European, which laws would he seek to change? He would inevitably draw on a long Western legal tradition to argue for, perhaps, stiffer penalties for various crimes, a tweaking of the law. Would Daniel call attention to this relatively minor change? I doubt it. His eye was caught by a man who will seek to install an entirely new (to the Western world) system of justice. The Beast will be given the latitude to change the law because of the threatening anarchy around the world and his undisputed position as benevolent world despot.

Chapter 8 continues with more visions of mighty kingdoms that prove difficult to comprehend. Assigning exact eras and leaders to these verses is risky and has earned more than one "expert" the title of crackpot when his or her analysis proves faulty. I do not wish to enter that not-so-exclusive club. I would offer a few thoughts on the appearances of these animals and horns.

Verse 9 tells us that the small horn's dominion will grow "exceedingly great toward the south, toward the east, and toward the Beautiful Land." This expansion approximates the spread of Islam, which has prospered in the southern hemisphere and towards the Far East, surrounding modern-day Israel. This horn, which could even symbolize Islam itself, will magnify itself to the point of equality with God, as in speaking for a god with a new name, the all-powerful Allah. Daniel goes on to say that the sacrificial system would be ended and the place of the sanctuary thrown down. As chapter 3 showed, Islam is the one faith that has built a magnificent edifice on top of the ancient Jewish temple, thwarting any attempt to revive infidel worship there.

Truth will be "flung to the ground" by this ruler, and he will perform his will and prosper, Daniel foresees. Islam tolerates no other truth than its own, in the process crushing all other versions of the truth. I also hear echoes of the Islamic Jesus breaking the cross into pieces to demonstrate the erroneous teachings of Christianity. Despite this rejection of truth, this ruler will live large. Prosperity as a mark of Allah's approval remains a central tenet in Islam, much as it was for the Jews and their relationship with Jehovah in Old Testament days.

Gabriel interprets more specifically what Daniel has seen as the chapter progresses. He describes the little horn in detail in verses 23-26. Verse 24, which says: "his power will be mighty, but not by his own power" indicates a supernatural enabling that I believe matches up well with Revelation 13. The end of this verse also mentions a thorough persecution of believers, as he will "destroy...the holy people." Christian people will not be his only target. I see in verse 25 a revenge of the poor on the rich, mirroring the coming "north-south" conflict that many have predicted for decades, when the have-nots avenge themselves on the haves. "He will destroy many while they are at ease," Scripture says, a possible reference to the Last Days being as the days of Noah (Matthew 24:37-39). This prideful, violent rule will lead to a confrontation against Christ, who will triumph "without human agency" (v. 25b). The antichrist will be so powerful and demonically aided that only the divine power found in Jesus will suffice to stop him.

Daniel 9 could be termed one of the most stunningly accurate chapters of prophecy in all the Bible. In this chapter, Daniel declares that 69 "weeks" will elapse between the declaration of Cyrus to rebuild Jerusalem, made in 444 B.C. (Nehemiah 2:1-8) and the coming of the Messiah. Scholars date Christ's triumphal entry at 33 A.D. A quick calculation of lunar years yields the exact 483-year gap between these two major events. Christ's death is also foretold in this passage (v. 26), then the mysterious 70th week is mentioned in verse 27, when "the prince who is to come" will "make a firm covenant with the many for one week, but in the middle of the week he will put a stop to sacrifice and grain offering." This has led to the predominant interpretation that the antichrist will break a covenant with the Jewish people midway through his reign.

An echo of Revelation 13:14 and 15 lingers in the second half of this verse, when "on the wing of abominations will come one who makes desolate," a possible preview of the famous "abomination of desolation," which has provoked much debate among interpreters. Christ also mentioned this abomination, saying that it would occur before His second coming (Matthew 24:15). He added that the erection of this abomination would introduce a period of tribulation unequaled in history, the more intense second half of the time of Jacob's trouble. The existence of a massive, gleaming mosque on the site of the former Temple tells me that the stage is already set for this abomination, the form of which no one can identify without reserve. Perhaps an Islamic antichrist would allow the construction of another Temple in another part of Jerusalem, and then turn that edifice, as well, into an Islamic place of worship.

Daniel 10 goes on to describe the rise and fall of various empires, a vision that continues into chapter 11. We then come to another description of the Beast after verse 29. We hear of the "abomination of desolation" again in verse 31, then gain insight into the antichrist's charismatic leadership, as verse 32 tells of "his smooth words" that "will turn to godlessness those who act wickedly toward the covenant." Remember such portrayals whenever the identity of the antichrist is discussed. This man MUST be a master of rhetoric, a powerful persuader of people, which is why I do not identify bin Laden as a serious candidate and lean toward a more refined Muslim person.

In contrast to those who are deceived by the Beast, "the people who know their God will display strength and take action," verse 32 continues. The next verse mentions again that those having this relationship with God will be persecuted unto death "for many days." Again, note the preponderance of verses detailing persecution of the godly by the Beast. I will return to some of these passages in chapter 11. Verse 36 tells us that this king "will do as he pleases," exalting himself above every god and speaking "monstrous things against the God of gods," sounding much like Mahdi and his assistant, who will first argue against all faiths but Islam, then suppress the practice of those religions. Mahdi and Isa will attack all the primary doctrines of Christianity, even as well-informed Muslims do today. In the midst of these verses on self-exaltation and theological persuasion, a curious phrase works its way into the prophecy. Daniel reports that this ruler "will show no regard for…the desire of women" (v. 37). What connection could possibly exist between self-glorification and women? Why are they even mentioned?

I'll answer a question with a question: what faith, despite its numerous attempts to cover up its true stance on women, remains a religion where the females suffer second-class status around the world? I have heard Muslim women argue for a balanced application of the Koran to include women in the faith as full partners. Indeed, some verses of the Koran talk of an *ummah* composed of both strong male and female components. But the practical, nuts-and-bolts administration of Islam in today's societies yields a quite different picture. One can pick up autobiographies from *Princess* to *Inside the Kingdom* to *Not Without My Daughter* to read of feminine heartache in Islam. Clearly, the Pharisee class in Islam, the scribes and judges, hold women in low esteem—they must pray behind the men in the mosque, their testimony equals only one-half of a man's in court, their rights in divorce add up to nil after the husband says, "I divorce you" three times. When theocratic regimes apply true Islam to modern societies, schools for girls are shuttered, head-to-toe coverings mandated and executions begun for those even accused of adultery.

No regard for women? The antichrist sounds like a member of the Taliban. Take it from a man who has received many a weeping and weary Muslim woman, beaten or run off by an angry husband for "sins" ranging from infertility to suspected thievery, Islamic women are often condemned to a life of misery that the rest of us can only imagine. As I remarked many times to friends in France, I never saw a veiled woman smile in my city. Most looked as if they carried the weight of the world on their shoulders as they made the four-block trek around the neighborhood, forbidden to travel outside that invisible barrier by protective husbands. Many of the Muslim women in my town, just a few miles from the Paris city line, had never even been to the City of Light.

I know that as soon as I write these paragraphs, numerous Muslim women will cry, "No, true Islam esteems women." I have watched their press conferences, read their writings and applaud their efforts. I only report what I have lived and seen. For the vast majority of Muslim women in the world, especially in countries considered Islamic republics, leaders show little regard for the desire of women, I'm sorry to say.

Verses 37 and 38 take us deeper into this final king's doctrine, telling us that he will have no regards for the "gods of his fathers" or "any other god," preferring "a god of fortresses, a god whom his fathers did not know." Again, I have had debate opponents point to these verses to nullify the argument for an Islamic antichrist, opining that the Beast will worship a new god not previously known, perhaps himself. These counter-arguments have some weight, but I can turn 37 and 38 to prove my own thesis just as easily. Muhammad certainly had no place in his heart or mind for the gods of his fathers. Rather, he was repulsed by the pagan gods of his people and must be given some credit for abolishing several cruel heathen practices as Islam grew, outlawing the burial of twins and idol worship, among others. Any Muslim could be said to have rejected the gods of his fathers in that he has turned his back on Arab, African and Asian polytheistic worship in submission to Allah.

As for a god of fortresses, would you agree that a holy book that includes the call to war as a crucial thread through its pages would qualify as the scripture of a warrior god? Verse 38 can at least help us to narrow the field in our search of the antichrist. He will not be a Hindu or Buddhist, that's for sure! The choice of words, again, I find intriguing. The god of jihad, the god who ordered worldwide submission by military conquest if necessary, would fit the bill of a god of fortresses, I believe.

Daniel 11 chronicles the Beast's battles, concluding with verse 45, which predicts a kingdom stretching into the Holy Land. Egyptians, Libyans and Ethiopians will follow in his wake, although he will experience resistance as he seeks to occupy Palestine. Sound familiar? One of the most astounding historical facts of all time has been the inability of Islamic nations with combined armories far greater than Israel's to destroy the Jewish state.

Chapter 12 once more mentions "a time of distress such as never occurred" with "everyone who is found written in the book" rescued to eternal life. Thus concludes a fascinating yet mystifying book of prophecy. I congratulate anyone who builds a coherent eschatology on this book; their minds are far sharper than mine. I would need decades of study to unravel Daniel's mysteries, but the clues I do understand point to a Muslim as final world ruler.

The New Testament alludes to the coming antichrist as well. 2 Thessalonians 2, for instance, represents one of the more extensive portrayals outside of Daniel or Revelation. This passage has echoes of Daniel, speaking of a time of apostasy, a son of destruction, a man who exalts himself as a god and will be followed because of his "power and signs and false wonders." It also presages Revelation 13, where the two-man coalition will use their supernatural abilities to convince many of their divine approval.

1 John 2: The Theology of the Antichrist

1 John 2 touches more on the theological core of the antichrist in an electrifying couplet of verses that stand as a neon sign advertising the Beast's essence. After the solemn warning, amusing in a spiritual sort of way, that "it IS the last hour" (John wrote 1900+ years ago), he writes that antichrist is coming. He then gives the litmus test for the Beast's detection in verses 22 and 23: "Who is the liar but the one who denies that Jesus is the Christ? This is the antichrist, the one who denies the Father and the Son. Whoever denies the Son does not have the Father; the one who confesses the Son has the Father also." In effect, John says that the antichrist's core belief will be a denial of the Trinity, a nullification of Jesus' divinity. Of all the doctrinal distinctives that Paul could have underscored (Polytheist?

Satan worshipper? Condoning immorality? Works righteousness?),
he chose this one: a repudiation of Jesus being the Anointed One of
the true God, a disavowal of God being three persons, Father, Son
and Holy Spirit. The Holy Spirit inspired John to accentuate this fine
point of theology in order to correct the Gnostic Christians that
denied the incarnation of Christ, reasoning that all matter was evil
and it would thus be impossible for a divine being to take on human
flesh. I believe another reason existed for this emphasis, in God's
amazing plan.

One of the chief beliefs in Islam is the denial of the Trinity, which
Muhammad understood to be God the Father, Mary the mother and
Jesus the son. Several Koranic passages hammer this idea, including
4: 172: "Speak nothing but the truth about God. The Messiah, Jesus
the son of Mary, was no more than God's apostle and His Word
which He cast to Mary: a spirit from Him. So believe in God and
His apostles and do not say: 'Three'. God is but one God. God for-
bid that He should have a son!" This verse, often repeated in the
mosque during Friday worship, unifies Muslims across the globe
and reaffirms a central doctrine, their belief that no man is to be
unduly exalted above another. Bingo! What other major faith regularly renounces the Trinity as part of its rituals? Buddhism has no
comment; Hinduism doesn't even mention the Christ, Judaism has
a Messiah figure. Islam alone rises above the crowd and decrees,
"Allah does not have sex with women! He has had no son."
Whomever we believe the antichrist will be, he will blaspheme the
Trinity. I think that 1 John 2:22 and 23 add another layer of credibility to the hypothesis of an Islamic antichrist.

Traces of Islam in Revelation

Continuing on to the Bible's final book, the Revelation to John, I
choose a few other verses for your consideration. Having already
touched on chapter 13 and the two-man alliance that will rule the
planet in the Last Days, I will avoid speculation about the plagues,
seals, trumpets, and fallen stars. Among other passages, I would note
that the Beast and his 10-king cabinet will not only hate the immoral
harlot of chapter 17, but will "wage war against the Lamb," only to
be overcome by the real Jesus, who throws them into the lake of fire
in chapter 19. Islam's zeal for feminine sexual purity is apparent to
anyone who has spent time in one of their societies, and the fact that

the Beast will hate sensuality, not promote it, could allude to his Islamic origin as well.

After the chapter 19 judgment, a 1000-year divine culture will rule on planet Earth and all the wondrous prophecies of the ancient seers of Israel will be fulfilled, lambs and lions in repose side by side, children next to serpents, bountiful crops feeding everyone and eternal joy rendering the tear duct obsolete (Interestingly, no mention of virgins for the pleasure of redeemed males). The governors of this messianic kingdom earn mention in verse 4 of chapter 20. Those who had not worshipped the beast or his image and had not received his mark upon their forehead or hand will receive special recognition, as does another group that I believe gives us an additional hint about the Beast's background. "And I saw the souls of those who had been beheaded because of the testimony of Jesus and because of the word of God," John says, and my mind races to those terrible videos of hostages in Iraq pleading for their lives before a sharpened sword swooshes down upon their necks. Could some of these martyrs, one of whom I know was a missionary from Korea, be the first of this group, "beheaded because of their testimony"? Of all the methods of execution that could have been ordered for these all-star Christians in chapter 20 (bullet to the head, hanging, obliterated by a bomb), the Holy Spirit through John mentions beheading, the favored form in Islam for slaying an infidel. I remember Muslim friends in the Paris area always mentioning beheading as the proper response to any threat to their faith and people. "*On va les égorger,*" they would say, "We will cut their throats," using a butcher's term for sacrificing an animal in Allah's name. Beheading remains part of the Islamic army's psychological terror. As the number of Christian martyrs grows, we soon will be able to put faces on the favored believers in Revelation 20 who are given special honor by God for their courage. They will have lost their lives at the instigation of an Islamic ruler who chose to dispose of them in traditional fashion, a swift blow to the neck.

For some reason, God has not chosen to devote a major portion of His Word to the depiction of Earth's final years. The verses that do touch on Armageddon are interspersed with other prophecies pertaining to times past. Even when long stretches of chapters concentrate on the Tribulation, as in Revelation, they do not lend themselves to crystal clear interpretation.

The Lord has, though, left enough in His record to help us assemble a portrait of the final king of this world. And, as I have sifted through those verses, I confess to an extreme case of the shivers. My mind would quickly race to my experiences in the Muslim world: a conversation I had, a missionary I had met, an imam I had heard, a video I had watched, a headline I had read or a conference I had attended. Too many "coincidences" arose for me to believe that the Beast will be a Catholic or an atheist or a Jew. When the grid of Islamic prophecy is laid over Scripture's forecast, the likeness emerges even more clearly, and I have indeed trembled in my basement while reviewing the correspondences between the two.

No matter what school of thought you subscribe to, there can be no doubt that the coming antichrist will be a powerful, militarily-inclined denier of the Trinity who favors beheading his enemies. He will have a miracle-working assistant and come from the Middle East. He will attempt to change the measurement of time and the governing law, and he will not include women in his decision-making process. Are you positive that he will be a Romanian? At the risk of incurring the wrath of a people I love, I put my money on a charismatic closet fundamentalist.

This king will have worldwide sway, but how will he possibly bring the most powerful nation on Earth to its knees? Why won't the United States escape this dreadful judgment allowed by God? Will it result from the sins of homosexual marriage, sex and violence on TV, stem cell research? What great American sin will actually power the push towards Armageddon, as the Beast uses his great riches to bankroll his movement (Daniel 11:38)? I doubt you have ever heard this crucial flaw exposed by radio or television preachers, perhaps not even by the pastor of your church. This immorality's corroding influence works almost silently in today's world, like an invisible gas that eventually suffocates its victims. It has faded to the background because it is not seen as contrary to God's law, yet every day that our society succumbs to this sin, Muslims rejoice to see us sink ever deeper into the mire that it creates.

Chapter Ten

The Sin That Will Cut America's Throat

Every culture in the world has an unwritten code that classifies wrongdoing from most serious to petty. Many times the oral history of a given people will reveal what values they hold dearest and which deviations from those values will earn the most severe sanctions, often in the form of tales told about bygone heroes. For instance, George Washington, America's founding father, was said to have never told a lie. We do not know, however, if he was selfish or prone to losing his temper, both of which would be considered far more serious sins than not telling the truth in other cultures. The emphasis on George's reluctance to lie demonstrates that repeating or inventing a falsehood constitutes a serious sin in our culture. Such an emphasis does not exist in many other societies, as any tourist fresh out of the airport who has employed a "guide" can attest. Americans are often exasperated while traveling overseas by the ability of non-Americans to stretch, hide, shade and conceal the truth. These people do so with ease because they have grown up in cultures where breaking a relationship represents a far more serious transgression than spitting out the entire truth. They often will tell another party what he or she wants to hear rather than the naked truth, which could lead to a broken rapport. Americans believe, however, that one should tell the truth "even if it hurts." We raise our children to speak honestly and swear in witnesses to "tell the truth, the whole truth and nothing but the truth," so help them God. Perjury represents a criminal offense, and a serious one at that. As someone raised in the U.S., I, of course, affirm this value and am rankled by verbal deception.

Other sins grade even higher on the cardinal list: sexual sin, cheating, perversion. Need evidence? Compose a list of people who have resigned from public office in the face of scandal in recent years and then research why they left their position. Sexual iniquity would rank as the primary buster, with financial hanky-panky pulling into second place. By contrast, I have lived in parts of the world where both of these practices are expected of politicians, and thus more readily tolerated by their constituents.

I do not wish to argue for or against my culture's (or any other culture's) checklist of serious sins; I only desire to point out the existence of such scales in all societies. The danger of grading sin, though, is the inevitable devaluation of certain forms of evil that offend God's holy nature but pass almost unnoticed in a given populace. Sometimes these overlooked vices can stealthily ruin a life or society. In this chapter, I want to draw your attention to a sin condemned in God's word yet encouraged by our culture on a regular basis. I believe this transgression will lead to our ultimate undoing as a nation, despite its widespread acceptance.

By comparison, this sin does, in fact, earn vehement condemnation in most other cultures of the world, and the American blindness to it fuels some of the fury that our country experiences at the hands of Islamic fundamentalists and other peoples bent on harming the U.S. This sin will lead to our doom because it steers our country into unsavory relationships that we will one day regret, and its hold has become so complete that it dictates our interaction with the rest of the world. It has, in effect, become our master.

The Problem of Greed

The sin of which I speak is greed, defined as "excessive desire, especially for food or wealth," a vice reviled by God, quite energetically so, judging from the number of biblical passages dedicated to its denunciation. Yet, somehow, this corrosive deficiency of character usually escapes censure in our nation; in fact, it is often celebrated, as lifestyles of the rich and famous draw oohs and aahs and millionaires write books sharing their secrets for acquiring wealth. You can turn on your television at just about any hour to learn about the fabulous life of some particular celebrity or see his house or ogle her car, and our out-of-control desire for more grows.

Part of the problem lies in our economic system. Many Americans use greed as a motivating factor to "get ahead" and "become somebody." Such drive powers capitalism and keeps a vibrant economy humming. One president, after enduring the greatest economic collapse in our nation's history on his watch, experienced the downside of this initiative. Herbert Hoover offered the memorable quote. "The problem with capitalism is capitalists. They're too damn greedy."

Greed manifests itself on many levels in the United States, from the millions who are obsessed with accumulating wealth to the families who plunge deeper into debt to buy bigger houses and more cars to the politicians who rarely ask for sacrifice to the ambassadors who insist that the "American way of life" be preserved in all international agreements. This sin so captures our country that many Americans have to travel to the developing world before having an epiphany regarding the reason for their existence. They return home sobered, changed, realizing that life is more than possessions and that they in fact have more than they will ever need. If it's not travel that changes people's perspective, it's death. How many testimonies have we heard of people escaping death's clutches to realize "what's important in life"? The answer is never money, as I recall.

In condemning greed, I do not want to sound insensitive to readers who barely make ends meet and often have too much month at the end of the money. As someone who has been in the ministry for 16 years, I know what that feels like, and I can relate to your worry and desperation. You might find yourself falling even further behind as the gap between rich and poor widens and greed divides our country into two ever-more-disparate categories.

That inequality grows worldwide as well, and scores of sociologists have predicted a North-South hemispheric battle in years to come, generated by dissatisfaction with the economic status quo and competition for scarce resources. The religious aspect of this battle has been underplayed, I believe; the fact that most of the world's richest countries have sizable Christian populations in contrast to many of the world's poorest nations, which are often Islamic, adds an interesting dimension to the conflict.

Sadly, the U.S. contributes greatly to the lifestyle gap that forms a primary cause in the fundamentalist revolution. We insist on the preservation of our "way of life" and aspire to greater monetary heights through our domination of such organizations as the International Monetary Fund and the World Bank, both of which are headquartered in our capital. Eager to amass more wealth, we struggle as a nation to share with the world, often believing that if others worked as hard as we do, they would be able to achieve as well. Meanwhile, we maintain the myth that we are a generous Daddy Warbucks to the world. Alas, the statistics reveal a different story: of the 22 most industrialized nations on Earth, the U.S. ranks 22nd in percentage of gross domestic product given in foreign aid, investing just .1 percent in the development of an often-hungry world.[270]

I do not wish to lambaste you, dear reader, for your lifestyle choices as you relax in your home enjoying the fruits of your labor. I do think, though, that we Americans should reflect on just how much of the world's resources we consume, and then seek to live a more simple lifestyle in light of the world's growing inter-dependency. We who claim to follow Jesus Christ especially need to discern how to imitate his unadorned mode of living in modern times. Christians should be the most radical examples of anti-greed, I believe.

How bad is it? Here are just a few numbers to chew on: Americans consume more than half of all the goods and services of the world, yet comprise just 4 percent of the world's population. We spend more than $10 billion annually on pet food alone, which is $4 billion *more* than the estimated sum needed to provide basic health care and nutrition for everyone on the planet. The $8 billion we spend on cosmetics exceeds by $2 billion the annual amount needed to provide basic education worldwide.[271] As two British authors put it: "Americans are happy to consume most of the resources of the world, insist on exceptionally cheap petrol, and expect to be provided with an endless variety of cheap, processed food—because America is the cosmos."[272]

Don't starve Rover or throw away your eye shadow just yet, but do be aware that some economists believe greed has created a major problem that will eventually bankrupt our country—debt. Nigel Gault, an economist for the Global Insight research firm, offers: "The U.S. as a nation is just living way beyond its means. There is a worry that at some point, U.S. spending growth will have to slow sharply to get this under control." He cites "soaring" household debt and a "ballooning" federal budget deficit as examples of greed gone wild.[273] As one social commentator summarized the cycle: "We live in an ambitious and striving society. Most Americans hope to get ahead. They work hard. They like to spend what they earn—and they also compete compulsively to show how well they've done. As a result, anxiety and angst become a permanent way of life, even when the economy is doing fairly well. Enough is never enough."[274]

That writer went on to say that the "squeeze" most Americans feel is actually self-created, citing three common areas of gross over-spending: eating out, vehicle purchases and home acquisition.

The Bondage of Addiction to Oil

Restaurant bills and flashy rides will not be the primary culprits when the inevitable collapse comes, however. McDonald's French fries and Ford Tauruses do not keep our economy pumping, no matter what their publicists claim. No, at the foundation of the ravenous economic machine seeps a resource that powers the entire apparatus, and our country's thirst for it has led us down dark streets like a junkie desperate for a fix. God has allowed this addiction as a precursor to the final drama He planned before the beginning of time. I refer, you realize, to oil, of which we slurp 25 percent of the world's supply, three gallons per person per day.[275] Our lust for this liquid has become so acute that it shapes our foreign policy and sends our troops into harm's way when the supply is threatened, often to Islamic countries, while we ignore other trouble spots that have no reserves under their soil. Muslims are well aware of this killer habit that we have, and one day they will capitalize on the shakes we get when our dependency becomes even slightly more expensive.

As our national consumption of oil skyrockets and continues to outpace global production by greater and greater margins, America becomes more and more dependent on imported crude, particularly from the Middle East. The graph lines separating consumption and production look like a "less than" sign (<). Reflecting our inability to pare down our lifestyles, this use will continue to distend, expanding nearly 50 percent in the next 20 years as SUVs, pickup trucks and minivans continue to replace thriftier sedans and wagons as the standard family car (accounting for 56 percent of new vehicle sales in 2003, up from 22 percent in 1980), and the auto industry revives production of muscle cars.[276] Since 1988, the average gas mileage of U.S. passenger vehicles has fallen precipitously, during a time when conservation should have been encouraged and even mandated to end our enslavement to the Middle East.[277]

Joined with the issue of declining supply is the delicate area of exploration. Experts in the energy field believe that vast deposits of oil do exist, but permission must be given to access these reserves, and many of them lie in the Middle East. Growing opposition to infidels living in Saudi Arabia, for instance, will limit entrée to these wellsprings, ensuring an impasse as energy-starved Americans eventually attempt to force their way into the fertile sands of the region. Al-Qaeda and related groups have a clear, publicized goal in Saudi Arabia, as mentioned in chapter 8: to drive out the 100,000 Western expatriates who help run the country's oil industry and whose military and technical support are vital to the government.[278] Judging from the recent rise in such attacks, the terrorists' strategy is gaining momentum, speeding the arrival of a direct confrontation between buyer and seller.

Thus, if and when fundamentalist Muslims control the Middle East, they will have two giant levers with which to manipulate the world economy; they not only will determine the amount of oil delivered to the world, they will also bar access to the billions of barrels that still lie beneath the earth's surface, if they so choose. This mastery of oil's present and future flow seems so thorough that certain energy experts believe the sole valid U.S. response will be to reduce demand, not hope for additional exploration in volatile regions of the world.[279] Few men or women of influence seem to have the guts necessary to address this ominous dilemma, however, preferring to encourage Americans to consume ever more natural resources to keep business booming while ignoring the menacing signs of a head-on collision between dealer and addict.

For a time, the U.S. did demonstrate it could conserve gasoline usage, soon after the energy crisis of the 1970s, when Arab leaders clamped an oil embargo on our country in retaliation for our support of Israel in the 1973 Mideast war. I remember the incredible lines at service stations in those days, the altered routines, the proliferation of cyclists on the roadways. The federal government mandated a 55 mph speed limit as well as gasoline efficiency standards, and research scientists dived into study of alternative energy resources. A Strategic Petroleum Reserve was created and many of us turned down our thermostats at President Carter's urging. Drivers switched to smaller, more economical vehicles and oil consumption fell by 10 percent between 1976 and 1985. The response was admirable, but the suffering incurred contributed to President Carter's exit from office, when the "malaise" of sacrifice was swept out by Ronald Reagan's preferred optimism. What true American really wanted to drive a four-cylinder car, anyway?

Lower oil prices in the '80s and '90s led to immediate backsliding. Americans returned to their beloved gas-guzzlers and demand for oil rose by almost 25 percent between 1985 and 2000.[280] But these "boom" years will exact a cruel price one day. We should be preparing for another possible crisis, because the country that guards half of the world's reserves, Saudi Arabia, cannot be considered a stable or reliable friend. If the booming group of Islamists in that nation seizes control of the petroleum infrastructure, they will no longer need to buy private jets for their distant cousins or bankroll raucous vacations to Monaco. They will be far more concerned with the extension of Allah's reign than living a lifestyle worthy of Robin Leach's reportage.

Even micro-steps, such as a simple tightening of the Corporate Average Fuel Efficiency standards, hardly touched since 1986, would help, cutting U.S. demand by a million barrels a day, two-thirds of which we import from Saudi Arabia. Yet, no politician is willing to risk Detroit's wrath.[281]

Optimists who brush off our yoke to Saudi, noting the multiplicity of oil providers in OPEC, fail to realize that the House of Sa'ud's good will alone sustains the global economy. As one Saudi observer stated: "It may not seem like much oil, but the surplus capacity is what keeps the world's oil markets from going on a facedown rollercoaster ride during periods of crisis. In other words, no matter what country you buy your oil from, Saudi Arabia determines world price by how much oil it chooses to produce."[282]

Did you read that last phrase? The Saudis fix the world price by determining how much oil they will produce. What happens when they turn the tap off? A world that consumes 82 million barrels of oil each day will be forced to alter its collective lifestyle as the new holders of the keys to the kingdom watch the formerly wealthy squirm and scream. Nonetheless, don't forget that God Himself has allowed Islam's holiest land to call the shots, for a time. As much as it cramps our style, we are thoroughly dependent on a liquid that flows primarily from a very tenuous part of the world, and that reliance will only increase as its share of the total grows to two of every three barrels produced on the planet by 2020, according to the Department of Energy.[283] Furthermore, for future reference, 80 percent of the world's proven reserves rest dormant in nearly 100 percent Islamic countries.[284]

Despite the Bush Administration's National Energy Policy Development Group report that warned that the "imbalance" of importing two-thirds of our oil "if allowed to continue, will inevitably undermine our economy, our standard of living, and our national security," little encouragement is given to curb our nation's craving. Why? Energy authorities cite a messy confrontation with "powerful commercial interests, solving difficult technology problems and convincing the American public that cheap fuel is not a birthright."[285]

I can attest to that last obstacle to cutback. Hearing Americans moan about paying $2 for a gallon for gas draws little sympathy from those of us who have lived in Europe and adjusted to life in a land where it costs more than twice that. Not surprisingly, the 15 most developed EU countries, despite having 100 million more people than the U.S., use one-third less energy.[286] Americans will always oppose the massive taxes that produce much skimpy energy use in Europe. The last increase was a paltry four cents a gallon, way back in 1993, when President Clinton ordered it to howls of protest. We prefer lower prices at the pump even if we have to pay hundreds of billions of dollars in taxes to support a U.S. military presence in the Middle East, a hidden tax that few take into account in our collective ignorance.[287]

Thus, the God-ordained right to life, liberty and the pursuit of happiness will permanently include the right to accumulate as much as one is capable of and driving the vehicle of one's choice, regardless of the long-term consequences. This has meant, more and more, the purchase of at least one sport utility vehicle or pickup truck, both of which get miserable mileage. In short, we live as if the calendar reads 1905, when the U.S. boasted vast oil reserves that kept gas prices minimal. In 2005, sadly, the lower 48 states produce less than half the oil that they did even 30 years ago, and northern Alaska's production continues to decline as well.[288] In the modern equation, we must either adapt or be held hostage as we come in 10th place in current reserves.[289]

As for those who tout alternative energy sources as a way out of being held captive to Arab whims, a transition to vehicles powered by electricity, natural gas or corn mush would require a huge investment that doesn't appear to be forthcoming. As one veteran oil industry executive, Robert Ebel, who now heads the energy program at the Center of Strategic and International Studies, predicts direly, "We cannot produce our way to energy independence, and we cannot use efficiency or conservation to achieve energy independence. It's just not going to happen, at least in my lifetime."[290]

In short, our greed has overpowered our will, the definition of addiction, and we are now stuck in an unseemly relationship with Muslim oil barons that will eventually cut our supply and watch us shiver as we go cold turkey. The world's proven reserves are concentrated, in order of quantity, in Saudi Arabia, Iran, Iraq, the United Arab Emirates and Kuwait.[291] How's that for a lineup? I challenge you to find a more Islamic region. Our gluttony for petroleum has led to an understanding with Saudi Arabia, among other oil-producers, summarized thusly by a CIA agent: "The bottom line is that what the Saudis really care about is driving home the message to Washington that it needn't worry: Sure, we've lost control of our country, and our citizens are slaughtering yours, but you can depend on us to keep your cars on the road and your houses warm."[292] I'm not a cynic, but I have to admit, that synopsis hits the mark.

As one detailed study of the problem notes: "But in the end the quest for more cheap oil will prove a losing game: Not just because oil consumption imposes severe costs on the environment, health, and taxpayers, but also because the world's oil addiction is hastening a day of reckoning."[293] Joseph Romm, former Assistant Secretary of Energy in the Clinton Administration, adds: "If people cared about oil imports they would buy different cars. In response to 9/11, people started putting flags on their SUVs and buying Hummers. That tells you something."[294] Indeed!

Our Role in Spreading Terrorism

The documentary "Fahrenheit 9/11" worked hard to prove the connection between American oil interests, big business and terrorism. The reporting was often sound, but the conclusions drawn proved to be a bit stretched, in my opinion. For instance, it takes a true skeptic to believe that President Bush fights the war on terrorism in order to promote businesses with which he has links. I can't go that far. The film did not go far enough, however, in detailing another aspect of the oil-terrorism connection—my personal gas consumption and the spread of fundamentalism. At one point during the film, I wanted to stand up and holler to the packed house:

"Let's not just blame Republican politicians for this scandalous link-age. We need to all look in the mirror, too. Our habits power this entire cycle!" For, it is our greed that not only will back us into a cor-ner, but actually feed the monster that will eventually eat us. Oil money has spread Islamist doctrine around the globe and helped that wing to seize the educational and publishing arms of the faith.

As Baer summarizes:

> "We buy oil from Saudi Arabia, refine it, and put it in our automobiles, and a certain small percentage of what we pay for it ends up funding terrorist acts against America and American institutions at home and abroad....a smaller amount will go to funding Saudi-based groups that intend to do harm to the West, because otherwise, those same groups might do harm back home in the sunny suburbs of, say, Riyadh."[295]

Bernard Lewis, the Princeton University scholar on Islam, offers this cogent summary: "Without oil and the creation of the Saudi king-dom, Wahhabism would have remained a lunatic fringe."[296] Brother Andrew, the famous Bible smuggler turned mission executive, echoed this point at a 1995 prayer conference, more than a half-decade before 9/11. He asked, "Who was the source of funding for the global expan-sion of Islam in the past 30 years?" then charged the industrialized West with the willingness to pay "any price" to maintain our mobility, which requires large quantities of crude oil. He went on to note that Muslims interpret this financial windfall as Allah's blessing and part of his will to bring the whole world under Islamic rule.[297]

As I envisioned in chapter 8, the current American-Saudi connec-tion could shatter at any time. As author Baer plainly states:

> "Terrified that the fanatics will one day come after them, the Al Sa'ud shovel out protection money as fast as they can withdraw it from their Swiss bank accounts. Never forget that it is the Al Sa'ud who ultimately sign the checks for the mosque schools. They fund militant Islamic movements in the Middle East, Africa, central Asia, and Asia for the same reason. It's hush money to divert Muslims' attention from the money the Al Sa'ud are stealing against the day when

they will have to flee the desert for their palaces strung out along the Riviera; their penthouses glowing against the night skies of Paris, London, and New York; their mountain aeries bathed by the cool evening breezes of Morocco. The House of Sa'ud, after all, knows what the West is beginning to learn: Horrors are out there waiting worse than Osama bin Laden."

About one fill-up in five contributes a dollar to propping up a corrupt government that would repulse most of us, Baer adds.[298]

This begs the question: would Americans be willing to settle for a lower standard of living and use alternative sources of energy (including foot power) to choke the worldwide dissemination of Islamic fundamentalism? Which congressman will articulate this choice to the nation? Would any have the courage to do so? I think you know the answers to these questions. The end result of our greed feeding this terrorism machine will be a sea change in our world. As Baer envisions:

"Take the rage in the mosques and the streets of Saudi Arabia; add weapons and a willingness to use them, not just against Western terrorist targets but against the House of Sa'ud and the petroleum infrastructure that supports it; continue to look the other way while it all happens; and we can take the last half century of oil-fired industrial prosperity and kiss it g-o-o-d-b-y-e."[299]

All booms have a bust one day. Just before He told the parable of the rich fool in Luke 12, Christ said, "Beware, and be on your guard against every form of greed; for not even when one has an abundance does his life consist of his possessions" (v. 15). The man in that story always struck me as quintessentially American. He sounds just like Donald Trump when he brags about bigger barns one day. But we all have a little of the Donald in us; what we have never seems to be enough, does it? Perhaps a fresh meditation on Luke 12:15 can help us to prepare for the coming chaos. With the knowledge you now have as a result of this chapter, how will your lifestyle choices, even down to your choice of vehicle, be affected? How are we supposed to live in light of the approaching gridlock in world affairs?

Chapter Eleven

A Proper Response to These Times

Now that you have read what could occur in the next few years, I hope and pray that fear and dread do not grip you. I realize the difficulty in swallowing the thesis that Muslims will one day direct world affairs through an antichrist who demands conversion or imprisonment or death. Yet, the fact is, such persecution and the ceding of absolute power to an evil, demonically inspired anti-God has long been predicted in the pages of our Bibles. No one in their right mind would wish these events on themselves or loved ones, but they will occur in God's plan, and part of the reason I have written this book is to prepare the Church for the fulfillment of these awful prophecies. In short, I am willing to deliver a Jeremiah-like message and risk being thrown into a pile of, uh, refuse. I'm a big boy. I can handle it.

Often when I share my theories in churches, people respond by asking, "Now what are we to do?" On one hand, I think that our response as followers of Jesus Christ is obvious. They have been outlined in Scripture for centuries: "Stand firm in the faith," "Love your enemies and pray for those who persecute you," "Let not your heart be troubled." On the other hand, I caution against an overemphasis on application whenever a truth is presented. This arises from our living in a society that is bent on doing, not being. Sometimes new thoughts should be allowed to sink into your mind. Reflect, first, on all that I have shared. Then, you will be better able to respond as the Holy Spirit leads. Do not skip such meditation; you will miss out on tremendous blessing. The Lord can speak to you in far more meaningful ways than I.

Even so, at the request of many of my listeners over the past few years, I include this chapter of preparation for the possibility of an

Islamic antichrist ruling the world for seven years, beginning some-
time near the end of this decade. For guidance, I will follow the outline of the pamphlet created by the Homeland Security Office and
distributed by the United States Postal Service entitled: *Preparing
Makes Sense. Get Ready Now.* Inside, former DHS Secretary Tom
Ridge states, "Terrorism forces us to make a choice. We can be afraid.
Or, we can be ready."

Amen to that! I would echo that counsel on a spiritual level.
Rather than being gripped by fright, followers of Jesus Christ need
to face the End Times courageously and be prepared to withstand
any storm that might come our way.

Preparing Makes Sense offers four simple steps for Americans to
take in order to survive a terrorist attack, making the analogy that
such groundwork resembles a working smoke detector that can save
one from a house fire. Rather than repeating the pamphlet, I will use
the four points as a launching pad for their spiritual equivalents.
Here goes:

Make an Emergency Supply Kit

Make an emergency supply kit of items ranging from batteries to
duct tape, from canned food to flashlights. Two such kits should be
assembled, the authors reason, one for those who are able to remain
at home and a more lightweight version for those who need to flee.
What would a spiritual survival kit look like? How about a faith that
is rooted deep in the Scriptures, for starters, a faith that will not waver
according to circumstance? I know that many of my readers have limited time and, as a result, they have long ignored the exhortations of
their pastors to plunge into Bible study. Think of this application
point as an emergency measure, and realize that reading God's Word
can be both stimulating and comforting. "Thy word is a lamp to my
feet, and a light to my path," David said. "Plead my cause and redeem
me. Revive me according to Thy word" (Psalm 119:105, 154). We will
all need such guidance in days to come. God's Word promises to give
it. No other book can fortify the soul as completely, either.

Your spiritual emergency supply kit should contain comforting
passages of promise, such as the Psalms or sections of Christ's teachings. Add to that a survey of biblical prophecy by spending time in
Daniel, Revelation, Isaiah and other prophetic books. I would recommend study tools to accompany such a perusal of these Scriptures. Top

off your reading with selected chapters from the New Testament letters that urge faithfulness in times of trial, many of which were penned specifically for us who live in the Last Days (Romans 8, 1 Corinthians 15, 2 Corinthians 5, Ephesians 6, Philippians 3, 1 Thessalonians 5, 2 Thessalonians 2, 2 Timothy 3, Hebrews 11 and 12, 1 Peter 4, etc.). These chapters will come alive as you remember that they were written precisely for the purpose of steeling the faithful, another example of God's grace to His church, which has faced persecution throughout its existence.

My Bible came alive as never before during my years in Africa for a multitude of reasons, one of which was the fierce persecution suffered by many of the Muslim men who made professions of faith. Each Tuesday night, we would meet for mutual encouragement under the stars in my neighbor's courtyard (rained out once in two years!). As a fellow missionary and I read to these precious brothers about God's guarantees to those on trial for their faith, the atmosphere turned both solemn and electric. The word for encouragement in the Jula language that we used translates "to harden the soul." We humbly strengthened these men who faced job loss, eviction, spouse theft and slaughter of their flocks for their newfound faith with verses like:

> "Who shall separate us from the love of Christ? Shall tribulation, or distress, or persecution, or famine, or nakedness, or peril, or sword? Just as it is written, 'For Thy sake we are being put to death all day long; we were considered as sheep to be slaughtered.' But in all these things we overwhelmingly conquer through Him who loved us." (Romans 8:35-37)

Contemplate such verses so that you will be ready when a zealous policeman knocks on your door and demands that you repeat the Islamic confession of faith or be thrown into jail. Through the digestion of such Scriptures you will build a faith that does not rest on American military power or economic prosperity. You will construct a belief system that rests on the faithfulness of the founder, not your present circumstances. You will assimilate key truths that will carry you through hardship, such as "God loves me," "God is in control," "God rewards those who stand true," "God said that all this would occur." Begin now to build your spiritual supply kit by carving out an hour or two per week to feed on the bread from Heaven in emergency preparation.

We will all learn much in coming years about the depth and strength of the American church's faith. Some question whether our country has what it takes morally and psychologically to withstand the threat of terrorists. *World* magazine cultural editor Gene Edward Veith said: "In some ways, the Islamists have a stronger culture than Americans do—not better, by any means, but more cohesive, more committed to their beliefs, more eager to accept hardship and death in the name of their cause."[300] Will his words be proven true? Construct your worldview based on an eternal perspective that remembers the end of the story during the terrible years before Christ returns, then act accordingly. "Therefore, let those also who suffer according to the will of God entrust their souls to a faithful Creator in doing what is right. For consider Him who has endured such hostility by sinners against Himself, so that you may not grow weary and lose heart. But realize this, that in the last days difficult times will come. You, however, continue in the things you have learned and become convinced of, knowing from whom you learned them" (1 Peter 4:19; Hebrews 12:3; 2 Timothy 3:1,14).

Make a Family Communications Plan

What a keen idea for the twenty-first century! *Preparing Makes Sense* argues for advance decisions to be made concerning an emergency shelter, escape plan, and a proper response if one is caught at school or work. Raise your hand if you have formulated a strategy covering these areas. I would imagine not too many families have. My brood has a tough enough time even eating together twice a week, let alone working out how to respond to a terrorist attack! Our communication ebbs and flows according to the packed schedules of four people 14 or older. The U.S. is a curious country in this way. Most other societies allow for a family meal time, no matter how busy each member is. One of the great revelations of my sojourn in Europe was the close family ties there, despite the predominant non-Christian worldview. This was a direct contradiction of the teaching I had heard for many years that linked abandonment of Christianity with the meltdown of the family and eventual societal collapse. I found French families to be far closer and spend much more time together than their American counterparts.

We live in a culture that speciously separates the family and we need to seize the initiative to disciple our children as God desires. I understand that much of what I have shared in this book would spook many young children, and I do not advise this book for family devotions. I do believe it is important that children in Christian families be told of how Jesus will return and set up His kingdom on Earth, including all the scenarios for that event (pre-Tribulation, mid-Tribulation and post-Tribulation), whether or not you agree with them. Rarely have I seen devotional aids that mention the Second Coming, in direct disobedience to the Bible's frequent commands to be alert. Given the rapidity of change in our world and the reality of permanent terrorism, we would be wise to include the End Times somewhere in our family discipleship. The goal is not to keep Johnny or Sally up at night with bad dreams, but to build a unit of Christian people that will stand together in difficult times, armed with the awareness that God has spoken about a violent end to our world. As the Great Tribulation approaches, we should not keep all prophetic passages a secret from our children. We owe it to them to give them at least a hint of the hardship that might arrive soon. It would be a shame to see children abandon the faith of their fathers and mothers because "you never told me about this and this world leader talks about one God, too," or, "I thought God loved us. Why are we suffering? Your faith is a bunch of bologna!" Persecution will either strengthen or destroy the faith of your family. Communicate in a way to ensure, as best you can, the first alternative.

The Homeland Security brochure also encourages people to "talk to your neighbors about how you can work together." Could we do the same, in a sensitive manner, on the spiritual level? If indeed there are witnesses for Christ left on this Earth when the trouble starts (and not just on videotape, as film versions of a pre-Tribulation rapture always show), we should take the lead in explaining what will unfold according to the Bible, at the risk of being labeled loony. Perhaps even this book would make a suitable gift for the neighbor or colleague that you care about. Granted, it is doubtful that we will see a great harvest when the price of conversion equals imprisonment or death, but I believe there will be a new openness among the lost as they see the Bible proved correct again and again. In fact, much of the apathy in America over the Gospel will dissolve when the stakes are raised. People will be clearly identified for or against

Christ, with the consequent rewards or punishments. There is nothing like persecution to cure the Church of "lukewarm" believers. I remember hearing a former Mau Mau-rebel in Kenya tell me of his conversion as a result of his participation in the execution of a Christian man who refused to pledge allegiance to the rebel movement above Jesus. Some of your neighbors will be attracted to a faith that stands strong even when the cost is high. We owe it to our friends and acquaintances to get the truth out as we see "the day" approaching.

Be Informed

Americans are urged to not only prepare an emergency supply kit and talk through response scenarios as a family, a toll-free number and Web site for additional information on terrorist threats is available as well. I am thankful for the professionals who monitor the terrorist climate, but it is impossible to track a giant army of extremists worldwide at all times and in all places. Terrorism's greatest weapon is surprise.

I repeat DHS's directive on a spiritual level. Even though Scripture tells us that we will never know the exact time and day of Christ's return, it does not discourage study of the signs preceding that day or frequent discussion of the coming drama. On the contrary, the Bible tells us: "Be on the alert, for you do not know which day your Lord is coming. Be on the alert then, for you do not know the day nor the hour. But you, brethren, are not in darkness, that the day should overtake you like a thief; so then let us not sleep as others do, but let us be alert and sober. For those who sleep do their sleeping at night, and those who get drunk get drunk at night. But since we are of the day, let us be sober, having put on the breastplate of faith and love, and as a helmet, the hope of salvation" (Matthew 24:42; 25:13; 1 Thessalonians 5:4,6-8).

Sometimes when I hear people talk about Christ's second coming, they speak as if we are to ignore it in order to avoid the sin of predicting the date. This backlash against misinformed prophets who have pinpointed dates in the past and urged retreats to the mountains goes too far. Christians should do all they can to be unlike the people in the times of Noah, who were eating, drinking, marrying and being married, oblivious to the coming disaster. That is one of the reasons why I wrote this book.

I also sense a lack of vigilance when I meet the "pan-Tribulationists," those who believe it will "all pan out in the end." I appreciate those who do not get dogmatic over a certain eschatological position, but a dismissal of the subject can lead to a similar "same old-same old" attitude that inflicted Noah's peers, who "did not understand until the flood came and took them all away" (Matthew 24:39). There is no sin in keeping a close eye on the newspaper and your Bible. If we prepare mentally for possible persecution, we will more likely emerge faithful and victorious. So, I say again, be informed. Read or watch a broad spectrum of news, track developments in the countries that I have mentioned in this book, and spend much time in prophetic passages, not to the neglect of other portions of God's Word, but as a regular part of your spiritual diet.

Read through Matthew 24, for instance, and ponder its implications. Join a study group that examines Revelation in all its mystery. Consider the doomsday proclamations of the major and minor prophets, get out a map and think about the ordained fate of much of the Middle East. God will be true to His word. Rather than simply attending worship services and reading Christian novels and self-help literature, every single follower of Christ in this day and age should be a self-taught aficionado of prophecy. The times demand it. Keep your lamp lighted, like the five prudent virgins in Matthew 25.

Remain Calm

After scaring the bejeezus out of its readers, *Preparing Makes Sense* concludes with two words: "Remain calm."

Most people who would take the information in the pamphlet seriously would be anything *but* calm after reflecting on the contents. Without Christ in my life, I'm sure I'd panic! After working through this book, perhaps you, too, are susceptible to fear. Often when I share these truths in churches, the pastor has to pick up the pieces for weeks after, calming the rattled flock after my departure. When I put the chapter 8 timeline on a PowerPoint slide, it all hits home and a God-created defense mechanism kicks in. In the face of the catastrophes that I have outlined in these pages, calm does not seem a normal reaction, and it is not. Remaining tranquil will require both supernatural resources given to us by the Holy Spirit and a knowledge of the end of the story.

When we watch a movie whose ending we already know, we are able to remain composed even when disaster strikes our favorite main characters. In the same way, when we consider the in-between time that debuts with world chaos and ends with the real Christ's return, we should never lose heart. We know, based on Jesus' promises, that "he who believes on Me shall live even if he dies. And if I go and prepare a place for you, I will come again, and receive you to Myself; that where I am, there you may be also. These things I have spoken to you, that in Me you may have peace. In the world you have tribulation, but take courage; I have overcome the world" (John 10:25; 14:3; 16:33). Chewing on these promises and others will enable us to persevere no matter who the antichrist is or when he appears.

A flurry of literature about the psychological effects of terror has appeared since 9/11, finding a particularly receptive audience in the U.S. One writer, who drew heavily on the Pulitzer Prize-winning book *The Denial of Death*, made the point that human beings create an illusory world so that they will not have to come face to face with death, even though it is as certain in life as taxes.[301] We Christians, though, do not have to formulate such a world. We who walk in the path of the one who said, "I am the resurrection and the life," can say calmly, "Yes, we all will die. But those who place their trust in Christ will live again because He did."

In other words, the man, woman or child who is freed from the fear of death is free to live life with gusto and meaning, without fear and trembling, even if his world collapses. David Livingstone, the great missionary and explorer, related that his life changed in the instant when a lion's jaws clamped on his arm and the beast swung him like a rag doll, permanently disabling him. Having looked death in the eye at that moment, Livingstone said that he no longer feared it, liberating him to accomplish the feats that earned him knighthood and a country's adoration. Similarly, if the events discussed in this book do take place one day, and the U.S. ends up in the jaws of an antichrist, we disciples of Jesus, of all people, should be the least ruffled, the calm guides needed in a time of crisis. When the illusions of immortality and an ever-growing GNP are burst, we who name the name of Jesus are to be the ones that people turn to for serenity. In fact, we will probably be the only ones who are able to "remain calm."

A present parallel can be found in Israel, where people live under the constant specter of terrorism. One journalist who wanted to explore the temperament of Israelis found a people who "live defiantly, indomitably, with a heightened intensity, as though each day might be their last."[302] Sounds like an excellent model for us in the End Times.

Certainly, there is a chance that none of the events described in this book will take place anytime soon. God might postpone His judgment another 2,000 years. It would not be the first time that His mercy stuns us. However, if in fact the world does darken for a time and the Church does remain on the Earth through that period, we will need a down-to-the-bones assurance that God is faithful and that His word is true. With that confidence, we can remain serene.

Preparing does make sense. We *should* get ready now. However, I am a realist and a fairly normal human being. I have little time for planning, and life's events often catch me by surprise. I do not expect you to begin a two-hour daily study of Biblical prophecy. I do pray, however, that you will see the world through a new lens. I pray that you will become a student of current events and Biblical prophecy, with a highly sensitive eye trained on the Islamic world. Based on my knowledge of Islam and my interactions with Muslims, I believe quite strongly that God will use this false religion for His purposes. It seems ideally conceived for this task.

May God grant us all the courage and faith to endure to the end. We will be tempted to believe the God talk of the antichrist who will speak of one God, submission to Him, and brotherhood with Abraham, Moses and Jesus. We will wobble when faced with the choice of conversion or prison or instant death. We will lose heart as friends and loved ones are killed by an angry enemy. We will be tempted towards self-preservation as our love for others grows cold. Yet, "in all these things" will we "overwhelmingly conquer through Him who loved us," as Paul did? How will we, as formerly comfortable Americans, react when we suffer for the first time as much of the world does presently, scrambling for food, robbed of our freedoms, surrounded by death? Just how tough will we be?

I pray that we will rise to the occasion, that we will draw on resources we never knew we had, that we will find the words to say, as Jesus promised, as we rely on the Holy Spirit as never before and remember His words:

"If the world hates you, you know that it has hated Me before it hated you. If you were of the world, the world would love its own; but because you are not of the world, but I chose you out of the world, therefore the world hates you. Remember the word that I said to you, 'A slave is not greater than his master.' If they persecuted Me, they will also persecute you; if they kept My word, they will keep yours also. But all these things they will do to you for My name's sake, because they do not know the One who sent Me. He who hates Me hates My Father also. These things I have spoken to you, that you may be kept from stumbling. They will make you outcasts from the synagogue; but an hour is coming for everyone who kills you to *think that he is offering service to God.* And these things they will do, because they have not known the Father, or Me. But these things I have spoken to you, that when their hour comes, you may remember that I told you of them. But when He, the Spirit of truth, comes, He will guide you into all the truth; for He will not speak on His own initiative, but what He hears, He will speak; and He will disclose to you what is to come. Therefore you, too, now have sorrow; but I will see you again, and your heart will rejoice, and no one can take your joy away from you." (John 15:18, 20, 21, 23; 16:1-4, 13, 22)

Despite the awful atmosphere of those times, it will be exciting to discover the power of the Spirit as He bears us along to our glorious eternal destiny. I do not wish this time of Jacob's trouble on anyone, even to prove that I am right, yet I do look forward to a deeper walk with God, and I know that suffering is one of His choice methods for drawing me closer to Him.

As the lines are drawn more clearly in our modern world, we also need to be careful not to give in to Muslim hating, which seems to be a popular trend these days. We need to turn a deaf ear to conservative talking heads who urge the carpet-bombing of the Middle East or the nuking of Mecca, both ideas that circulated widely in conservative publications read by many evangelicals. We need to reject the idea that the Middle East should be made into a parking lot, as one worship team member recommended to me during my visit to his church. Just because the antichrist could be a Muslim and

Islam contains several insidious elements that threaten world peace and our very nation, we Christians must separate the faith and its leaders from its followers. Those of us who have lived among and loved Muslim people do not blame them for having been born into a lie. We marvel at how deeply God loves them as He appears to them in dreams and calls them to Himself. We wonder also at the love He passes on to us when we pray for His patient affection. We pity the enslaved of this faith to the point of committing our lives to their salvation. Muslims, too, deserve a chance to hear Christ's fantastic news for them, that they can be freed from the tyranny of feared judgment, that martyrdom is not the sole, sure way to Paradise. Rather, that someone *else's* sacrificial death has opened Heaven's gates.

We Christians are the Americans who must love Islamic people, though not blind to their ideology or intentions. Even as they increasingly become our primary enemies, we need to apply the difficult commands of Christ's Sermon on the Mount, praying for those who persecute us, giving our coats to them, walking a second mile. That, my friends, earns you admission to the graduate school of Christianity.

When we stand to pray for our troops in Iraq, we must not stop there. We must intercede also for Muslims, for bin Laden, for zealous, misguided terrorists who could be transformed as completely as a killer named Saul once was.

I close with a Scripture and a Jula blessing.

The verse stands as a final assurance that the Lord will safely see us home no matter what transpires on our planet. It comes from the pen of that old war veteran Paul, who destroyed forever the myth that being in the center of God's will was the safest place to be. Paul followed the Spirit's promptings right into beatings, imprisonments, shipwrecks and, eventually, martyrdom. Near the close of his life as he wrote to his protégé Timothy, he thought back to a betrayal and near-death experience, and realized again how trivial both were compared to the eternal glory that awaited him. He wrote: "The Lord will deliver me from every evil deed, and will bring me safely to His heavenly kingdom; to Him be the glory forever and ever. Amen."

The blessing is one that I often gave to brothers and sisters who lived in desperate circumstances and sometimes suffered additionally for their faith, people who didn't have enough to eat, couldn't find a job despite their best efforts, lost their employment, friends and even family members as a result of their conversion to Christ. This prayer seems appropriate in light of all that you have now learned, as it includes the verb I mentioned earlier in this chapter.

"Ala ka I ja gbeleya." May God harden your soul. Amen.

Endnotes

1. Neil MacFarquhar, "Syria, Long Ruthlessly Secular, Sees Fervent Islamic Resurgence," *The New York Times,* October 24, 2003.
2. Joyce M. Davis, *Martyrs: Innocence, Vengeance, and Despair in the Middle East* (New York: Palgrave Macmillan, 2003), p. 176.
3. Anthony Shadid, "Old Arab Friends Turn Away from U.S.," *The Washington Post,* February 26, 2003.
4. Ziauddin Sardar and Merryl Wyn Davies, *Why Do People Hate America?* (New York: The Disinformation Company, 2002), p. 7.
5. Kenneth R. Timmerman, *Preachers of Hate* (New York: Random House, 2004), p. 308.
6. International Institute of Strategic Studies report cited by Barry Renfrew, "Report: Al-Qaeda Ranks Swelling Worldwide," *Associated Press,* May 25, 2004.
7. Ed Hotaling, *Islam Without Illusions* (Syracuse University Press: Syracuse, N.Y., 2003), p. 163.
8. Article from Strategic Forecasting Incorporated, www.stratfor.com, March 19, 2004.
9. Joshua Hammer, Richard Wolffe and Christopher Dickey, "The War Through Arab Eyes," *Newsweek,* May 31, 2004.
10. Maggie Michael, "Fugitive Vows to Assassinate Iraqi Leader," *Associated Press,* June 23, 2004.
11. John Mintz and Douglas Farah, "In Search of Friends Among the Foes," *The Washington Post,* September 11, 2004.
12. Robert Killebrew, "Al Qaeda, The Next Chapter," *The Washington Post,* August 8, 2004.
13. Ibid.
14. V.S. Naipul, *Beyond Belief: Islamic Excursions Among the Converted Peoples* (New York: Random House, 1998), p. 224.
15. V.S. Naipul, *Among the Believers: An Islamic Journey* (New York: Vintage Books, 1982) p. 164.
16. Lewis, *The Crisis of Islam* (New York: Random House, 2003), pp. 45-46.
17. Ibid., p. 114.
18. Robert Baer, *Sleeping With the Devil* (Crown Publishers: New York, 2003), p. 127.
19. Jean-Christophe Mounicq, "The Islamization of France," www.techcentralstation.be, August 28, 2003.
20. Steve Pearlstein, " 'Old Europe' Unprepared for New Battles," *The Washington Post,* July 21, 2004.
21. Christophe Dubois, "Des candidats terroristes recrutés en France," *Le Parisien,* December 10, 2003.
22. Christophe Dubois, " 'Nos banlieues représentent un vivier de volontaires,' " *Le Parisien,* December 10, 2003.
23. Ibid.

24. Christophe Dubois, "Plongée chez les ultras de l'Islam en France," *Le Parisien,* April 19, 2004.
25. Mounicq, "The Islamization of France."
26. David Ignatius, "Are the Terrorists Failing?," *The Washington Post,* September 28, 2004.
27. Ibid.
28. Jim Hoagland, "Straight Talk—In French," *The Washington Post,* October 15, 2004.
29. Valérie Mahaut, "Encore Une Salle de Prière Musulmane Fermée," *Le Parisien,* July 21, 2004.
30. Craig Whitlock, "Moroccans Gain Prominence in Terror Groups," *The Washington Post,* October 14, 2004.
31. "Une crèche saccagée, des cocktails Molotov ...," *Le Parisien,* December 24, 2003.
32. Olivier Bossut and Frederick Mouchon, "Traitement de choc contre la violence," *Le Parisien,* January 27, 2004.
33. Naipul, *Among the Believers,* p. 36.
34. Davis, *Martyrs,* p. 22.
35. Hotaling, *Islam Without Illusions,* p. 152.
36. Gene Weingarten, "Fear Itself," *The Washington Post Magazine,* August 22, 2004, p. 20.
37. David Brooks, "Cult of Death," *The New York Times,* September 7, 2004.
38. Lewis, *The Crisis of Islam,* p. xv.
39. George Otis Jr., *The Last of the Giants: Lifting the Veil on Islam and the End Times,* (Tarrytown, N.Y.: Chosen Books, 1991), p.130.
40. David Brooks, "War of Ideology," *The New York Times,* July 24, 2004.
41. Ibid.
42. Davis, *Martyrs,* p. 188.
43. Peter G. Peterson, "America's Image Problem Carries Grave Risks," *International Herald Tribune,* August 17-18, 2002.
44. Iraq Culture Smart Card, Marine Corps Intelligence Activity, February 2004.
45. Maureen Dowd, "Right Axis. Wrong Evil.," *New York Times,* July 22, 2004.
46. Richard A. Clarke, "Honorable Commission, Toothless Report," *The New York Times,* July 25, 2004.
47. Don Richardson, *Secrets of the Koran,* (Ventura, CA: Regal Books, 2003), p. 28.
48. David Gates, "The Pop Prophets," *Newsweek,* May 24, 2004.
49. Women's International League for Peace and Freedom Web site, comnet.org
50. Globalsecurity.org Web site
51. Ibid.
52. Robert Kaplan, *The Ends of the Earth,* (New York: Vintage Books, 1997).
53. www.bread.org
54. www.prb.org, the Web site of the Population Reference Bureau
55. www.fao.org, the Web site for the United Nations Food and Agriculture Organization.
56. Tim Dickinson, "Diary of a Dying Planet," *Rolling Stone,* June 10, 2004.
57. Colum Lynch, "Chronic Hunger is Increasing," *The Washington Post,* November 27, 2003.
58. usgs.gov, U.S. Geological Survey Web site.
59. "Quakes Grow Deadlier," *San Diego Union-Tribune,* September 28, 1999.
60. Paul Marshall, *Their Blood Cries Out* (Dallas: Word Publishing, 1997).

61. www.ransomfellowship.org Web site.
62. Quote from catholiceducation.org Web site of Catholic Educator's Resource Center
63. www.ransomfellowship.org
64. Ibid.
65. Dr. Anne Eyre, "Religious Cults in 20th Century America," American Studies Today Online, www.americansc.org.uk.
66. www.americanreligion.org.
67. Dr. Robert J. Lifton, "Cult Formation," *The Harvard Mental Health Letter*, Vol. 7, no. 8, February 1981.
68. David Barrett, "*World Christian Encyclopedia: A Comparative Survey of Churches and Religions in the Modern World*" (New York: Oxford University Press, 2001).
69. U.S. Department of Justice Web site, www.usdoj.gov.
70. www.whitecollarcrimeinfocenter.com.
71. www.glocal-challenges.org.
72. Ibid.
73. Ibid.
74. www.joshuaproject.net. The Joshua Project is dedicated to "bringing definition to the unfinished task" and draws on several reliable databases for its figures.
75. Eyewitness report from a Christian and Missionary Alliance missionary, France and North Africa missionary conference, Houlgate, France, September 2001.
76. www.wycliffe.org.
77. www.joshuaproject.net.
78. Ibid.
79. Ibid.
80. Campus Crusade for Christ President's personal letter to supporters, June 2004.
81. Ibid.
82. Campus Crusade for Christ staff member Denise DiSarro personal letter to supporters, Spring 2004.
83. For details on this supernatural direction of the Chinese church, see David Aikman's fine book, *Jesus in Bejing*, Regnery Publishing, 2003.
84. www.joshuaproject.net.
85. MacFarquhar, "Syria, Long Ruthlessly Secular, Sees Fervent Islamic Resurgence."
86. Otis, *The Last of the Giants*, p. 69.
87. Ibid., p. 205.
88. Ibid., p. 47.
89. Neela Banerjee, "As Oil Prices Soar, OPEC Says 'Not Our Fault,' " *The New York Times*, June 6, 2004.
90. "International Business Notes," *The Washington Post*, November 15, 2004.
91. Otis, *The Last of the Giants*, p. 71.
92. Ibid., p. 205.
93. Hotaling, *Islam without Illusions*, p. 98.
94. Ibid, p. 99.
95. Otis, *The Last of the Giants*, p. 61.
96. See the Naipul books for a start, as he interviews Muslims around the world and they echo this theme.
97. Otis, *The Last of the Giants*, p. 70.
98. Hotaling, *Islam Without Illusions*, p. 82.

99. Shadid, "Old Arab Friends Turn Away From U.S."

100. Dafna Linzer, "Poll Shows Growing Arab Rancor at U.S." *The Washington Post,* July 22, 2004.

101. Ibid.

102. Fareed Zakaria, "The Good, the Bad, the Ugly," *Newsweek,* May 31, 2004.

103. Philip Kennicott, "An About-Face on America," *The Washington Post,* August 24, 2004.

104. Ibid.

105. Sardar and Davies, *Why Do People Hate America?,* p. 46.

106. Samina Ahmed and John Norris, "A 'Moderation' of Freedom," *The Washington Post,* June 15, 2004.

107. Neil MacFarquhar, "Islamic Parties Gain at Expense of U.S.," *The New York Times,* Jan. 18, 2002.

108. Kennicott, "An About-Face on America."

109. Sardar and Davies, *Why Do People Hate America?,* pp. 47-48.

110. Kennicott, "An About-Face on America."

111. Ibid.

112. Caryle Murphy, "Grappling With the Morals on Display in Abu Ghraib," *The Washington Post,* May 29, 2004.

113. Sardar and Davies, *Why Do People Hate America?,* p. 64.

114. Kennicott, "An About-Face on America."

115. Sardar and Davies, *Why Do People Hate America?,* pp. 103-136.

116. Ibid., p. 55.

117. Hotaling, *Islam Without Illusions,* p. 175.

118. Samuel P. Huntington, *The Clash of Civilizations and the Remaking of the New World Order* (New York: Simon & Schuster, 1998), p. 119.

119. Ibid.

120. Alan Sipress, "Arabs Feel Sting of Yet Another Bitter Setback," *The Washington Post,* April 23, 2003.

121. Ibid.

122. Ibid.

123. Thomas L. Friedman, "A Hole In The Heart," *The New York Times,* October 28, 2004.

124. Killebrew, "Al Qaeda, The Next Chapter."

125. Camille Pecastaing, "The Secret Agents: Life Inside an Al Qaeda Cell," *Foreign Affairs,* January/February 2004.

126. Human Development Report 2004, www.undp.org/hdr2004.

127. Rajiv Chandrasekaran, "At the Ready to Answer Sadr's Call," *The Washington Post,* August 28, 2004.

128. Marc Sageman, *Understanding Terrorist Networks* (Philadelphia: University of Pennsylvania Press, 2004).

129. Jose T. Almonte, "How Poverty Becomes Dangerous," *International Herald Tribune,* July 26, 2002.

130. Otis, *The Last of the Giants,* p. 120.

131. Hotaling, *Islam Without Illusions,* pp. 143-44.

132. Otis, *The Last of the Giants,* p. 70.

133. Huntington, *The Clash of Civilizations and Remaking of the World Order,* p. 117.

134. Baer, *Sleeping With the Devil,* p. 161.

135. Mahmood Mamdani, *Good Muslim, Bad Muslim: America, the Cold War, and the Roots of Terror* (New York: Pantheon, 2004)
136. Killebrew, "Al Qaeda, The Next Chapter."
137. Ibid.
138. Daniel Benjamin and Gabriel Weimann, "What the Terrorists Have in Mind," *The New York Times*, October 27, 2004.
139. Killebrew, "Al Qaeda, The Next Chapter."
140. Ibid.
141. Otis, *The Last of the Giants*, pp. 69-70.
142. Thomas D. Segel, "The French-Muslim Connection," May 3, 2004.
143. Dubois, "Plongée chez les ultras de l'Islam en France."
144. Jean-Christophe Mounicq, "The Islamization of France."
145. Patrick E. Tyler, "Officials Investigate a Qaeda Suspect's Shadowy Life," *The New York Times*, August 13, 2004.
146. Craig S. Smith and Don Van Natta Jr, "Officials Fear Iraq's Lure for Muslims in Europe," *The New York Times*, October 23, 2004.
147. Wade Davis, "For A Global Declaration of Interdependence," *International Herald Tribune*, July 6, 2002.
148. Danielle Pletka, "Arabs on the Verge of Democracy," *The New York Times*, August 9, 2004.
149. Ibid.
150. Hotaling, *Islam Without Illusions*, p. 164.
151. Jason Burke, "Think Again: Al Qaeda," *Foreign Policy*, May/June 2004.
152. Ahmed and Norris, "A 'Moderation' of Freedom."
153. Jessica Matthews, "Match Iraq Policy to Reality," *The Washington Post*, September 28, 2004.
154. Gene Weingarten, "Fear Itself," p. 21.
155. Daniel Pipes, "Arabs Still Want to Destroy Israel," *The Wall Street Journal*, January 18, 2002.
156. Mortimer B. Zuckerman, "Graffiti on History's Walls," *U.S. News and World Report*, November 3, 2003, p. 45.
157. Timmerman, *Preachers of Hate*, p. 2.
158. Richard Cohen, "Return to Wannsee," *The Washington Post*, October 22, 2003.
159. Ibid.
160. Ibid.
161. Thomas Segel, "The French-Muslim Connection," May 6, 2004.
162. *Le Parisien*, June 9, 2004.
163. Craig S. Smith, "Neo-Nazis in Paris Vandalize and Burn a Jewish Community Center," *The New York Times*, August 23, 2004.
164. Hotaling, *Islam Without Illusions*, pp. 69-70.
165. Richardson, *Secrets of the Koran*, p. 50.
166. Thomas L. Friedman, "Jews, Israel and America," *The New York Times*, October 24, 2004.
167. Shadid, "Old Arab Friends Turn Away from U.S."
168. Sachiko Murata and William C. Chittick, *The Vision of Islam* (New York: Paragon House, 1994), p. 202.
169. Ibid., pp. 327-328.
170. Sheik Muhammad Hisham Kabbani, *The Approach of Armageddon? An Islamic Perspective* (Canada: Supreme Council of America, 2003), p. 228.

171. Ibn Kathir, *The Signs Before the Day of Judgment* (London: Dar Al-Taqwa, 1991)
172. Hotaling, *Islam Without Illusions*, p. 102.
173. Ibid., p. 94.
174. Burke, "Al Qaeda: Think Again," p. 19.
175. See alislam.org, among other Web sites, for further information about this sect.
176. Benjamin and Weimann, "What the Terrorists Have in Mind."
177. Sunan Abu Dawud, Book 36, Number 4271, narrated by Umm Salamah, ummul Mu'minin.
178. Kabbani, *The Approach of Armageddon? An Islamic Perspective*, p. 233.
179. Muhammad ibn Izzat, Muhammad 'Arif, *Al Mahdi and the End of Time* (London: Dar Al-Taqwa, 1997), p. 9.
180. El-Kavlu'l Muhtasar Fi Alamet-il Mehdiyy il Muntazar, 42, as quoted by Harun Yahya, http://www.endoftimes.net/08mahdiandtheendtimes.html.
181. Sunan Abu Dawud, Book 36, Number 4273, narrated by Umm Salamah, Ummul Mu'minin.
182. Sideeque M.A. Veliankode, *Doomsday Portents and Prophecies* (Scarborough, Canada: 1999), p. 277.
183. Ayatullah Baqir al-Sadr and Ayatullah Muratda Mutahhari *The Awaited Savior* (Karachi: Islamic Seminary Publications), pp. 4,5.
184. Izzat and Arif, *Al Mahdi and the End of Time*, p. 4.
185. Ibid., p. 15.
186. Ibid., p. 44.
187. Mohammed Ali Ibn Zubair Ali, *Aalalaat-e-Qiyyamat aur Nuzul-e-Eesa*, http://members.cox.net/arshad/qiyaama.html.
188. Izzat and Arif, *Al Mahdi and the End of Time*, p. 40.
189. Sahih Muslim Book 041, Number 7015.
190. Veliankod, *Doomsday Portents and Prophecies*, p. 351.
191. al-Sadr and Mutahhari, *The Awaited Savior*, p. 3.
192. Kabbani, p. 237.
193. Mufti Mohammad Shafi and Mufti Mohammad Rafi Usmani, *Signs of the Qiyama and the Arrival of the Maseeh* (Karachi: darul ishat, 2000) p. 60.
194. Kabbani, p. 237.
195. Sunan Abu Dawud, book 37, Number 4310.
196. Veliankode, *Doomsday Portents and Prophecies*, p. 358.
197. Hotaling, *Islam Without Illusions*, pp. 81-82.
198. Muhammad Ali Ibn Zubair, *The Signs of Qiyama*, http://members.cox.net/arshad/qiyaama.html.
199. Sunan Abu Dawood, book 37, Number 4310.
200. Mufti A.H. Elias, *Jesus A.S. in Islam, and his Second Coming*, http:www.islam.tc/prophecies/jesus.html.
201. Yahiya Emerick, *The Complete Idiot's Guide to Understanding Islam* (Indianapolis: Alpha Books, 2002), p. 108.
202. Ibid., p. 347.
203. Ghaida Ghantous, "Alleged Bin Laden Tape Offers Europe Truce, Not U.S.," *Reuters*, April 15, 2004
204. Douglas Jehl, "New Qaeda Audiotape Urges Muslims to 'Carry on the Fight'," *The New York Times*, October 2, 2004.
205. MacFarquhar, "Arabs Feel Sting of Yet Another Bitter Setback."
206. Emerick, *The Complete Idiot's Guide to Understanding Islam*, p. 171.

207. Hotaling, *Islam Without Illusions*, p. 153.
208. Peter Bergen, "Crude Relations," *The Washington Post*, March 14, 2004.
209. Burke, "Think Again: Al Qaeda," p. 24.
210. Bergen, "Crude Relations."
211. Michael Duran, "The Schizophrenic Saudi State," *Foreign Affairs*, January/February 2004.
212. Baer, *Sleeping With the Devil*, p. 162.
213. Ibid., p. 154.
214. Craig Whitlock, "Saudis Facing Return of Radicals," *The Washington Post*, July 11, 2004.
215. Ibid.
216. Baer, *Sleeping With the Devil*, pp. xix, xx.
217. Whitlock, "Saudis Facing Return of Radicals."
218. Baer, *Sleeping With the Devil*, p. xxviii.
219. Ibid., p. 16.
220. Ibid., p. 17.
221. Ibid., p. 161.
222. Ibid., p. 180.
223. Carmen bin Laden, *Inside the Kingdom* (New York: Warner Books, 2004).
224. Neil MacFarquhar, "The Saudis Fight Terror But Not Those Who Wage It," *The New York Times*, June 6, 2004.
225. Ibid.
226. Baer, *Sleeping With the Devil*, p. 202-3.
227. Ibid., p. xxvi.
228. John Cassidy, "Pump Dreams," *The New Yorker*, October 11, 2004, p. 46.
229. Ibid.
230. Ibid., p. 43.
231. Ibid., p. 45.
232. Michael Klare, *Blood and Oil: The Dangers and Consequences of America's Growing Dependency on Imported Petroleum* (New York: Metropolitan Books, 2003), p. 5.
233. Robert J. Samuelson, "Oil Fantasies," *The Washington Post*, October 6, 2004.
234. Tim Appenzeller, "The End of Cheap Oil," *National Geographic*, June 2004.
235. Jad Mouawad, "Oil Above $46 and Far Above OPEC's Ceiling," *The New York Times*, August 14, 2004.
236. Edward Helmore and Kamal Ahmed, "Outrage as Pentagon Nuclear Hit List Revealed," *The Guardian*, March 14, 2002.
237. Mahdi Obeidi, "Saddam, the Bomb and Me," *The New York Times*, September 26, 2004.
238. Mariam Abou Zahab and Olivier Roy, *Islamist Networks: The Afghan-Pakistan Connection*, (New York: Columbia University Press, 2004).
239. Salman Massod, "Pakistan Official Unhurt as Five Die in Attack," *The New York Times*, July 31, 2004.
240. John Lancaster and Kamran Khan, "Pakistan Losing Grip on Extremists," *The Washington Post*, August 27, 2004.
241. Killebrew, "Al Qaeda, The Next Chapter" .
242. Peter Slevin, "Libya's Uranium Linked to Pakistan," *The Washington Post*, May 29, 2004.
243. Nicholas D. Kristof, "Twisting Dr. Nuke's Arm," *The New York Times*, September 25, 2004.

244. Kristof, "Twisting Dr. Nuke's Arm."
245. Dan Eggen and Dafna Linzer, "9/11 Commission Offers Critiques On Many Fronts," *The Washington Post*, July 22, 2004.
246. Nicholas D. Kristof, "An American Hiroshima," *The New York Times*, August 11, 2004.
247. Ibid.
248. Ibid.
249. Graham Allison, *Nuclear Terrorism: The Ultimate Preventable Catastrophe*, (New York: Times, 2004)
250. George Will, "Holocaust in a Suitcase," *The Washington Post*, August 29, 2004.
251. Joby Warrick, "Libyan Nuclear Devices Missing," *The Washington Post*, May 29, 2004.
252. David E. Sanger, "Pakistan Found to Aid Iran Nuclear Efforts," *The New York Times*, September 2, 2004.
253. George F. Will, "The Iran Dilemma," *The Washington Post*, September 23, 2004.
254. Craig S. Smith, "Europeans Offer Plan to Ease Dispute on Iran Nuclear Issue," *The New York Times*, October 23, 2004.
255. Jim Hoagland, "Challenge From Iran," *The Washington Post*, June 17, 2004.
256. Nicholas D. Kristof, "The Nuclear Shadow," *The New York Times*, August 14, 2004.
257. Maureen Dowd, "White House of Horrors," *The New York Times*, October 28, 2004.
258. Robert Samuelson, "Nuclear Nightmare," *The Washington Post*, October 20, 2004.
259. Anonymous, *Imperial Hubris: Why the West Is Losing the War on Terror*, (New York: Brassey's, 2004).
260. Kristof, "The Nuclear Shadow."
261. Neil MacFarquhar, "Feeling of Frustration Makes Arab World an Explosive Region," *The New York Times*, September 13, 2002.
262. Hotaling, *Islam Without Illusions*, p. 157.
263. Ibid, p. 158.
264. Ibid, p. 159.
265. Pipes, "Arabs Still Want to Destroy Israel."
266. Craig Whitlock, "Grisly Path to Power in Iraq's Insurgency," *The Washington Post*, September 27, 2004.
267. Zuckerman, "Graffiti on History's Walls," p. 51.
268. Dough Struck, "Official Warns of Iranian Infiltration," *The Washington Post*, July 26, 2004.
269. Raymond Ludwigson, *A Survey of Bible Prophecy*, (Grand Rapids: Zondervan, 1951), p. 14.
270. Sardar and Davies, *Why Do People Hate America?*, p. 79. (See this book for a full discussion of how the U.S. benefits from eight types of manipulations to maintain our economic supremacy in the world)
271. Ibid., p. 82.
272. Ibid., p. 204.
273. "U.S. Trade Deficit Increased 19% in June" by Nell Henderson, *The Washington Post*, August 14, 2004.
274. Robert J. Samuelson, "Pressure of the American Dream," *The Washington Post*, July 26, 2004.
275. Appenzeller, "The End of Cheap Oil," p. 85.
276. Samuelson, "Pressure on the American Dream."

277. Appenzeller, "The End of Cheap Oil," p. 88.

278. Whitlock, "Saudis Facing Return of Radicals."

279. J. Robinson West, "Paying the Pumper," *The Washington Post,* July 23, 2004.

280. John Cassidy, "Pump Dreams," *The New Yorker*, October 11, 2004, p. 47.

281. Ibid., p. 46.

282. Baer, *Sleeping With the Devil,* p. xxiv.

283. Cassidy, "Pump Dreams," p. 42.

284. Appenzeller, "The End of Cheap Oil," p. 91.

285. Cassidy, "Pump Dreams," p. 43.

286. Jeremy Rifkin, "America, Wake Up to the European Dream," *The Washington Post,* October 31, 2004.

287. Cassidy, "Pump Dreams," p. 47.

288. Appenzeller, "The End of Cheap Oil," p. 85.

289. Cassidy, "Pump Dreams," p. 43.

290. Ibid., p. 44.

291. Ibid., p. 45.

292. Baer, *Sleeping With The Devil*, p. 46.

293. Appenzeller, "The End of Cheap Oil.," p.108.

294. John Cassidy, "Pump Dreams," p. 47.

295. Baer, *Sleeping With the Devil,* p. 151.

296. Sens. Jon Kyl and Charles Schumer, "Saudi Arabia's Teachers of Terror," *The Washington Post,* 2004.

297. Notes taken from address by Brother Andrew, Spring 2004, included in a Youth With a Mission prayer letter, May 20, 2004.

298. Baer, *Sleeping With the Devil,* p. 11.

299. Ibid., p. xxx.

300. Gene Edward Veith, "Peace Talk," *World,* May 1, 2004, p. 35.

301. Gene Weingarten, "Fear Itself," p. 23.

302. Ibid., p. 40.